SOUL SURVIVOR

Immortals of the Apocalypse: Book 1

DANIEL DE LORNE

For Nikki
For getting me here
and for keeping me here
(in a good way).

❧ I ☙

SCREAMS SHATTERED EMRYS'S DREAMS, AND THUNDERING footsteps trampled the remains into dust. His eyelids flickered open into the darkness of his living quarters while in the corridor beyond his door, the bellowing continued, a multitude of voices stampeding into his blood and kicking his heart into a frenzy. He bolted upright, threw back the sheet, and swung out of bed. His bare feet hit the floor and the vibrations rose up his legs. The lights activated, and the closer he got to the door, the more the screams and shouts swelled. He hesitated, not wanting to see what madness had struck Endurance.

"You're only waking now? You'd sleep through Judgement Day."

He spun at the sound of Nimue's voice as she crawled out of the hole in the back wall of his room. The diminutive and child-in-looks-only Darisami had her almost-black hair fashioned into a high bun. Her hazel eyes were wide and alert on her white as alabaster face.

"What's going on?" And why had none of the others woken him?

"It's Absolon. He's lost it."

That could mean anything. Absolon was nothing more than a barbarian, and from the sounds coming from outside, it wasn't unrealistic to assume he was sacking the place. "Lost it? Lost it how?"

"He fed on some souls. Went mad. Fed some more." She chewed her bottom lip. "Out in the open. The humans saw him and freaked. Some tried to kill him. Others ran and that started a panic."

Emrys swallowed a curse and looked at the closed door. What would he find on the other side? Five thousand humans lived in Endurance, a city their government had built into and below a mountain when the end of the world came sixty-five years earlier. He and a group of Darisami had snuck into Endurance with the humans before it sealed shut. One of the last cities left on Earth, Endurance was an ark to ensure the survival of the human race and, unwittingly, that of the Darisami.

And now Absolon had broken the covenant.

"Where are the others?"

"Ragnar, Yusef, and Denari are trying to subdue Absolon. Clara and Wyatt are at the exit, trying to keep the humans inside. It's a bloodbath out there, Emrys. They're killing humans to quell the uprising, but it's making it worse."

How many would be left when they were finished? This had to be stopped. The humans wouldn't survive if they got outside, and that meant he and all the other Darisami would starve.

"Where did it start?" He pulled on a pair of trousers and his boots.

She held out a shirt to him. "Lower levels but many of the humans are rushing to the top."

He went to the door.

"What are you going to do?" she asked.

"We need to keep the humans in, so I'm going up top too."

"I'm coming with you."

He raised an eyebrow.

"What does it matter if they see me now?"

She'd lived fifty-three years pretending to be a ghost flitting through the hidden parts of Endurance, and now it was time to come back to life. And if she was going to be seen as she truly was, he may as well too.

He paused and breathed deep, letting the wrinkles and age spots fade. His gray hair returned to its natural brown. He stole his body back from the ravages of time, so he no longer appeared as a sprightly ninety-year-old but as a fit and healthy thirty. The reclamation returned some of the energy he expended in maintaining a semblance of ageing. Considering the chaos he was about to walk into, he'd need every ounce.

He swiped the touchpad, and the door slid open. A man dashed past, a human following a herd of humans. The hallway outside his quarters on level four was nearly empty, but a cacophony filled the facility. He peered over the balcony to find the floor far below strewn with bodies, some bloodied, others simply lifeless, twisted, trampled. A battlefield in the pits of Hell.

A mob surrounded an armed Yusef. Wasn't he meant to be capturing Absolon? Yusef released a round of machine gun fire, and the humans fell like wheat beneath a scythe.

Nimue joined Emrys. "They'll all be slaughtered if we don't do something."

He looked above him at the throng on the upper levels. "We need to get to the control room."

But the control room was also on the top level with the

exit. The elevators would be jammed so they had to muscle their way through the stairs. Even then, they'd be clogged with the living and the dead.

"Come on. We have to hurry."

They joined the exodus of humans belting for the top levels, keeping their heads down and running as far as they could in the hope that no one recognized them in the confusion. Rattles of gunfire followed them. Who else had guns: more of his kind or the humans? It didn't matter. They needed to get to the control room before too many more humans died.

They ascended the stairs, pushing and shoving the crowd aside, easier to do with their supernatural strength. But when they reached the level beneath the top, they slammed against a bottleneck. The crowd jostled as it continued to grow, and he and Nimue had little room to fit. They got separated but he kept going, and Nimue rejoined him at the head of the stairs, sandwiched between one crowd and another, the gathering no less dense, no less jittery.

The humans pushed and shoved at him as they surged towards the exit, but he needed to go in the other direction. He grabbed the woman next to him, picked her up, and used her to push his way through, letting her go when she hit him in the face. He lifted body after body, and each time he touched a human, the symbol that would separate them from their souls buzzed inside his skull like a firefly trapped in a bottle.

One soul and this would be easier. He'd be stronger. He'd be sated. And they'd fall away from him in terror.

He ground his teeth together. He wouldn't kill. Not yet. Not until it was necessary.

He held onto the symbol as hard as he held onto the man in front of him. More shouted at him, demanding that he go the other way. The cleared space behind him soon filled as more people swarmed out of the stairwell, and he and Nimue were forgotten. Gunfire in the distance turned heads and bodies to greater danger.

He navigated a path through the crowd, some parting out of fear, others unsure of what had happened. Most people had fixated on the airlock to the outside, but others, perhaps smarter, perhaps more desperate, had targeted the control room. A wall seven people deep surrounded the room. He and Nimue joined them. Its thick glass windows held, despite the banging and the bullets and the begging.

"We need to clear a path to the door." His insides tugged, demanding a soul, tempting him with an easier solution, the urge that was always there, even after sixty-five years of restricted diet.

"There's another way." Nimue grabbed his hand and pulled him to the left, running down the empty hall while everyone's attention was focused elsewhere. She pulled him into a dark room. The lights winked on and the door slid shut, muffling the sounds like he was back in bed. That seemed like hours ago.

They were in a supply room with bare shelves. Nimue ran towards the back. Halfway along, she dropped to the floor, crawled to the right through the bottom shelves, and lifted aside a plate from the wall to reveal an opening. She slid in, and he followed.

They continued for a few feet, turned left, then right, then right again. Voices permeated the walls. Nimue stopped and spun, putting her legs in front of her. He grabbed her arm before she kicked in the grill.

"Do it gently," he whispered. "We don't know who's in there."

She tutted, spun back around, and lifted the grill aside

with her hands. Light filtered into the tunnel. He held his breath.

The tunnel exited beneath one of the control desks, and Nimue slipped out and hid while Emrys inched forward. Anybody could be in the control room—and they could be armed. And while he wasn't worried about himself, if bullets were fired, they could damage the consoles.

From his crouched position, he saw one set of legs. Darisami or human? He summoned the harvest symbol and climbed out from under the control desk.

Dark brown skin, broad shoulders, close shaved head. He banished the symbol in a puff of breath. "Hey, Wyatt."

The Darisami spun, leveling his gun at Emrys. "For fuck's sake, Emrys. Where the hell have you been?"

"He was sleeping." Nimue climbed out and dusted off the front of her trousers.

Emrys let the comment slide, his eye drawn to what was happening outside the booth. The realization that Emrys, Nimue, and Wyatt were all on the same side crashed on the faces of some. Others figured there must be a secret entrance. Wild hope entered their eyes, and it spread as one mouthed to another that they should look for a different way in.

"We don't have much time. Wyatt, guard the tunnel. They'll come through any minute."

Wyatt swore. "What are we going to do? We can't kill them all."

"The tunnel should slow them down. Shoot a few and they'll be wary. What's more important is finding…"

Emrys looked down on the control desk. All the buttons and screens were still intact, but it'd been so long since he'd looked at it that he struggled to remember how it worked.

"What are you looking for?" Nimue asked.

"I'm going to gas everyone."

"You can't be serious."

"Not to kill them, just knock them out."

Nimue paused. "Why didn't I know this was possible?"

"Take it up with Clara. Or Ragnar. Whoever. We just need to find it."

Rumblings echoed in the tunnel as too many people tried to come through on their suicide mission. He blocked out their noise and pressed his palm to the screen. It asked for his password.

He entered it.

Wrong.

His heart thudded.

Second attempt…

His hand slipped.

Error message.

Thud again.

Third time…

Access granted.

Wyatt fired a round into the tunnel.

Emrys breathed hard and fast. He wiped the sweat from his forehead. What he needed wasn't immediately visible. He had to search. One menu, then another. In case of emergency… No, that wasn't it. More menus, more delving, more disappointment.

Gunshots. A wet palm slapped the floor, followed by gasping breaths and a gargled plea before a bullet cut it short.

There! He found it buried down a select pathway that his fingers remembered and his brain had tried to piece together.

GOD.

He slammed his palm on the button, and gas released

out of the air vents, including those in the control room. He turned and watched the humans panic as white mist filled the corridor. They sought refuge, held their breath, but there was no escape. Gas suffocated every part of Endurance within seconds. A perfect solution to quell the maddest of uprisings.

It was a miracle it hadn't been required before.

The humans collapsed, unconscious, but he and Nimue couldn't stop. Subduing the humans was only part of the problem. The next mission wouldn't be so easy.

He swallowed hard to smother the disquiet over what he would soon be required to do, regardless of its necessity. He grabbed a couple of two-way radios from their cradles and gave one to Nimue. He left one on the console tuned to channel four and called Wyatt over to the screen.

"The gas will cut off in another three minutes, and everyone should be out for at least four hours. If we find anyone awake or it looks like they're starting to stir, we'll call you and tell you to press the button again."

He showed Wyatt how to get to the GOD button and gave him his access code.

"Where are you going?" Wyatt asked.

"To catch Absolon."

2

Ragnar and Clara flanked Emrys as he entered the cell. He clutched the hilt of the golden knife, fist squeezing around the leather that protected his skin from the burning touch of the precious metal. Even so, his palm itched.

Wyatt and Yusef had wrestled Absolon to the ground, forcing all their weight and strength on top of him. He'd always been a brute of a thing but now, filled with the souls of who knew how many, he was a force of nature that two Darisami struggled to contain. Twisting and writhing in their grip, he threatened to break free, and it was anyone's guess whether he went for them or returned to feeding on human souls.

Emrys only needed to stick his head outside the chamber to see the damage Absolon had wrought. Denari was still out there, dragging live but unconscious humans back to their quarters, and Emrys and the remaining five sane Darisami needed to help her. Absolon's execution had to be swift.

"We're all in agreement on what must be done?"

Clara's crisp, clear, condescending voice sliced through Absolon's babbling.

Apart from Denari's absence, the factions were evenly represented: Clara with Yusef, Ragnar with Wyatt. Absolon would have been counted on Ragnar's side had he not turned berserker and shattered Endurance's peace. Emrys was undeclared, as was Nimue, who perched on a bench at the back of the chamber, so still and composed that she may as well have been invisible.

"Absolon has destroyed what we've worked so hard to save. He must pay the consequences. Don't you agree, Ragnar?"

Ragnar's face was a mask fashioned of steel. "I still maintain he can be rehabilitated."

"It's too late for that. He has lost his grip on whatever restraint he once had and endangered us all."

Ragnar stepped closer to Absolon, to his friend, ally, and lover. He shook slightly, his jaw locked. Absolon bucked. Ragnar tensed, but he wasn't so stupid as to intervene. Emrys mourned for Ragnar, but he had to lock up his heart for what he was about to do. It had been decades since he'd had to act as executioner. He tightened his grip on the knife.

Absolon's ranting was the only sound while they waited for Ragnar to make his peace. When he nodded, Emrys stepped forward. Ragnar turned and left. His departure shocked Wyatt into slipping his grip. Absolon unseated the Darisami and got a leg underneath him, ready to spring forward. Emrys braced to slam his body into Absolon's, but Nimue leapt from her seat, onto his back, and knocked him down. Wyatt and Yusef dove onto Absolon and pinned him to the floor. Nimue's hand slipped through Absolon's matted locks, gripped his hair, and wrenched his head back.

"Finish this, Master Emrys." Nimue's command was a push to his back, her tone flat, firm, and insistent, forcing him to his task.

He'd been dubbed the Master—or his full title, Master of High and Low Works—even before they'd entered Endurance, feared for his willingness to execute their kind. It was a title he'd earned on numbers alone and a mantle no one else wanted to shoulder.

"Kill them, want them, mine, mine, mine." Absolon's voice rose and fell, loud then soft, a breathy rush powered by the inescapable desire for more.

How many souls had he harvested? They'd forced themselves to live on the minimum requirement of one every thirty days since humanity became scarce, but the sudden surfeit of souls after such a drought had fried his brain.

Emrys knelt out of reach of Absolon's snapping, slathering jaws. He'd been a handsome man, young, blond, brutish yet jovial. In another life, he was a Swedish peasant and soldier before receiving his gifts of immortality, strength, and a hunger for human souls. His sad eyes had danced with a mischief that many in this room had envied. He'd been Ragnar's human lover and his maker. Emrys also shared kinship with Absolon, the two of them born of the same Darisami father who had betrayed both their lives and their hearts.

But that was in the obliterated past. Emrys sighed. For all their differences, Absolon had still been one of them. Emrys hoped Absolon would find peace in death.

Emrys raised the gold knife, intimate with the nicks and scratches on its blade. He remembered every Darisami he had ended with his prized possession. Every name. Every face.

He'd add Absolon's to the list.

Emrys pulled back the knife ready for the thrust. The others in the room held their breath, the Darisami holding Absolon stiffened in preparation. Emrys's heart braced. "I'm sorry it's come to this, Absolon." He drove the blade of fatal gold through Absolon's right eye and into his brain.

Absolon screamed one long, sharp-toned shriek as if the thousands of souls he had fed on in his almost five hundred years as a Darisami were being dragged out of his throat. Wyatt, Yusef, and Nimue slipped off his shuddering body, jerking in the torrent that swept over them all and shivering from the ecstasy. Feathers brushed Emrys's skin like a flock of swans, strong and soft, beating and buffeting his own soul in their haste to be home. The electric lights flickered and sparked with the release of energy, and his eyes drifted skyward as the souls flew away. A smile stretched his face.

To behold such beauty!

It made him hungry.

That thought tipped a cold bucket of slime down his gullet and drowned his appetite.

He shunned the euphoria and stood guard in front of the door. Joy shone on the faces of the assembled. Some bit their lips to stop a moan or keep the drool from dripping down their chin. Darisami were bags of grain filled to bursting. Split the sack and all the goodness spilled out.

"Snap out of it! Enough souls have been wasted today."

Their eyes refocused, and they cast sheepish looks at one another. Clara, composure regained, raised her slender, sharp nose into the air. She crossed in front of Absolon's decaying corpse, casting a sneer for the pile of dust he would soon be. She surveyed each of them. Emrys sensed a speech.

"Thanks to Absolon's deeds, we are faced with a crisis

the likes of which we haven't seen for more than sixty years."

What Clara was about to say had been spoken of before. The Darisami had flooded into Endurance as an uneasy pack of ten when the underground citadel had gone into operation and its doors sealed to the outside world. Wherever the humans went, the Darisami were forced to follow. If they wanted to live.

They had worked to gain positions on the Council, effectively taking it over except for a few harangued humans who became nothing more than puppets. And so, the Darisami had ruled without revealing their nature, attempting to guide the humans and thereby ensuring the supply of souls wouldn't end.

But now the Council was obsolete, and the Darisami had whittled down from ten to seven. The humans were confined, but that would not help anyone in the long run. Prisoners rarely bred. There were *things* to discuss.

But with Ragnar and Denari not in the room, and Absolon barely disintegrated, Emrys would be damned if he let Clara twist the moment to her advantage.

"Now is not the time, Clara."

She spun like he'd slashed her.

He continued in as conciliatory tone as he could manage, but he couldn't blunt the edge in his voice, honed after such a day. "We all know something has to be done, but we have lost a comrade today. A friend."

She opened her mouth to speak but he held up his palms.

"Regardless of what some of us thought of Absolon, he was one of us. What happens next should be decided with *all* Darisami present. Don't you agree?"

Clara breathed in and the air smoothed lines, tension, and the naked ambition from her face. "Of course. We will wait for an appropriate time but be mindful we must act lest we perish."

With eyes for no one but him, she glided with a queen's composure towards him and the door. He stepped aside, and she departed. Yusef followed close behind. Wyatt dropped a sad look to the shimmer of dust that was Absolon, kissed his fingertips, and let them fall like rose petals cast on a grave. He sighed and left to seek out Ragnar.

Emrys and Nimue remained. He waved his hand over the sensor and locked them in with Absolon's corpse. He slid to the floor and rested his back against the wall.

"Don't let this break you, Emrys." She crouched by Absolon's empty clothes and trailed her fingers through his dust. She rubbed the powder between her fingertips, held it to her nose, sniffed, then wiped him off her skin. "There is nothing left. The dust on old books holds more memory."

Emrys cranked out a weak smile. Despite what he knew her true age to be, she seemed like a girl squatting on a riverbank and peering into a gently flowing stream. An innocent struck by the wonders of a world still to be discovered. She looked like his daughter Sian, dead nearly five hundred years thanks to his foolishness.

But instead of watching tadpoles and splashing in the shallows, Nimue played in the remnants of a creature that defied the natural order and survived on human souls. Her mind was sharper than his, definitely more devious. She had used her eternal childhood for ends that made him shudder. A scourge, that's what she'd called herself, but he found comfort in stroking her dark chestnut hair.

"Perhaps one day we will all become this." She rose and walked towards him with the surety of a woman who'd baited and bested barbarians. "After all, how can we say we'll live forever if no one ever has?"

He snorted at her sentiment. He wouldn't argue with her. In the past, he'd tried. And failed. Like he'd failed to end her life centuries before.

He'd hunted Darisami across the globe, wanting to destroy his kind for their wickedness and to assuage his own guilt, but when he saw Nimue, he could not take her life. They had become friends, and from then on, he'd only slain the wicked. There had still been far too many of them through the years.

She had moved on from Absolon's demise with callous speed, but he shouldn't have been surprised. Absolon had forgotten the boundaries too many times for him to be graced with her friendship. It had been a mark against him that Emrys could never accept.

And now I have killed him.

The thought jolted his head.

"You did what had to be done." She sat and rested against him. He put his arm around her shoulders and squeezed her close.

With his head leaning back against the wall, he listened to Endurance. The whir of the ventilation. The hum of lights. The austerity of metal and glass. Missing were the sounds of people talking, fighting, an occasional laugh, the expected hubbub of existence. All gone.

This is what he and his kind did. They destroyed everything they touched.

The humans were being dumped in their apartments and sealed in from the outside. They'd be kept alive until a Darisami chose them. How many had survived the frenzy of Absolon's terror only to find themselves subjected to the banal and dispassionate execution of an abattoir?

All because Absolon couldn't control himself.

He clenched his fists and unleashed a growl at the back of his throat.

Nimue hushed him and rubbed her hand across his stomach. "Anger is useless, Emrys. What's done is done. You could do no different."

Absolon had known the rules for the Darisami in Endurance.

Order. Restraint. Survival.

Those were the words they'd forced themselves to live by. One soul every thirty days, enough to stay alive. They had meant to encourage the humans to multiply so one day they could all leave and scuttle across the face of the Earth.

Order. Restraint. Survival.

Death to those who opposed it.

"But something has to change, and you know what Clara is thinking." She unwound from his embrace, and his gut reached for the withdrawn comfort. "We should be the ones to go."

Leaving Endurance had been on everyone's mind—Darisami and human—ever since they'd closed the doors and sealed themselves inside, but very few dared speak of it aloud. Except for Nimue. His old fears bubbled up. What if they found no other survivors? What if they did? He opened his mouth to speak, but she pushed to her feet, away from him and his arguments.

"I'm not listening to your objections again. I've lived here like a specter too long and, even with all the *food* locked away, I'll not be content wandering halls where only Darisami eyes disdain me."

She'd probably decided what she was going to say the moment they wrestled Absolon into the cell. For decades, she'd lived out of human sight lest they become suspicious of why she hadn't grown into a woman. She could change her features, but her eighteenth-century mortal life, subsisting on a diet that lacked adequate nutrition and her own genetics, had kept her small and under-developed. No amount of make-up could make her into a grown woman.

Confined to her quarters or abandoned corridors, she lived in the shadows. She had bent the rule on occasion and given birth to tales of a ghost walking the halls. Some —though not him, never him—had berated her, as if she were a disobedient child. They had even threatened her with execution.

Order. Restraint.

But she was the one who survived.

"And what if we do take the journey?" he said. "The same thing will happen there. Eventually you'll have to go into seclusion."

"Then we'll do the same again and find somewhere else. The human race won't become extinct. They're a plague that cannot be expunged. In the meantime, they might yet return to the Earth's surface and we'll reap the benefits."

Reap…like the Reaper.

"What if the others don't agree it should be us?"

"You'll convince them. You're well placed among this rabble. The Master instead of a murderer. That means you're impartial, beholden to no one, yet part of everything. They respect you. If you declare, they'll agree."

He tallied who would stand for him. Ragnar might hold a grudge, and Clara may find a way to make him pay for speaking against her. The others would fall in line with how those two voted. He would have to convince them he was acting for their benefit. They needed to trust he would lead them to a new fertile field. Any of them could have planned to be free of Endurance in the hope they'd discover some crop of humans ripe for harvesting. Fear of not finding one kept them guarding rations.

"What if I don't want to go?"

"Do you really want to stay and rot with the rest of them? You hate them as much as I do, Emrys. We could be free."

"At least for a little while. But they would follow us."

She snorted. "I'll take whatever freedom I can get. And you should too."

"I'm still not sure."

"Then do this for me." She got onto her knees. "Tell them I'm the one who has to go. I want to do this with you, Emrys, but if you cannot, then please don't hold me back."

Losing her would be like losing Sian all over again. But could he really leave Endurance and risk never finding another supply of humans? Did he have the courage to die?

"I need time to think."

"Fine, but we'll all have to meet soon to determine the next course. You need to encourage the idea that someone has to go in search of a new supply—and it can't be any of them." Her eyes sparkled with the flare of burning magnesium and turned his worries to cinders. He'd give her anything to keep seeing those eyes every day.

His decision was made.

"What do you want to see most outside?" he asked.

She laughed and slumped against him. "Everything."

Her response was simple enough, but her determination seized his spine and squeezed. He was trapped, and he wouldn't be free until she'd gotten her way.

The door to the cell opened and Ragnar entered. He paused and stared at them, as if willing them to not be there. Nimue bristled under his regard and slipped out of the room without a word. Ragnar's brow creased as he looked after her before he turned back to Emrys.

"You're still here." His voice rumbled low, and he

straightened his stance. He loomed over Emrys, his jaw set and eyes deep in shadow.

Emrys resisted the urge to rush to his feet, but even as he made a slow ascent, he stumbled and was forced to save himself against the wall. Ragnar's lip twitched, bristling his red moustache and beard before he turned away. Ragnar had once been a nobleman—or so he said. At the least, he'd been a soldier, perhaps of high rank. Either way, he'd assumed a level of power in their commune, and Emrys was happy enough to let him lead.

"Do you want to be alone?" Emrys said.

Silence dragged as Ragnar stared at where Absolon had been slain. Assuming that meant yes, Emrys took a step through the door.

"How many of us have you destroyed?"

Accusation pricked Ragnar's words, and thick serrated thorns hooked Emrys's skin. "I do what needs to be done."

"That's not what I asked."

He turned back into the room. "You want a number?"

"Yes."

"Forty-seven."

Ragnar absorbed the number like a sponge soaking up blood. He sat on a bench. "I remember Carys and Evander. Who were the others?" They'd been the other two Darisami who'd entered Endurance. They had failed to adapt to confinement.

Forty-seven Darisami shuttered through his head, starting with Lysander—everything always started with Lysander—then every name, every face, every death.

"An assortment including plenty who would have taken Endurance for themselves."

Anyone who wasn't part of their uneasy alliance was forfeit. They had qualms about letting Emrys in, a well-known killer of their kind, but his reputation for being just and measured—as well as ferocious and merciless—had overcome their hesitation. His kinship with Absolon and his pact with Nimue had also helped.

In addition, when the end came and they were all scrambling for a spot inside Endurance, he had fought hard for the ten of them, slaying as many Darisami as were foolish enough to try to take their place before the doors closed. The seven Darisami inside Endurance might be the only immortals left in existence.

And good riddance too.

"You killed your fair share." Because Ragnar would not allow another to rule him.

"Do you think we deserve to live like this?" Ragnar gestured to the space on the bench beside him, his eyes seeking Emrys and demanding he accept.

Though he was needed to help drag humans into make-shift prison cells, now was as good a time as any to work on Ragnar and get his consensus despite how hard it would be. It always was with Ragnar. Except when it came to Absolon. It was difficult to imagine Ragnar anything other than this austere, humorless, and rigid man with dark red hair, but he must have been something else when he was younger. Emrys struggled to think of him as warm or soft, but Absolon had gotten through that armor. It was too horrific to think neither of them had ever been loved.

"To say we deserve it implies we have done something to be rewarded." Though they had all done much to be punished, him included.

Ragnar grunted. "We try to live by one simple rule. Order. Restraint. Survival. Those words are engraved on the inside of my skull, yet they're a lie."

"They are a means to an end."

"I never thought I'd hear philosophy from our executioner." He hacked out a laugh. "I don't know how you can live with the guilt."

He wasn't referring to all the Darisami lives he'd taken, just one. But Emrys wouldn't let Ragnar cloak himself in false humanity.

"I have other sins to atone for. Killing those who flout the law and endanger our survival are very low on the list. Absolon was not the only one to crack under the pressure, and perhaps it's just as well he's gone. The human race is barely hanging on, and we don't have the luxury of gluttony."

Ragnar shot to his feet and headed for the door.

"You know I'm right, Ragnar. I understand Absolon meant a lot to you, but he wasn't the same, even before his end."

Ragnar stopped. Emrys thanked God he did. If he'd left, Ragnar would oppose him, and Nimue would not be pleased.

"He couldn't survive this life," Emrys said. "He was forged in a time of plenty where he didn't know famine. To remain as long as he did is a testament to the comfort *you* showed him, the strength *you* gave him to hold on, but he couldn't last forever. You only prolonged the inevitable."

Ragnar rounded on him, his mouth stretched in a snarl and his eyes blazing.

He forged his arguments in Ragnar's fire. "You asked me if we deserve to live like this, and if I was forced to answer, I'd say yes. Because we must do whatever it takes to hold on. We have a duty to survive and live as witness to this world. We have a duty to be steadfast against despair. We have a duty to hold on for those who have gone before to show our strength, to show that we are Darisami and we deserve life."

If only I believed that.

Ragnar unclenched his fist. His eyes sparkled from the wetness that coated them.

"Please, Ragnar, today's pain will pass. I am not your enemy. I am your brother."

He edged towards Ragnar and took hold of his hands. They were coarse, strong hands filled with life. Ragnar glared at him, but his hate could not outshine his grief. He lifted Emrys's hands and kissed the back of each.

"Brother."

His voice, his lips, his touch were so warm and tender that Emrys felt held by a lover, sharing a moment so private that few others had been privileged to enjoy. The gesture would have weakened anyone else, but it made Ragnar stronger. Is that why Wyatt and Absolon had been such ardent followers?

"Do you want me to stay?" Emrys said.

"No." Ragnar retracted his hands. "I'd like to be alone."

"Very well. I will see you later. Clara is anxious for a decision to be made about our future."

Ragnar grunted, took his seat and leaned forward over clasped hands to study Absolon's dust. Emrys left him. He had others to woo.

OUTSIDE THE CELL, EMRYS MET YUSEF DRIVING A transporter, its flat tray normally used for transferring one or two patients to the infirmary laden with seven unconscious bodies.

"Where's Clara?" Emrys asked.

"Top level. Giving out orders." Though Yusef was in Clara's camp, he wasn't above an occasional independent thought. Perhaps it had something to do with his human lover.

"Is Yeleni…"

Yusef narrowed his eyes, but the warning in them wasn't strong enough to hide his fear.

Emrys stopped. He didn't want a fight either way. "I'd better find Clara."

But Denari got to him first and forced him into service. Talking to Clara took second place to carting unconscious humans to their apartments-cum-cells. The gas began to wear off, and a call over the two-way to Wyatt soon had him racing to send a second stream of the toxin pumping through the vents. The woman he'd been carrying went slacker than before. How long had she been awake and hoping for her moment to escape?

After another four hours, the living had been secured and the dead were taken to the incinerator. He was waiting at the elevator doors when they opened to reveal Clara alone. She straightened her spine, her pointed nose ever so slightly lifted. Her eyes bulged more than usual. He nodded to her and entered the elevator, hand going to the panel as if to press a button then retracting. It wouldn't hurt for her to think he intended to go to the third floor as well.

The doors closed. He didn't have long to talk. "Clara, I apologize if earlier I spoke out of turn."

She didn't respond.

"I've seen crowds like that before. Decisions could be made, and while people might agree then, there would be grumblings later."

She'd heard him—how could she not?—but she kept her silence.

One more level to go.

"I agree something has to be done," he said.

"Do you?" Her voice raised and lowered in time with her eyebrows.

He almost sneered at how obvious she was. Show her resistance, and she'd cut you down. Agree with her and she was your best friend. He'd known sledgehammers with more subtlety.

"Of course. Absolon's actions have forced us to do what has been needed for a long time," he said.

"And what do you suggest?"

He had to be careful. If he appeared too eager, she was likely to become suspicious he wanted something that might go against her own interests.

"It's not for me to plot our course forward. However, what we have discussed on other occasions seems the only possible plan. We must find fresh supplies. These humans will not last long. Imprisonment—forced imprisonment such as they undergo now—will break most of them. They may be cowed but they will not breed, and we will run out of souls."

"At least we agree on one thing."

The elevator stopped and they walked out together, though Emrys lagged a little behind. They marched down the corridor without another word to each other, and the gap their voices left filled with the banging and muffled shouts of the prisoners.

Yusef met them coming from the other direction. Though he'd cast off the wrinkles of age, he remained stooped and sullen. "They'll scream until their throats bleed."

The shouting behind the door next to them grew louder.

"We should bind and gag them," Clara said.

Emrys ground his teeth and his empathy. "We don't have the supplies to do that. We can show some mercy."

Clara ignored him and paced down the hallway, looking at the doors like she was grading cattle. Would any break free?

Though Yusef didn't move a lot, he vibrated with a nervous energy that prickled Emrys's skin.

"Where is she?" he whispered to Yusef.

Yusef's eyes darted towards Clara before jerking his chin further down the corridor. Somewhere, in one of these rooms, was the woman with whom Yusef shared his bed.

Screwing the humans was acceptable, but forming a bond was frowned upon. Especially when it might mean a female missing out on falling pregnant. But Yusef had found one who was infertile. Since their coupling some twelve years earlier, he had shone amid the gloom that permeated Endurance. He'd asked the Council—humans excepted—if he could make her Darisami and was denied. He took the refusal in stoic silence. If he hadn't, the penalty would have been death for both of them.

Now he was forced to keep Yeleni prisoner.

Yusef would have to be watched.

Emrys put his hand on the man's shoulder. "I'm sorry for what has happened."

"It doesn't make it any easier." Yusef's tone had bite but no teeth.

Denari met them. The gray in her black hair was gone, the wrinkles faded back into youthful ebony skin. She was as lithe and as supple as a birch rod and her eyes delivered the sting.

Clara returned.

"Imprisonment isn't the end of our troubles with the humans." Denari's words were crisp and cut like the staccato of a machine gun.

"What do you mean?" Clara said.

"They'll need to be fed. If we open the door, they'll attack us or injure themselves trying to escape. We'll be lucky if any survive."

Emrys swore. She was right. The humans would prove difficult to maintain without using force. They had access to water from their bathrooms, but how long could they go without food? If they were weaker, would they be more compliant? He hated the thoughts for their heartlessness.

Yusef winced. "That is no way to live."

Yes, he would have to be watched.

Clara whipped her head around and glared until he cowered. "Yusef, I think you should go help Wyatt."

With a lost look for Emrys, he disappeared down the hallway towards the elevator.

"Denari, I trust you are unconcerned?" Clara asked.

Was ice cold? Forced feedings. Beatings. Torture. Death. Throw in a hip-hop beat and that had once been Denari's Saturday night. She tilted her head to the side as if surprised by the question.

"It is an adjustment but nothing we cannot overcome. Order. Restraint. Survival." She bowed her head to them and left to patrol, a lightness and rhythm to her step like the prisoners' torment had been set to music.

Emrys did not share Denari's confidence. Thousands were now imprisoned in Endurance. Even with Absolon gone, there were still seven Darisami who required a soul every month. Almost ninety humans per year would die by their hand. At the best case, that would last them about three decades. But that wasn't guaranteed. Could seven Darisami maintain Endurance that long? Not just the humans, but the running of the city? They knew a lot about its operations but the list of things they didn't know had no end.

Alternatively, they could let the humans loose and see

what happened, but how soon before they made for the exit? Nimue's plan was the best option. While the remaining Darisami fought over scraps, he and Nimue could get out. He needed Clara's backing.

She swept past and headed for the elevator, setting a fast pace, and he wondered if hearing those people unsettled her. Back in the elevator, she was once again composed.

"Another of us may be lost before this over," he said.

Her face closed—eyes narrowing, lips pursing, cheeks tensing—as if it all came to a point to stab his conclusion through its heart. "Yusef will see sense. He did before and will again."

He hoped so. The last thing he wanted to do was kill another Darisami so soon.

"Perhaps. We need to meet. All of us."

"I agree. We will congregate in the council room at seven tonight."

"I will inform the others."

The elevator stopped at the fifth floor where Clara kept her rooms. "Please do." She walked away. He'd been dismissed.

3

When Emrys entered the low-ceilinged council chamber, Ragnar and Wyatt were seated on the left side of the round table. Endurance's architects had wanted to inspire its inhabitants to live in a way that was more cooperative than the one that led to the ark's creation. As such, a circle was chosen because it had no start nor end, and therefore no single leader. They'd learned nothing else from the rest of the legend of King Arthur, and the Darisami were no better. Division was obvious. Ragnar's band—Absolon's seat empty—on one side, Clara's on the other. Yusef was the only one of her allies already present, keeping his head down and biting at his thumbnail.

The seats the humans had occupied were now unnecessary and vacant.

Emrys took his place between the two factions that kept him out of the way of the glares that Clara and Ragnar lobbed at each other. He nodded to Ragnar and smiled at Wyatt. Wyatt smiled back. Yusef was lost in his own thoughts, but Emrys didn't sense any lingering mistrust and malevolence from the group for having killed one of their comrades. As the hours had passed and he had talked to them, the execution became less a real event and more a story to use as he saw fit.

Nimue arrived, her hair flowing and free around her shoulders and framing her pale skin and large doe eyes. She climbed into an empty chair almost opposite him but two off to his right. Smart girl.

He castigated himself.

Not girl, woman.

Denari arrived with such bounce in her step that she could have come from a carnival. She sat beside Clara's spot, then the woman herself arrived. Clara always liked to make a grand entrance, her slender chin upwards, her back curved in an elegant line to give her more length to look down her nose. Ragnar ignored her until she stopped behind her chair. Six empty seats remained with no one to fill them.

"Thank you all for coming," Clara said, as if they served for her pleasure. "It has been a trying day, but we cannot delay. Absolon's rashness has forced us into a new direction." Her gaze scoured the Darisami. Emrys stopped himself from cringing as her steel-gray eyes grazed him.

"We cannot restore Endurance to its former function," she said. "And, without action, we are destined to cower in these monstrous cocoons and starve to death. If we are honest, Endurance has been broken for a long time. The humans have not bred as much as needed. If not barren already, they will eventually become so, and considering what we have had to do to them today, I doubt they will be receptive to procreating. Plans for returning to the surface stalled years ago, and we cannot revive them on our own. We must find a new source of souls or perish. I for one have not survived this long only to die like a rat in a trap."

The group murmured consent. Emrys leaned back in

the uncomfortable chair to observe the Darisami. They all focused on Clara, even Ragnar, who slouched nonchalantly, with a scowl darkening his face. Agreeing with Clara would bring him pain.

"We know there are other arks out there. Until recently, we were in communication with one. It has since gone silent, but I refuse to believe humanity has died out. We need to find a new ark that is free of Darisami and claim it. Do you agree?"

Free of Darisami...

What if the Darisami's presence brought about the ark's failure?

Clara sat, assured her words had the desired effect.

Ragnar leaned forward. "We all see the need to find a new source, but who are you willing to sacrifice to the outside for this mission?"

"It is a concern, Clara," Denari said. "There is no guarantee of success. Whoever goes may perish before they find a soul to replenish their life force."

"Or maybe they'd keep the new ark for themselves." The soft way Yusef said it and the stunned look on his face when everyone swiveled to him revealed he hadn't intended to speak aloud.

"You raise a good point, however unsavory." Clara turned back to Denari, then directed her comments to the room. To Ragnar. "This is a difficult mission, but it is not our only hope. While one of us searches for a new source, the rest must attempt to sustain Endurance. These humans must last as long as possible. Meanwhile, Yusef's point is sound. Whoever goes must be trustworthy."

"In that case it won't be you." Wyatt's low blow earned him a reprimand from Ragnar.

Nimue rolled her eyes at Emrys.

"And I wouldn't trust you to stay and watch the prisoners for fear you'd go as mad as Absolon," Clara said. "Have you already forgotten to whom he held allegiance?"

Ragnar slammed his fist against the table. "You *dare* to burden me with Absolon's guilt when it is the decisions of the entire council that led us here? Our bickering and fear kept us locked inside, unable and unwilling to maintain contact with the rest of the world. We restricted the humans and lied to them, telling them communications were down or the arks had fallen silent well before they actually had, all because we feared an attack from other Darisami. So don't insult me, Clara, as we are *all* culpable."

They shouted across the room at each other, joined by Wyatt and Denari. Yusef kept his head down.

Then there were Emrys and Nimue. A slight smile painted her petite lips. When she met his eyes, she nodded.

He rose, breathing deeply to steady himself. "Darisami!" His voice boomed above their squabbling. He gestured to Clara. "We have a proposal to go forth and find a new source. Despite our differences, we can all agree—can we not?—that the time has come for a new field to harvest. I would have a show of hands."

All raised their hands except for Wyatt. "But that still doesn't solve—"

Emrys cut him off. "These arguments are easily overcome. There is division in Endurance. We cannot deny it, though it shames me to speak it. Watching the prisoners is a necessity, and we must find a way to lessen their suffering."

Denari sneered.

"There are many of them. We have subdued them, and many behave like frightened sheep. But among the sheep may be wolves who plot an attack. I do not say this to inspire eradication. I say this as a warning. Only two of us should go on this mission. The rest must stay behind to guard and, if required, slay them should they break free."

He softened his voice now that they were all so attentive. "Our secrets have been kept since our creation. The humans here are marked for death. They will not see a new world. But until the day we find a new source, they must remain alive, and we can harvest until then."

"If you have a suggestion for who should lead this mission, out with it. But I warn you…" Ragnar pointed at Clara's camp. "I won't accept one of them."

"Likewise," Clara said.

"I offer myself," Emrys said.

Ragnar grimaced.

Did he think he'd been played?

"You?" Denari blurted.

"Yes. I am not tied to a faction. I am the Master, impartial yet acting for the good of our community, fractured as it is. And admit it, some of you would prefer I was no longer around."

Clara fixed him with a look worthy of a starved python. "Good. The Master of High and Low Works, what a fitting choice."

Nimue stood. "And I will go with him."

"You?!" Ragnar and Clara shouted together before turning back to glare at each other.

Wyatt's mouth opened on a laugh that was more breath that sound. "No offence, Nimue, but what makes you think you'd be suitable?"

Nimue's eye twitched as it so often did when she was mistaken for an actual child. She gave a tight approximation of a smile, ducked her eyes, and looked at the floor. "Who else would be better? If you send two adults, the other ark may turn them away for fear they are bandits.

Send a man with a child and they are more likely to show compassion."

She swept her hair behind her ear.

"Emrys and I can concoct a story that would make anyone offer us their bed and rations. And a child can move freely without raising suspicions. They can see what adults don't. Brothers and sisters, you know this is our best hope."

"I never thought I'd hear the day you'd willingly *pretend* to be a child." Clara's patronizing tone chipped at Emrys's resolve to attempt consensus. What was it doing to Nimue?

She smiled but it had all the warmth of an LED. "Think of it as a sacrifice for the good of our survival."

"What say you, Emrys?" Ragnar asked. "Could you and Nimue pull this off?"

"When we find more humans, the pretense of her being my child will lead to our quick acceptance."

"Very well. Is anyone opposed?"

Some shook their heads. None raised their hands.

"It seems we have reached an agreement," Clara said. "Emrys and Nimue will go forth to locate a new ark and a fresh supply of humans. Once they have infiltrated the group, one will return for the rest of us, and we will seek asylum. After our admittance, we will guide the humans to rebuild their shattered civilization and venture out of their dead-end burrows." She turned to Emrys. "You leave tomorrow."

He bowed with a hand to his heart, accepting the council's dictum. His body warmed with the knowledge he'd guided them to accept him as the choice to go forth. It hadn't been as hard as he'd expected. And Nimue was going with him.

Only then did he allow himself to really wonder how much of the outside world remained after a confluence of tragedies had brought about its destruction. A worsening of the climate led to a scarcity of resources, combined with a few pandemics, and a fuckload of fear. War had been inevitable. As inevitable as death.

Darisami started to rise but Ragnar held up his hand. "Wait. They must be bonded."

Nimue's eyes flared, but Emrys spoke first. "You do not trust us?"

Bonding among the Darisami was rare and had never been done inside Endurance.

"It is not a question of trust, Emrys, but of necessity. We must know what happens to you. If you fail and perish, we must know. If you succeed, we can come sooner."

"Ragnar speaks sense for a change," Clara said. "So, either you agree to bond, or you don't go."

His skin crawled at the idea of having another inside his head, but he resisted a shiver. "Of course. Nimue and I will submit to bonding. Who shall share a soul with us?"

"Me." Ragnar's mouth opened enough to flash his teeth at Clara.

"Me too." Clara tried to make her response sound light and easy, but a tension weighed in her voice, like she was annoyed Ragnar answered first.

Emrys didn't care about their power play. The outcome was what mattered. Bonding one soul between three Darisami was unusual, let alone four, but it had its benefits. The more they shredded a soul, the less time the connection lasted.

"Very well, we agree. However, I demand Nimue and I be allowed to harvest a complete soul each to replenish our strength. We need to have as much time on our side as possible."

They agreed, and their agreement broke the dam restraining his hunger. It flooded into his stomach, like water smashing into parched earth, dried and resistant. Unable to take the deluge, he tried to hold on through his hunger's pounding. He'd fed eighteen days earlier, and the anticipation of feasting on a fresh soul almost swept his feet out from under him. The past sixty-five years had used so much of his mental energy in resisting his overwhelming need. He'd been disciplined and forced himself to believe that if feeding was not an option, then he could not feed. Simple as that.

But the feel of a soul as it swelled through him drenched every other thought in his mind. With a start, he realized he'd been thirsting. He'd been promised nourishment beyond what he was normally allowed. A treat! His body slavered to get it. Saliva filled his mouth, and he gulped it down. He mustn't make it look like a ploy to get his teeth into a new soul.

Who would it be?

Who would he choose?

The young ones were off limits. It would have to be someone old, of course, near the end of life. No reason to abandon that edict. He wanted a male, one not too defiant but not one that had been broken. One who showed a little bravado. That would be like swallowing elderflower wine.

"You will have a soul each but only because of your mission." The last Ragnar added lest any of the others thought they could take advantage of this situation. No doubt some of them had reaped a soul or two during the day's mayhem.

"Thank you," Emrys said.

Nimue bowed her head. The Darisami stood and departed. Ragnar left with Wyatt, and Yusef hurried out. Clara and Denari remained and approached Emrys. Nimue joined them.

"We are putting a lot of trust in you." Clara ignored

Nimue, who only came up to her shoulder. "Expending souls and losing two of our number are actions that should not be taken lightly, but I have faith in your abilities. Return to me with good news."

Did she say 'me' on purpose or was it a slip? Either was possible with Clara.

"We will do the Darisami proud," he said.

"Yes, and we will make sure *you* are the first to know of our success," Nimue added, the stress undeniable.

Emrys gave her a querying look.

"I look forward to hearing from you, Nimue." Clara's smile streaked across her face, then she rounded to leave with Denari by her side.

"Oh, Clara, before you go." Nimue ran over to her. "Watch Yusef. He needs our help at this time, and it would not be good for him to follow Absolon's path and defy our law. It wouldn't be good for you either."

Clara nodded, worry clear in her eyes even if her face remained stone.

When Clara and Denari were gone, Emrys took hold of Nimue's arm. "What are you playing at?"

"Let. Me. Go." If her eyes had been fire, he'd have third-degree burns.

He released her, regretting his rough handling. He uttered a sincere sorry.

She waved it away. "I do what is required."

"You're going to start a war."

"It won't come to that. If anything, I'm preventing one."

He choked on her words. "How?"

"If Yusef does what you and I think he's going to do, Ragnar's camp won't be able to control themselves and will blame Clara as she blames Ragnar for Absolon. Ragnar is too weak right now to lead on his own, and he's too raw from losing Absolon."

"But if you provoke Clara into thinking she's in charge, that will make things worse. We need Endurance secure as a backup."

"Clara won't act until we have succeeded. Ragnar will be able to keep her in check until then, and she'll do everything in her power to make sure she is seen as the reasonable and sensible choice for leader."

"Shaky, Nimue. Very shaky. If you go on like this, there won't be anyone left."

"Oh, Emrys, you do exaggerate." She laughed, slipped her hand into his, and squeezed. "Let's prepare for our journey. Who knows how long the road ahead will be? Or even if there's still one to walk."

⚜   4   ⚜

Emrys and Nimue rested overnight while the others patrolled. When he rose the next day, Nimue and Clara were waiting outside his door. Nimue was dressed in similar fashion to him, simple travelling gear that would last long enough through harsh weather. Their boots were solid and stopped midway up their calves, though these were hidden beneath dusky gray trousers. Their torsos were covered with a thick gray tunic, a hood hanging at their back. And underneath they wore long, white-sleeved shirts that hugged their skin.

Clara's thin frame was draped in a deep crimson skirt with a hem that hovered just above the floor. Wrapped around her thin middle she wore a belt of darkest black fabric with not a speck of dust. Long sleeves hid her hands.

"You always were such a late sleeper." Clara unfolded her arms, spun on her heel, and strode for the elevator. He and Nimue followed.

The ride up four floors stretched for an age, his insides twisting until they sang. He dug his nails deeper into his palms, hoping the pain would distract him. It couldn't look like he wanted this.

Nimue slipped her hand into his, smoothing out his fingers and holding tight. It helped. A bit. He could crush her hand, and she wouldn't flinch. She'd crush back. The need eased and settled in the base of stomach, ready to launch.

Soon.

The elevator stopped. Denari was waiting. Wyatt walked the corridor.

"We have chosen for you, but if there's anyone you'd like in particular…" Denari's voice was level as if she had asked him what he'd like to drink.

He shook his head, and she smiled. He wished he could see through the doors to who suffered inside. He would have known who to choose then and make this as easy as possible on them and him.

This was a lucky dip, and his excitement turned rancid.

Denari led them down the corridor and they stopped outside apartment 8143. The room's inhabitant was banging on the other side.

Ragnar approached them. Like Clara, he was dressed in his most formal clothing—sturdy black trousers and a white shirt that hugged his built frame. Considering how he'd looked the day before, it was a marked improvement. The forlorn expression was gone and replaced with his usual hardness, eyes carved from granite.

"Emrys, you take this one," Clara said. "Nimue, next door. Then Ragnar and I will split a third with you. Agreed?"

They nodded. The banging got louder.

"Good. Denari." Clara gestured for her to proceed.

Emrys readied himself. The Darisami formed a wall to stop anyone rushing out, and Denari pressed the sensor to open the door. Emrys's gaze met the startled eyes of a man he didn't know. His victim staggered back, and Emrys charged him. His hand wrapped around his victim's throat. The door closed behind them.

The man looked about fifty-five but had enough fight within him to try to tear Emrys's iron grip from his neck. So many of those born inside Endurance were weak and poorly. Perhaps it was the lack of sunlight. But not this one.

"It's okay." Emrys tried to inject a soothing tone into his voice, but hunger stripped it raw. "Everything's going to be okay."

The man's eyes pleaded with him. Emrys didn't want to see his pain. Murder was best performed in the dark. He closed his eyes.

The harvest symbol formed in his head without thought, without trying. He'd remember that symbol even if he forgot his own name. Lines and curves interlocked until they glowed the color of blue sapphire, vivid and clear. He imagined the symbol in the palm of his hand and so it was. He let it go, and it touched his victim's skin.

The man choked on his cries.

And his soul connected with Emrys's hand, a light brush against his palm. He sucked in a rapid rush of breath. The soul was pure, no matter what trauma the man suffered. A cool but forceful breeze swept into him, and the human sagged as his flagging vitality entered Emrys. His grip on the man's throat was all that held him up. In the blessed darkness, in his private world, Emrys drew the soul into his ravenous body.

Daylight twinkled beneath his skin as he took all that the man had been. His name was Henry. Flavors of his life filtered into him—a bleak thing stuck in Endurance yet not discontent. He caught oil on his tongue like it had landed on Henry's skin and he'd kissed it off with a tender brush of his lips. He inhaled a woman's scent, his lover, and a surge of worry for her wellbeing. On a better day, Emrys could have lingered and dissected every aspect of Henry's life and found who that woman had been and what their love had been. He could have pieced together their life and written a biography deeper than anything anyone—including Henry—could have constructed.

He breathed in essence, untarnished with fallacies and affectation. What he tasted was the freshness of a down-to-earth man who got on with life despite his troubles. Any other day, he would have explored that further. Any other day, he would have celebrated all that Henry had been. Any other day, he would have been gentle.

But he did not have another day, and he consumed Henry in half a minute, dragging every last shred of the nourishing soul into his body.

Henry's heart stopped. Emrys lay him on the floor and swayed, energy coursing through his blood, as refreshing as the morning spray off the ocean. It swept away the crustiness that stuck to his insides. How had he coped through sixty-five years?

Order. Restraint. Survival.

But that was then. Now he was awash in this beautiful soul as it fluttered through him. He breathed deep, the air pushing the soul to the very edge of his body.

He moaned.

"Could we get on with this?" Ragnar's gravel-toned voice intruded.

His eyes shot open, and he spun to face Ragnar and the others. The door had opened without him noticing. Fury scorched his gullet, and the loving caress of the soul turned to a fire's brand. They could have had the decency to give him this moment of solitude. He hated feeding where others could see him, but he had to control himself.

Nimue was looking at him, but her eyes were slightly unfocused, and she had a small smile in the corner of her mouth. She'd been quick. He'd follow her lead next time. Suck out the soul and savor it while looking as if your mind was present. He was rusty.

Too rusty.

Ragnar gestured for him to follow, and he joined the procession down the hall.

"Do you all remember the symbols for bonding?" Clara couldn't hide her condescension.

"Do you?" Ragnar said.

Clara pursed her lips before stopping outside the door to apartment 8145. A look passed between her and Denari.

"We won't have any trouble with this one." Denari's words were as soft as snow, her eyes were as sharp as sleet. Who had she chosen?

Denari opened the door. A small solitary boy sobbed in the far corner of the room. He couldn't be more than six years old.

Emrys's chest hollowed out. "Clara, no! Not him."

"Yes, him." She pushed up her sleeves and entered the room. The others followed.

What happened to their compact, their *honor*?

"He's too young. We only take the old ones." He forced air and authority into his words.

"Normally, yes, but the younger the soul, the stronger the bond. We can't have you slipping your shackles before you complete your task."

"Not. Him." He stayed as far from the boy as he could while still standing in the room. He crossed his arms over his chest and cleared his mind of any symbol. They couldn't force him to take a child's life.

"You'll eat steak but not veal?" Clara gestured at the

boy with a flat palm. "Your sentimentality is foolish. He will die anyway."

The boy pleaded for his mother.

"Ragnar, you can't agree with this."

"Why can't I? Clara speaks true. We need some reassurance, and the younger the better." He and Clara approached the child who cowered and hid his eyes.

"Nimue? Do you accept this?"

"I do." Her eyes, face, tone blank.

"And yet I do not," he said.

He'd not killed a child since the night Sian died.

Clara pulled the gold knife from out of her sleeves. "You have a choice—do this or die in Endurance."

When had she taken the knife from his room? That was *his* knife, and if anyone was going to be threatened with it, it was going to be her. Could he snatch it from her and slaughter them all? Or would he be overpowered despite his recent soul injection? Denari moved at the edge of his vision. He would not get far.

I am a foul thing.

He gave a small nod, but even that tiny movement made him nauseous.

"Very well." Clara slipped the knife back from where she'd drawn it. "Ragnar, pick him up."

The boy was too terrified to resist. He didn't even squirm as he was lifted off the floor and held by both arms against Ragnar's chest. Clara and Nimue each took hold of one of the boy's hands. Ragnar's palms were already on the boy's bare skin.

Emrys's gorge rose at the back of his throat, saliva flooding his mouth until he thought he'd be sick.

I do not want to do this. I do not want to do this.

"On the count of three." Clara glared at Emrys.

Nimue hissed at him to hurry up. "The boy is doomed anyway."

Perhaps I can make something of his sacrifice.

Emrys placed the heel of his palm against the boy's forehead, sweat plastering his fringe.

I'm sorry.

"One…" Clara said.

It had begun.

The boy peeked up at him. Fear twisted his face.

Emrys closed his eyes.

The first symbol…

"Two…"

The second…

He lingered at the end of it, not wanting to go forward.

"Three."

His pulse quickened.

God, how he hated this. God, how he wanted it.

The symbols lit and shot down his hand. The boy shrieked. No soft sigh for him. No peaceful passing. They sliced his soul into four parts, and the trauma they inflicted would be revisited on themselves and have them all retching in the corner when it was done. He held on to the hope the snippet he'd score would outshine the bitter after-taste of such an unholy act.

The boy's soul unlocked from his body and became fluid. Emrys braced while the four Darisami struggled to hold on. They weren't fighting each other—they were fighting the soul. They tugged and stretched, until the soul split like the ripping of a piece of cloth. The boy's scream shook Emrys to the core. He kept his eyes slammed tight, blocking his ears to the wailing. Thread by thread, the soul came apart, and the momentum broke it into four.

One piece embedded itself in him.

He snatched back his palm as if burned, and the boy's

head slumped forward. Emrys staggered to the wall and leaned against it, but it wasn't enough to keep him upright. He couldn't stay with the little corpse. He stumbled through the door, his insides twisting with the poisoned morsel of the destroyed young soul, and collapsed to the ground, heaving, focusing on the scuffs and dirt. He sucked in breath like it was the last bit of oxygen on Earth and readied himself for the final part of the bonding.

He sought the shard, *hunted* it, and strove to reach its golden light while avoiding the sharp edges. It rebounded against the hollowness of his chest and sparked wherever it hit. He grasped it and cursed as it sliced his mind. He imagined bringing it to his lips like a leaf that held a few drops of precious water while he drifted on an endless sea. It touched his tongue, and he thirsted no more.

Blessed be the Creator.

He sighed. The worst had passed. He slowly sank back on his ankles. The vileness of what they'd done curdled in his stomach. How could they do that to a child? How could *he* have done that to a child?

Clara appeared, smoothed her dress, and brushed aside Denari's helping hand. Ragnar was tense. Nimue wasn't in his eyeline.

His mind buzzed, a fuzziness spreading across it. Awareness. He focused.

Are you all right? Nimue's voice chimed in his head.

I will be. The fuzziness increased in intensity. Ragnar and Clara insisted on his attention. He opened to them while projecting into them. Thoughts melded, and his mind added their unique voices to set them apart. Without the voices, he still could have known who was who.

Ragnar's thoughts were earthy and colored crimson. Clara's were crisp and made of glass. Nimue's were black and solid. She stepped out of the room and frowned at him. Emrys got to his feet. The bodies of the men and the little boy were in the corridor bound for the incinerator. Bile surged at the back of Emrys's throat, and he swallowed hard to keep it down.

"Ugh, being in your head is like traipsing through a smoky brothel, Ragnar." Clara screwed up her mouth.

"Something you'd know a lot about."

Clara glared at him.

Be quiet, both of you. Nimue's voice thundered inside Emrys's head.

Clara's mouth opened, but Emrys spoke first. "I think we're done. It works. It's time we left."

Clara nodded, cast a disdainful look at Ragnar, and led the way to the elevator.

Denari sidled up to Emrys. "How does it feel?" Her voice crawled into his ear.

He sealed his lips, and she chuckled and ran to catch up to Clara. How Denari had survived the past six decades was beyond him.

They entered the elevator and ascended to the uppermost level in silence, but their thoughts were not still. He didn't pry into their minds, but he sensed an electric hum like those bug zappers that used to hang from porches on summer nights.

Ragnar's nostrils flared like a bull preparing to charge. Clara's smile was honed, and her eyes wide and round. She strummed her fingers across her folded arm. He checked himself. He'd been biting his bottom lip and tracing the eternity symbol on his thigh. He stopped both, straightened his stance. He could not show uncertainty. He could not show remorse. The child was dead. He had to live with his part in that. Getting away from Endurance would help.

The doors opened onto the entrance hall on the top

floor, and they filed out. Yusef was waiting and offered each of them a pack. "A few things for the road."

The packs were shabby but that was part of the costume. They'd been pulled out of storage in pristine condition but been rubbed in grease with a few holes cut in them for good measure. Inside was a knife, some dehydrated food, a canister filled with water, a gun in a holster, a few magazines, a compass, torch, and a pair of sunglasses. Wyatt had suggested a doll for Nimue, but she'd scowled the suggestion out of existence.

Emrys pulled the gun and holster out of the bag and strapped it around his waist.

"And my knife?" He held his hand out to Clara.

She didn't move. "It's staying."

That was *his* knife. He'd carried it for five centuries and slaughtered dozens of Darisami with it. It belonged to him. It was part of him, and he'd be damned if he'd leave it behind. "What if I need it?"

"Improvise."

"See sense, Emrys." Nimue clipped a steel bowie knife to her waist. "How would it look for a survivor wandering the world carrying a knife of solid gold?"

Clara's smile widened in direct proportion to Emrys's glower. That knife was his protection, his ward against being just another Darisami parasite.

"I want it back."

"Then you had better succeed," Clara said.

He slipped on the sunglasses. The knife would be his payment for never seeing these Darisami again.

"If there's nothing else?" Clara smirked.

Emrys and Nimue were escorted to the giant entry doors. They hadn't been opened in years, not since some humans thought the world must have changed and sought to test their theory. The Darisami hadn't stopped them but they had stopped them returning. Once out, they were out for good, and a suggestion that they might have been cont-aminated meant their pleading went unanswered.

Wyatt and Denari said goodbye. Yusef hugged Emrys for a long time, then took his hands, raised them to his lips, and kissed them. He looked into Emrys's eyes. "I wish you a safe journey."

"Thank you, brother."

Yusef knelt to Nimue and repeated the ritual then moved away, not staying to watch them leave. A thought resonated inside Emrys's soul with the certainty of death. Perhaps it was better the knife stayed behind.

Clara and Ragnar came forward and assessed them like they were a secret weapon about to be launched on an unprepared enemy.

"You both know how important this mission is to all of us," Clara said. "You go with our faith and with our hope."

"We expect to be kept informed." Ragnar raised his eyebrows, letting them convey his warning: desert us and I'll come for you.

Farewells and orders given, the doors opened onto a long dark tunnel that stretched for half a mile. They'd walk it alone. With a final look to the group, Emrys slung his pack over his shoulders and proceeded with Nimue by his side.

Lights flickered on as they walked, dispelling the hollow darkness. The doors slid behind them, scraping against the railings, and sealed them in. And out. Like a tomb, leaving those five Darisami locked in Endurance.

"Race you?" Nimue disappeared down the tunnel. The lights couldn't detect her fast enough and the blackness swallowed her.

He laughed despite himself, and the sound echoed,

spurring him into a run. His feet barely touched the ground, unhampered by fallen scraps of metal.

It felt good to run. Though Endurance had been large, he hadn't been able to stretch his legs. The place was so closed that the walls towered in and over him. Sheets of metal curled around his body and bound him in place. Running, and at such speed, was a freedom he'd missed.

Wait until I'm in the open air.

He reached the end of the tunnel.

"You're slow, Emrys."

"I'm not slow. You've got lower wind resistance." He chuckled.

She kicked him, and he cursed. The lights detected their presence and sputtered to a dim glow. When he could see again, she wore a sweet smile that acid couldn't melt.

The giant metal doors separated, and a wedge of bright light broke through. Even with sunglasses on, Emrys shielded his eyes with his hand.

So much light!

The world was his once more.

❃   5   ❃

THE YELLOW-TINGED SKY SPILLED ABOVE EMRYS AS AN untroubled pool of toxic water. Ahead lay sand and rocks. In the distance lay mountains. A haze hung low, skirting the horizon like a smear of shit. Endurance had been built in the desert, far from rising tides and fault lines, carved out of the side of a rock face and buried. Nothing much had changed over sixty-five years except the heat. It felt hotter.

No footprints or tracks directed their path towards a new home or supply. Someone else had to be alive. Somewhere. The hairs on the back of his neck raised. What if Endurance contained the last sorry remnants of human civilization? The Darisami would be even more endangered than he'd thought. The stark sky left nowhere for delusions to gather. This could be his end.

The left side of his brain buzzed, insistent yet ignorable. Not that he would. Not yet.

Yes, Clara?

Her thoughts whipped him as if she was surprised at the contact. She recovered, though being farther away from her, he felt superior. He was free—in a way—and he was strong enough to withstand this unforgiving land for at least a month.

Have you found anything?

Nimue looked at him, her forehead creased. He rolled his eyes and pointed to his head. She pursed her lips. Clara hadn't contacted her.

Patience, Clara, we're only just outside the gates.

Well, hurry!

We will take as long as required and will be in touch when something important happens.

Her thoughts seemed to draw back breath, but he jumped in before she could argue.

Tell Ragnar, too. I don't want you two buzzing in my head at all hours. Do you want me to go mad?

Silence stretched.

See that you don't, she said.

She left with such speed his mind burned. Getting used to her consciousness would take time.

Nimue waited for an explanation.

"Clara. Wanting to know what we had found so far."

"She tries my patience."

He laughed, but the sound sank. Talking aloud made him uncomfortable. Too much space, no walls to keep the sound in, and only one person to hear it. Talking mind-to-mind was almost a comfort as it provided a boundary. How easily he'd become caged. Thinking on the exchange with Clara, he noticed she'd appeared on the left side of his head.

"Think something to me."

She flinched as if the sound spooked her. Perhaps she'd thought she was alone. "What?"

"Think something to me. I want to test a theory."

She sighed a deep, heavy sigh laden with the irritability

of the elderly. She fixed him with a stare that had him shifting to scratch an itch between his shoulders. Those old eyes in her young face…

Her thoughts intruded like she'd driven a tank into his head. It didn't hurt, not in the normal way of pain, but it pressed against his brain. If she'd tried harder, could she have broken through and rummaged through his thoughts? He'd always believed the bonding was built on reciprocity and an imposed respect. A mind couldn't be violated against its will, as if it were read-only. Now he wasn't so sure.

What he did know, however, was Nimue's thoughts nestled in the back of his skull, in a place separate from Clara's. It was discrete and distinct. Ragnar might appear on the right. He smiled. Now he'd know who to block, imagining a steel wall that sealed them off and kept him safe.

"What did you discover?"

Rather than speak he projected into her mind. It was like picking his way through nettles and low-hanging thorns. He lost what he wanted to tell her, distracted by the shadows of an overgrown forest. He couldn't pierce the darkness, but he knew menacing beasts lurked within. He'd always known she was tough, deeper than the others, and hid more than she revealed, but this worried him.

What? she said.

He shook himself and told her what he'd found out about the positioning of the others' thoughts.

Excellent. Dull gray tinged her thoughts. He suspected she'd already worked this out and neglected to tell him.

That was his own fault for not thinking of it sooner. Like a chastened child, he retreated from the briar patch of her mind and set his sights on the unmarked path ahead.

According to the maps they'd pulled up on the central computers in Endurance, the nearest ark was about four hundred miles south-west. They needed to get moving. It would be better if they reached shelter before the moon showed her face and caught them.

He hefted the pack onto his shoulders. "Let's run." He broke into a sprint with Nimue following behind, her short legs in no way a hindrance.

His stride lengthened the more distance he covered, and his muscles rejoiced at being free. The land passed beneath his feet in a blur of browns and yellows, and air filled his ears.

Speed erased conscious thought, so there was just him and the earth he pounded. He pushed himself faster and the landscape changed. The mountains neared, and the sun dipped. They ran on the bed of a dried lake. Dirt turned to mud, and mud turned to an inch of water then two. He longed to submerge himself, but it never got deep.

They reached the mouth of the stream that had once been a raging river, a trickle compared to a flood. Ancient and fallen trees lined the edge like crumbling sentinels, their craggy arms devoid of the fat of fertility. They were bones ready to crumble into splinters. They watched as Nimue and Emrys followed the river.

Silence persisted. If he made a noise, it would turn unwanted eyes on him, nebulous though they were. Like the eyes of God seeking the sinner, there wasn't anywhere to hide. How far and how long they had run, he didn't know but somewhere beyond the mountains and on the plains, Nimue hissed and brought him to a sharp halt.

"What—" But he didn't need to finish.

The sun had dropped beneath the horizon and turned the sky a deep orange. Twilight had arrived, and the first pinpricks of starlight pierced the dark canvas. The moon was a waning crescent, a time of rest.

And surrender.

A gentle phosphorescence rose beneath Nimue's skin. It was gentle at first, a slight hue that brightened her skin and eyes, a fuzzy light in the gathering gloom. He held up his hands and light broke through. As the sun set and night settled, the glow intensified. The souls they'd recently imbibed shone through their skin by the light of the moon. They stood as beacons.

He swore and searched for shelter. They couldn't approach any human that night without frightening them —or worse, sparking some guff about divine beings coming down to the earthly plane to deliver a miracle. Any Darisami walking the land would spot them too and wonder why they were so healthy. They hadn't long left the mountains and though he hated to double-back and lose ground, they provided the only surety. They could hide in a cave and wait out the night. He ran, knowing she would follow.

Though only small parts of his body were exposed— his face, hands, and neck—the strength of the souls illuminated far more of his form, projecting an intense glow around those parts for half a yard. The dread of night settled upon him. It was an old, forgotten pain he'd avoided living in Endurance from a time when he'd been unwilling to walk abroad on a moonlit night for fear of inspiring the blighted masses. The illumination served no purpose to the Darisami. All it did was warn others and hold Darisami captive to the daylight hours or those few blessed nights when the moon hid her face.

With each fleeting footstep on the ground, he ran into his memories of the night Sian died. He couldn't run fast enough to save her. He hadn't known Robert saw him kill

Lysander with the golden knife. Emrys had glowed so brightly that whatever Robert had seen could only have been part of the truth. Emrys killed that Darisami, that Lysander, for his threats to his daughter's life, for his false declarations of love, but it had been for naught.

He had saved Sian from Lysander, but not from the villagers' superstitious madness. The flames ended her screams the moment he arrived. The people who had been his friends and community charged him with their pitchforks and halberds.

He emptied the village of souls, then dropped in front of his shop and home's burning wreckage. The top floor had collapsed, and his house became a bonfire that leapt to the next and the next until the village was blackened and burned to the ground, and all his tears had dried.

They reached the foothills of the mountains and found a cave to bunker down in until the moon passed.

"That could prove problematic," she said.

The light had always been a problem.

He sat on the ground with his back leaning against the rock wall, and tiredness covered him like a chainmail blanket. She sat, and he put his arm around her. In the darkness, she almost felt like Sian.

�֎ 6 ֎

THE SHARP LIGHT OF DAWN STOLE INTO THE CAVE'S MOUTH and woke them. They'd slept, a merciful blessing Emrys had always been thankful for. To never sleep, to never dream, to never escape the horror of what he was would have been intolerable. He was sure sleep wasn't necessary, nothing needed to be regenerated or renewed—Darisami were built to be unstoppable—but he felt rested.

Nimue wore a smile, warm like the morning, as she lifted her head off his lap. "Are you ready?"

He nodded, and they raced from the cave.

Dawn vanished. They sped across a scorched land, desolate and blighted by drought. They needed to get out of the mountains and cross the plains to reach the closest ark.

What hope did they have of finding anyone alive out there? Endurance was an anomaly. It had survived as long as it had against the odds but even it couldn't hold out forever. Inevitability had crept in and rusted it from the outside in. Doomed. Like the rest of the planet. He fixed his eyes ahead, aware of the thoughts that slid between his joints and popped. He had a mission. The sun beat down as it rose to claim the sky and force him to his knees. He couldn't fail.

But maybe failure was the only option.

Onward they ran and hours passed. The right side of his head vibrated, and he stopped short.

What is it, Ragnar?

Emrys couldn't keep the biting tone out of his thoughts, and Ragnar snarled. Emrys would have to watch himself, but the intrusion into his head tested his patience.

I'm checking you two are still alive.

Emrys looked at Nimue. Her eyes were pointed right and up. He gestured for her to jump into his head so they could share thoughts. She bloomed at the back of his skull, and he let her in.

Yes, we're alive, she thought.

Emrys sighed. She brought him a comfort he would be ashamed to admit to aloud. He had a companion to stand with him against outside forces. She held the line with him against the power-hungry duo.

I'm glad to hear it, Nimue. Have you found anything yet?

It's deserted. Nothing lives out here, but we're not far from Fortitude.

Let's pray there is something there worth finding.

How is Endurance? Emrys asked.

Some humans refuse to eat. Nearly all of them cry.

Emrys didn't have anything to say to that lest the color of his thoughts betray him.

They'll quieten down eventually, Nimue said.

That or they'll die. Ragnar's thoughts were resigned but lacked sympathy. A name flickered through his mind, not strong enough to form completely but they knew he'd been thinking of Absolon. *God speed.* Then Ragnar was gone.

"We're better off out here," she said.

Emrys's mouth screwed up like he'd eaten the soul of a rapist.

The sun breached its zenith and dipped down the other side. As soon as they noticed the dipping of the solar sentinel, they pushed themselves harder. He didn't want to admit the moon frightened him or that a need to get back beneath some sort of structure invaded his stomach.

Fortitude was smaller than Endurance, capable of holding a couple of thousand. Like many other arks, it had been carved into rock. The great construction phase in the dying days of the American Empire had brought together monstrous diggers to rip the bowels out of the earth and create a haven for humanity's remnants. The work had expanded quickly but expertly. Emrys had avoided the builders and planners, architects and ministers who had overseen the project, but he saw what it had done to the people living in the area.

As construction continued and they could see an end, people panicked. Tension filled the air like quick-drying cement. Human emotions were never rational at the best of times. Faced with their extinction, they went raving. No amount of placating or reassurances that there would be a place for all, that no one would be left behind, kept them from vying for the limited places they believed—or perhaps knew—existed.

They were right.

In those final days, taking souls had been a mercy for the humans. Too many were spoiled with the thought of abandonment and distress over what was to come. The Darisami picked off a few before the end, as an act of mercy, and snuck into the arks before the doors closed sixty-five years ago. They invested themselves in the robes of normal citizens and civic responsibility, committing themselves to seeing the human race—and the Darisami —survive.

As Emrys and Nimue crested a small hill, they found what they'd been looking for.

But it was hopeless.

The iron gates that protected Fortitude were bent open like they'd been attacked with a giant can opener. Rusted and sharp edges protruded outwards revealing a black-as-coal belly. Communications with Fortitude had gone silent decades ago and now they knew why.

"Should we keep going?" he asked.

"There might be someone left. They might have a better idea of what is going on with the other arks." He caught the glint in her eye like that of a wolf stalking a wounded stag, but she glanced away, and it was gone.

They stepped across the threshold. The wind had blown sand into the entrance and scattered it down the tunnel. She pulled out a torch and lit the tunnel's internal organs. Pipes and conduit ran like veins and arteries but no heart pumped life through them. Only their boots on the sand, stone, and concrete made a sound. It echoed too loud for a space too large. It oppressed them and kept them silent. He examined the edges of the light for any movement but there was none.

They reached the opened elevator doors, a seemingly endless drop inside the shaft.

"Is there any point?" he asked.

She scanned the hallway with her torch, the spotlight shining on the remains of a home abandoned. A few benches for the people to sit on and wait, a scarf strewn across the floor next to a sandal and a satchel. Other bits of detritus. Musty. Empty.

"Let's have a quick look." She hooked the torch

through the handle of her backpack and climbed into the shaft, finding the ladders that scaled its walls. The light jerked and swung, shining randomly though casting enough light to see the rungs. Emrys followed and fell into a rhythm, his hands and feet finding a safe route. The doors were closed on the second and third floors down but open on the fourth. They exited.

"Just like home." He eyed the sleeping quarters, their contents thrown out of the doorways and scattered on the floor. The residents had left in a hurry, but where had they gone? Or maybe it was rats. The blasted oversized things had caused trouble in Endurance by getting into the wiring. Perhaps they'd done the same there.

She leaned over the balcony, shining her light over the ark's bones.

No flesh.

"Where are the bodies? Where is anything to show what happened?" Her voice strained.

"Who knows how long it's been like this? Everything could have rotted, and scavengers come to take the remains."

"There should be something." She scanned the depths with the torch and sucked in her breath. "There." Her whispered word fired into the dark.

"What was it?"

"A shadow moved. Quick." She dived off the edge of the balcony, her descent taking his stomach with her, and he forced the rest of himself to follow.

Slicing through the stale air, he sped towards the ground then rolled at the last second and came to his feet. Nimue was already running with the torch in her hand. The shadows shortened and lengthened as the light waved while she chased the lone survivor. Emrys saw the man.

His terror-stricken face kept turning back to the light

that hunted him down. He sobbed and shrieked, his long greasy brown hair flicking back and forth and framing wide open eyes. Nimue launched herself on him, and he collapsed to the ground in a wailing mess. Begging. Pleading. Crying.

"Stop that noise!" She rolled him over and sat on his chest to pin him to the ground.

What must he have thought, being beaten by a child he should have by rights been able to brush aside with no more than a firm wave of his arm? Then again, looking at the man, it was doubtful he could have even managed the thought, let alone the deed.

He was emaciated, his arms stripped of muscle, the skin having nothing to wrap itself around except bone. The rest of his body wasn't much better, and his skin was a pale yellow. He had a small head, or it would have appeared so on a filled-out body but on him it was over-large, bulbous, and slightly triangular. His beard was matted and full. He definitely wasn't Darisami.

The man blubbered louder.

Emrys crouched. "Hey, we're not here to hurt you. We're after information."

He continued to cry like an infant.

Nimue slapped the man, and his mouth closed. He choked on the tears and snot that clogged his throat. "Much better. What's your name?"

"A-a-a-Andrew. Please don't hurt me."

"Hello, Andrew. I'm Nimue, and this is Emrys. We're not here to hurt you." She spoke in a sing-song voice that prickled Emrys's skin. "Where is everyone?"

Andrew ummed and ahhed and searched for a way out.

Emrys clicked his fingers in front of Andrew's face. "Hey, focus!"

"They're all gone."

"We can see that. Where?"

"Nowhere. Just gone. One day, here. Next day, not."

"Were they here when you arrived?"

"Who?"

"The people."

"What people?"

"The people who lived here."

"No one lives here. Can't you see we're all that's left?"

Emrys grabbed the torch from Nimue's bag and shone it in Andrew's face. His eyes were unfocused, shifting constantly like he chased the movement of moths. Had he been there when Fortitude was still alive, or had he turned up later?

A putrid smell assaulted Emrys's nostrils. Andrew had soiled himself though he didn't seem to notice or mind.

"We won't get anything useful from him now," Nimue said. "We could wait to see if he has a lucid moment, but I doubt it."

Emrys grunted.

"Do you want him?" she asked.

Mercy. That's all they could give him. Even if it was plainly self-serving.

"You can have him." He stepped away.

"Who are you people?" Andrew asked. "Do you have permission to be here?"

"It's all right, Andrew," she said. "We're going to help you find them."

"Really? Mother's been dead ten years. I think she'll be the hardest to find, but then again she was awfully good at cribbage."

Was it really mercy when they didn't know they were in pain?

He sensed her forming the symbols and Andrew's soul

unlocking. She drew it in rapidly, and Andrew died. She sighed with endless contentment. Then she smiled like a stoned teenager and staggered up from the corpse. A rat squeaked in the darkness. At least Andrew would provide a meal for more than one.

"What now?" she asked.

"Keep searching? Andrew might not have been alone."

They searched Fortitude but found no one else. Andrew was the last. They looked for any signs of what had happened, but other than a general sense of abandonment, Fortitude kept its secrets. The network systems had been fried, but they couldn't tell whether that was what led to Fortitude's collapse or came afterwards. A thick layer of dust coated everything.

They spent the night inside Fortitude, and he gravitated to what would have been his room in Endurance on the fourth floor, apartment twelve. Nimue didn't join him. After he said he was going to rest, she turned away, calling back from the gloom that she'd wake him in the morning.

Freedom was next.

Next.

He was even less pleased at the idea than before. What did they have to look forward to? Maybe the next place would have skeletons, some sign it had survived longer than Fortitude. They knew of no Darisami in Fortitude, so did that mean having Darisami had saved Endurance from collapse?

He laughed as he lay down on the still-made single bed. Endurance was finished as well.

<hr>

Coarse rope tightened around Emrys's wrists and burned his skin before morphing into the feel of Nimue's small fingers stroking his hand and enticing him into wakefulness. The world fell into gloomy form, but he cast her hand away. He knew there was no rope but not until he checked its absence with his own hands could he dispel the feeling.

"How did you sleep?" She perched on the edge of his bed.

"Well enough. And you? Did you sleep?"

"Some, after I searched again."

"Nothing?"

"Andrew was the last."

He swung his legs out of bed. "Let's go then." He headed for the door, and she followed. Scooping his backpack up from the floor, he left the sleeping quarters and they made it back to the exit.

The sun had just risen but already it had bite. Dewy mornings with the pleasant call of larks and robins were a thing of the distant unreachable past. He looked back to where they'd come, hills blocking the way, forests of skeletons crossing his view. It had taken them a day and a half to reach Fortitude, though it would have been less if the moon hadn't shone. Freedom was about five days from where they were, larger and therefore able to take in a greater number of people. It seemed a long way to go for disappointment.

"Have you spoken to Endurance?" she asked.

He shook his head. He should have done it yesterday when they'd reached Fortitude but, in the face of such emptiness, he couldn't stand to have Clara and Ragnar scratching around inside his brain. Now that he was outside, he wished he'd done it earlier. The two voices seemed like a couple of prisoners locked in a cell and, though he knew they couldn't take control of his body, doubt gnawed at him. What if the inmates could take over the prison? If they could see through his eyes, they might attempt to break out, safely exploring the surroundings by controlling his body.

I'm being paranoid.

Ragnar and Clara would stay in Endurance until the other died. There would be no ground ceded in that war.

He sighed. His mind touched Nimue's first, the dark forest of thorns less spiky today, before reaching out to the other two. They unfurled in his skull.

What have you found? Clara's serrated voice sawed against his synapses.

And it's a pleasure to hear from you too, Clara.

Her mind darkened just as when she narrowed her eyes.

Are you two all right? Ragnar asked.

Emrys analyzed the concern in Ragnar's thoughts and found it weighted more in his favor than Nimue's. Interesting.

We're fine, Nimue said, *but Fortitude is an empty shell. We found one survivor who couldn't give us any useful information.*

What did you do with him? Clara's thought was wary and shrewd.

Do you really need to ask?

Let's hope you two don't get your full appetites back.

It was a mercy killing, Clara, he replied. *His mind was gone, but we thought it best not to leave witnesses.*

We can live with that, Ragnar said. *So, you found nothing of use?*

Nimue delivered a brief report of their explorations. Clara and Ragnar paid hungry interest to what Emrys considered useless trivia. Perhaps they thought Fortitude could be restored. He doubted it.

Freedom is next, Emrys said. *It will take us at least five days.*

Why so long? Clara's question fired like a machine gun.

The moon, Nimue said. *We're too exposed at night when it shines. We don't want to give rise to any panic, and who knows if humans have ventured out of the arks. The land hardly seems able to support anything so it's unlikely but not impossible. The air is clear enough, wouldn't you agree, Emrys?*

Yes. It's best we travel by day and shelter at night. Even then we can't run too fast. It would look unnatural.

I don't think you have— Clara said.

This is how we're doing it, Clara. Unless there's some urgent news you need us to hear, we're going to get on our way. What of Endurance?

The prisoners have mostly quietened down, Ragnar said. *All except a few have accepted food, but we're monitoring those who refuse.*

No sorry or pity laced his thoughts. He merely gave a clinical assessment of the situation, with a touch of bother that there should be some pockets of resistance.

Very well. Until we talk again.

The voices faded from his head like a fog disappearing from a moor.

"That was unpleasant," Nimue said. "I don't like having those two in my head."

He laughed. "What about me?"

"Oh, you're all right. Clara is just so sharp, and Ragnar's like an avalanche. The sooner this wears off the better. Then we'll never have to hear their voices again."

"You think they won't come after us even after we lose contact?" he said.

"It depends how it all plays out."

"True. Besides, I think we have a couple of months before the soul dissipates and we're left alone."

"And who knows what might happen by then?"

"Yes, I wonder."

Nimue laughed in a high pitch befitting a young girl,

but the maturity behind it revealed a woman much wiser than her form suggested. He loved to hear her laugh, even if it was never as carefree as he expected.

He turned his back on Fortitude and started to run. Five more days, six at the most, then Freedom.

❦   7   ❦

Freedom...

No survivors, but plenty of bones. They reported the news to Ragnar and Clara, then kept going. Their footsteps hastened, worry catching at their heels as they kicked up the dust of a country gone silent.

🙦   8   🙤

INDEPENDENCE...

Doors blasted open from the inside. Dried blood on the walls.

They spent the night huddled in the entrance, the wind shrieking at them like banshees. The moment the sun rose, they fled Independence. They didn't speak much. They had to keep going.

Nineteen days before he needed a soul.

❦ *9* ❧

Liberty…

The ark had succumbed, and they didn't stay longer than they had to. They ran until moonlight forced them to hide, and as soon as the moon faded, they ran again. His body squeezed the soul he'd had in Endurance of every bit of sustenance.

Fifteen days 'til harvest.

❦ 10 ❦

Salvation...

Another ark abandoned. Ragnar and Clara shouted inside his head to move faster, panic in their thoughts as time ran out and not a soul roamed the dead earth.

Victory...

Fallen.

Providence was their last hope but that was still three days away, and he was weakening. Nimue had fed on Andrew, so she had two days more of survival, but she didn't gloat. Her eyes set on the next ark. Her lips thinned into a hard line. Her assumptions that someone survived outside of Endurance were tested.

Seven days until he had to feed.

❧   12   ❧

MUCH OF THE CITY OUTSIDE PROVIDENCE HAD COLLAPSED since humanity sealed itself away, but some skyscrapers still pierced the clouds. The shadows lengthened as he and Nimue ran down corridors of ruined buildings. Though he needed to feed in fewer than four days, he suggested they seek shelter. They didn't want to be stuck at Providence's gates beneath a shining moon.

Their heels clicked on the asphalt as they passed jagged spires and cracked ruins. Burned-out and rusted cars barricaded streets. Spindly weeds had pushed their way through the cracks.

Reclamation.

That would have been a good name for an ark. As good and as useless as any of the others.

Street after street was silent and solemn. Glass blown out of windows left sparkling teeth to slice looters. Not that there were any. The place felt as abandoned as it looked. No sense of any people remained, no matter where they walked, through suburban bungalows or inner-city apartments and office buildings.

They climbed one of the taller towers, one with stairs intact, its floors solid except for a few holes. The silence hung heavy around them as if it wanted them to leave. They persisted, and on the twenty-eight floor, they got their view across the city to Providence.

His stomach rumbled at the mere suggestion of souls for harvest, then recoiled from its unwarranted hope. Why should Providence be any different? Why should it have survived when all the others had fallen? Four days remained. Emrys was going to die.

Unlike Endurance and the others, Providence was not built in isolation or into the side of a mountain but instead sat partly above ground on a mostly flat plain. Thick concrete walls formed a circular, gray mausoleum that from this distance appeared whole. Nothing moved around its base, but that signified neither life nor death.

"There has to be someone still alive in this city." Nimue's voice sounded so loud. They'd taken to sharing thoughts more than words over the past month, and to hear her speak rattled him like a stone inside an empty and dented tin can.

"No, there doesn't."

"I'll find someone for you, Emrys. You won't be free of me that easily." She walked to the other side of the room, while he kept his eyes fixed on Providence.

She talked of their plans for when they got inside. He raised a concern about quarantine, but she dismissed it. Darisami registered the same as humans, no matter the tests. They'd pass as healthy humans.

She talked of how soon it would be before Ragnar and Clara attempted the crossing. They had been less insistent of late, despite detecting a note of resignation from them that he and Nimue would perish. Their thoughts hardened against the idea of leaving Endurance, but that suited him.

He stared, gave monosyllabic answers, and she stopped talking. She stayed at the back of his head, a warmth that attempted comfort but grew to be unbearable. They could have been the last two beings roaming the Earth.

Another hour passed, and nothing outside Providence changed. Then a shadow shifted around one of the corners of the city on a street not too far from their position. Emrys pressed his hands and nose against the window. The shadow moved.

And another.

And another.

And they were coming towards them. He signaled to her.

What is it?

I don't know yet, but we might have company.

It was a quick flash, something substantial and solid whereas before it had just been shadows. But it was human. Or at least in human form. And the human was armed, holding a machine gun steady as they slinked through the streets.

He searched and found more shadows.

Long shadows.

The sun was slipping towards its rest. His fingers retracted into claws, and the hair on the back of his neck prickled. How many were coming? He'd counted four but didn't know for certain. There could be more.

Another flash of a black uniform, a protective vest, boots, helmet. Guns. A military unit.

How did they find us? She looked around, but if there were security cameras, they wouldn't spot them. They could hide cameras in anything nowadays. Or then. Before it had all gone to shit. *The sun's setting. We don't have much time. We could kill them. You need to feed, Emrys.*

No, they might be from Providence. We need to get inside.

But we could take these ones now, then approach.

Not if their command already knows we're here. They'll never let us in.

He lost the soldiers as the building in front blocked his view of their approach. He watched the street at the base of the skyscraper and waited.

They reappeared and filed into the building.

They're coming. We have to go downstairs to wait for them.

What if we get stuck out here, Emrys? The moon will give us away.

Then we kill them, but we have to try.

He held out his hand, and she took it. They ran, pretending they were ordinary, frightened humans, down the stairs through a darkened concrete shaft. They descended floor after floor until they heard boots on concrete, jiggling metal pins, and magazines rattling in guns.

We have to let them know we're here, he said. *Remember to act frightened. Let's find a spot where they're bound to find us and beg for mercy. That means tears.*

I hope you know what you're doing.

He pulled her onto the thirteenth floor. It was gloomier down there. The sun didn't penetrate that low. The sounds of an approaching army grew louder. She squeezed his hand, and he nodded.

"Hello?" she called down the stairwell. Her voice quavered with the fear of a little girl lost.

The sounds stopped.

She tried again. "Is anyone there?"

The marching started again but slower. They were getting closer. Wary.

They'll shoot us before we have a chance to explain.

"There are two of us," he shouted. "We just want some help. We're waiting on level thirteen."

It sounded childish, begging for them to come find them, but how else would they be found and taken into Providence? He dragged over an old chair and propped open the door. They backed up into the foyer and positioned themselves in front of the reception desk like they were awaiting dignitaries.

They knelt on the tiled floor and put their hands behind their heads. This was no guarantee of anything. Someone might have an itchy trigger finger and shoot them as soon as they saw them. Or Providence's policy may be to exterminate any person found outside its walls. He told himself he didn't fear bullets.

As much as I hate to suggest it, we might need to pretend to be a lot more subservient than we're used to. She eyed the dust.

He followed her example and put his forehead to the floor. His hearing strained, and soon enough the echoes took on a definite shape, less reverberation, more presence, then the guards stormed in.

A soldier forced his knee onto Emrys's back and pinned him down. It took all his self-control to stop himself from fighting, even more to keep from killing the one who manhandled Nimue up off the ground.

"Don't move," the soldier said.

He ground his teeth.

Relax! she shouted inside his head.

He forced his shoulders to soften and his jaw to go slack. There was no pain, just pressure as he was pushed into the floor. Another soldier picked up his rucksack and emptied it. He grabbed the gun from its holster, grunted, and tucked it into the back of his waistband along with the knife. He stuffed the rest of his things back into the bag.

The soldier who had him pinned eased back. "Don't try anything stupid, or we'll shoot you and the girl in the head."

He wanted to fight back, not just from the gnashing of his hunger but because this debasement was beyond him or anyone. Surely, no real survivor would give in so easily.

Nimue's sobbing reached his ears, and he spun to find her. He glimpsed her with her face buried in her hands before the soldier kneed him in the stomach and clobbered his back with the gun, forcing him to the ground.

"Move that fast again, and I *will* shoot you." The gun barrel nuzzled into the base of his skull.

"Please, don't hurt my father." Her plaintive plea made a neat little incision across his heart, one that stung like a paper cut but bled like a severed artery. *Calm down!* her thoughts commanded. *We'll be fine.*

"Hey, it's okay. We're not going to harm you." A soldier with three stripes on his lapel crouched to her height, unhooking the knife from around her waist and handing it to another soldier. "We just need to know a little bit about where you're from."

"We're from Endurance."

The soldier turned his head to Emrys and smiled, a patch of skin amidst black efficiency. "That's a long way." He signaled to the soldier leaning on Emrys's back. If the opportunity ever arose, Emrys was going to tear out that one's soul.

He was hefted to his feet and dusted himself off. "Look, I'll answer all of your questions but, please, may I have my daughter back?"

"Not until we're sure this isn't some con," his tormentor said.

"Stand down, Brink. We've got their weapons." The one with three stripes and the nice smile guided Nimue towards Emrys, and she ran into his arms and buried her face into his chest. He kissed her hair.

"There, there, it'll be okay." His stomach soured as he played the doting father.

Emrys was about to suggest they move on, but the leader stepped forward. He was taller than Emrys, about six-one, and filled his uniform with muscle. He removed his helmet to reveal dark blond hair and vibrant green eyes that held more life in them than anything human Emrys had seen in Endurance. The leader was clean shaven, showing off a strong jaw, but even more than that, it amplified the genuine, welcoming smile. Combined with those eyes, it was radiant like warm sunshine before the nuclear blasts. This was someone who the apocalypse had not ruined.

Emrys forgot his need to leave.

"I'm Captain Galen Rhodes of Providence. What are your names?" Galen extended his hand to shake. His friendliness was unexpected but welcome.

The other three soldiers raised their weapons in warning, but Emrys clasped Galen's hand. His grip was warm, strong, and in no hurry to let go.

"I'm Emrys Stone, and this is my daughter, Nimue."

Galen's smile broadened.

Brink cleared his throat, and Galen withdrew his hand.

"We saw you come in," Galen said. "What are you doing here?"

"Seeking shelter. Endurance is falling. We thought Fortitude or Independence might help, but they're both dead." It wasn't worth telling them about the others now. Already their journey from Endurance would be hard enough to accept. "Providence is our last chance. We're nearly out of food and water. We just want a home."

Nimue wailed like a hungry, frightened girl.

"You are from Providence, aren't you?" Emrys asked.

Galen nodded. At least they'd confirmed that. And it must be doing well enough to have an operational militia with surveillance on the nearest city. A militia meant training, order, control—it meant survival.

"Why should we let you in?" Brink said. "You might be dangerous."

Emrys rounded on him. "Then why investigate? You could have let us starve, or if we got to Providence, kept the doors barred. You must have known there were only two of us or you would have sent a larger force. And why should survivors be treated with such hostility?"

"We don't mean to be suspicious." Galen's face dropped none of its goodwill. "But there are protocols we must follow to keep our people safe." Galen's tone was softer than Brink's, cautious yet curious.

"We're not tainted, if that's what you think. Endurance limps along but we had to find somewhere else. In time others will follow."

"All the more reason to not let you in." Brink's words fired in rapid jabs.

"You would turn away survivors?" Contempt thickened his voice. The soldier's equipment rattled as they moved under the spotlight of the uncomfortable question. "The human race is hanging by a thread, and you'd turn people away when you could do something to help?"

"Don't worry, we've got orders to take you to Providence," Galen said.

Brink interjected, but Galen stared his subordinate into disgruntled silence before focusing on Emrys. The smile returned. "Are you both fine to walk?"

Emrys nodded.

"Excellent."

Why was Galen so happy to see them when Brink was

so sore? The other two soldiers held their tongues, but their tense stance seemed more in Brink's favor than theirs.

Galen flicked up his chin at the rest of his unit, and they marched down the stairs and towards Providence. The sun was dangerously heavy in the sky, like it would drop any moment and shatter like a lightbulb.

They set a steady pace. Galen marched with one soldier in front, while Brink and the other stayed at the back, keeping Nimue and Emrys in the middle. Brink's attention and his gun remained trained between Emrys's shoulder blades, but Emrys was more concerned about the moon and when and where that inconstant harlot would show her face. Only Nimue's fingers entwined with his own stopped him from sprinting. But it wasn't enough to keep panic stealing the air from his lungs and play tricks on his eyes. Slashes of light darted at the edges of his vision. Did they come from him or her?

They headed down the main drag, but Providence was still too far away for them to make it in time. Had these soldiers been stationed in the city and holed up in a bunker?

Their steps quickened. The soldiers didn't want to be caught in the dark any more than he did, but they had no idea what they really had to fear. Could he and Nimue break from them? Claim they needed to rest for the night? He tried to think of a way out. The skies darkened.

After six blocks, they turned right and headed towards what used to be a warehouse: three stories high, red brick walls with broken glass windows. Each one looked like a gaping maw with jagged teeth. The blackness within eager to swallow them whole.

Galen slid aside a panel on the wall to reveal a keypad. After pressing buttons, he gripped the handle on the large warehouse door and pulled it back. The wheels squealed as the door slid to the left, and they stepped into an almost empty building. There were no levels above to obstruct the view to the ceiling, and the whole ground floor stretched out like a hangar, but empty of planes, people, or the assorted detritus of a factory used for manufacturing. Instead the only thing to break the monotony of nothingness, the eerie absence of stuff, was a small squat room, with concrete walls, in the center of the warehouse.

The door rumbled closed behind them and locked. Perhaps they would rest there the night. They'd have to stay far from the windows.

The soldiers turned on their flashlights. The spotlights bobbed along the floor as they walked to the small building. Nimue and Emrys followed. They stopped outside another steel door, and Galen punched five numbers into the dimly illuminated keypad. The lock clicked, and he turned the handle.

Emrys held his arm up to shield his eyes from the sudden flood of light pouring out of a white room. Nimue did the same. Unease nipped the back of his neck. His shoulders rippled to dispel the feeling, but it sank into the pit of his stomach. It looked like a padded cell, and he knew how humans liked their experiments.

"What is this?" The sharp fear in his voice was no act.

"This is how we get into Providence. Don't worry, you're safe." Something about Galen's voice lulled Emrys into feeling a certainty he hadn't known for hundreds of years. A certainty that had none of the dread of death.

Unfriendly hands shoved him in the back. Startled, he fell into the room, pulling Nimue with him. They landed hard on the ground and he spun, worried they were about to be locked in, but the soldiers followed and shut the door behind them. They lowered their guns. Brink's mouth was crooked with an evil smile.

Galen pressed a series of numbers on the keypad, and the room started to move. They were in a goddamn elevator. It fell fast, but steadily, smoothly, silently. It slowed, then paused for the barest of moments before it took off sideways away from the city.

And towards Providence.

❧ 13 ❧

NIMUE HUGGED EMRYS TIGHT. *SINCE WHEN DID PROVIDENCE get tunnels? Imagine if more of us had come. Imagine if we'd been stuck out there at night. Glowing like fucking Christmas trees!*

"Shhhhh." Emrys smoothed her hair. "We'll be okay."

The whole thing could have been ruined. How did we not know about this?

Her rabid thoughts bit into him. He tried to protect himself, half-tempted to block her, but instead he breathed as deeply as he could and imagined a shield that she could batter all she liked without hurting him. When she came up against it, her mind flinched.

Don't worry, nothing is ruined. This has just taken us by surprise. We're still on course. He paused for her to speak but received a wave of cold. *You've stopped crying. Sniff or something. They have to believe you're distraught.*

Her mind snarled, but he ended the communication. She let out a couple of long sniffs, and he hugged her tighter, harder. She dug her nails into the back of his neck, and his muscles stiffened. She was far too strong for her own good.

"When we arrive, you will be taken to quarantine and processed," Galen said.

Icy fingers gouged the base of his spine and sent a chill spiking into his skull. He had four days left to get a soul. How long would quarantine last?

"What about you?" Emrys said. "You've been exposed to us."

He smiled, that strong mouth again. It was like magic. "It's unlikely you've got anything we haven't had shots for."

"I admire your confidence. What will happen to us then?"

"That's up to the council to decide."

"And what's the likely outcome?"

Brink chuckled. "Hopefully, they'll turf you and your urchin back outside."

"Quiet," Galen said.

Brink stepped back from the dangerous tone in his captain's voice.

"I imagine you'll be accepted into the fold, but I suggest telling them how useful you can be."

"Any suggestions?" Emrys said.

"I'm sure a man who's made it this far across dangerous terrain has plenty of skills."

The elevator slowed to a halt, and the doors slid open. Behind the soldiers, he could see more guards, their guns at the ready, pointing at their comrades' backs. So many souls…

"Follow me." Galen turned out.

Emrys hugged Nimue tighter.

The white of the elevator ceded to a gray steel and blue paneled hallway—the ass entrance of Providence. This was the back way, where secret missions to the surface were conducted, where the upper echelons of their diminished society would escape if anything went wrong.

Guarded, locked up tight, protected. It would be the way he and Nimue would flee if necessary. How many of Providence's inhabitants knew of its existence?

The soldiers were only distinguishable from one another by their height and build. Most were about six foot. A couple were taller. Twelve in all, some thinner than he would have expected on a soldier. Then again, soldiers were made for war. Without one, they spoiled. The arrival of two strays was probably the highlight of their decade.

Two sets of hands hooked under his armpits, and Nimue was pulled from him. He broke free, forgetting to show restraint, and rushed for Nimue. They armed their guns and the butt of one drove into his back. The first attempt bounced off, but when the second came, he remembered to succumb and dropped to the floor.

A foot hooked under his stomach and flipped him onto his back. Ten muzzles pointed at his body, one belonging to Brink. "I warned you not to try that shit."

He'd be fucked if he'd allow them to take her away. His head buzzed. It would be her scalding him and telling him to ease off. "Where are you taking her?"

"I'm sorry, Emrys. You have to be separated." Galen's voice sounded behind the muscled goons. "For testing. If it were up to me, you'd be housed together, but it won't be for long. I promise."

Emrys growled. "Endurance made promises too and look what happened to them."

"We're very interested to hear about Endurance's problems, but you have to understand that we have our way of doing things. We don't mean you any harm, but we have to protect Providence above all else, and I have orders I must follow."

Soldiers hoisted him to his feet. A soldier held Nimue

with one hand around her skinny arm. Her eyes downcast, her mouth bowed in an unhappy crescent, her face was a perfect mask of a broken child. All she needed was a rag doll and a dirty, torn orphan's dress.

"Go with them, Nimue. We'll be together again soon."

She sniffed and nodded but didn't look at him. His head burned with the force of her thoughts. It was like trying to keep the door closed on an out-of-control furnace. He didn't dare relent until she'd calmed down.

The soldier led Nimue away down one corridor, and Emrys was hustled along another. "Don't worry." Galen put his hand on Emrys's shoulder, and Emrys hated how much the gesture soothed him. "We're not monsters. She'll be perfectly safe."

"She'd better be."

A small number of guards accompanied him, enough to keep one man—though strong—from doing something rash. Had anyone seen him take that first hit? Whoever clobbered him must have noticed he refused to buckle. He hoped no one would check for bruises. All his vitals might register as human, but his body wasn't going to turn purple from the beating, no matter how savage the blow. He might be able to use that to his advantage. He could join the military. At least then he'd have a chance of visiting the surface. That would be a way to serve.

As an outsider, they'd consider him expendable so no great loss if he were killed—though what Providence needed protecting from he had no idea. Yes, he could see that working. As far as they knew, he'd demonstrated great tenacity and survival skills in getting there. He'd oil up those lies, not too much so as to make them unbelievable, but enough to command some respect and show he was an asset.

He studied his guard. For all their uniforms and equipment and discipline, they were probably an untested force, and that allowed for weaknesses.

Brink, for example.

That asshole should have been kicked out long ago, but with no actual battle to fight, what harm could he do? Yes, Emrys could see the reasoning for all of this. Jobs for everyone, an army befitting a country in exile. It would all work perfectly.

They marched him into a white padded cell with three soft walls. Inside was a bolted-down table and chair, and a bed with a mattress and gray blanket. The fourth wall was floor-to-ceiling glass with a section that slid open to allow access. He had a space of about twelve square feet in which to move, but not large enough for his four guards to stand side by side. They staggered themselves to form a human barricade.

"What next? I get strip searched?" Emrys laughed.

"That won't be necessary." A voice rose from behind the wall of military might. It parted to reveal a thin, short woman in blue scrubs. Her black hair was tied in a ponytail, her cream skin smooth and unblemished, her expression clinical. She did not look like someone who thought laughter was the best medicine. She carried a small tray holding a butterfly needle, collection tubes, and a tourniquet. "Are you afraid of needles?"

"Would it stop you if I said yes?"

Her lips pursed. "Please take a seat." She placed the tray on the table.

He sat and rolled up the sleeve on his right arm. She applied the tourniquet, found a vein, swabbed it with alcohol, and pierced his skin. It had been a long time since anyone had done this to him. Blood had been taken when Endurance was first established, and the first council had forced everyone to be screened. The Darisami had been fascinated to learn that there was no difference between them and the humans, at least nothing in the blood. Or nothing that the machines could register. Perhaps one day a new secret would be revealed. He prayed Providence hadn't already found it.

The tube filled with crimson. She replaced it and slotted in another.

"What's your date of birth?" the medic asked while keeping her gaze intent on the blood.

"Why do you need that?"

"We need to vet you, so what's your birthdate?"

"How are you going to vet me? I wouldn't have thought you could access Endurance's records."

"Everything was centralized in the beginning. You don't look old enough to have been in the first intake. After that, who knows what we might find. Date?"

The Darisami had wiped themselves out of Endurance's public system after they'd gained control of the ark and maintained a hidden level of access, using false names and identities to control everything. They'd limited their connections to the other arks in case they got hacked. Officially, he didn't exist, which was fortunate. Otherwise, his record would have shown him to be in his late nineties.

And Nimue…well, that wasn't even worth thinking about.

"September 15, 2111."

"Thank you." The doctor finished drawing his blood and left the cell. The soldiers followed her out. Galen was the last to leave.

"The tests shouldn't take long, then the Council will decide what should happen to you. I think they'll at least want to know how you travelled so far."

Another story he'd have to concoct.

"I look forward to it."

Galen, with his strong chin and plump lips, studied Emrys, seeming on the verge of asking questions, but something flickered across his eyes, and his smile faded into a sad facsimile of its former self. Galen nodded at him, left the room, and sealed him in. Emrys mulled over what he'd witnessed.

He should have been thinking of other things, not trying to discern the meaning behind a human's facial expressions. He needed to get out of the cell fast and find something to eat. He needed to ensure Providence let him and Nimue stay. But he wanted to know more about Galen. He wanted to see those lips again and hear more of that voice.

Starvation had made him crazy.

He sat on the chair when what he really wanted to do was pace. He rested one arm on its back and the other on the table, his finger circling a figure eight on the tabletop. He widened his peripheral vision but couldn't see the cameras he knew to be there. They'd be trained on him, and the room was probably fitted with heat sensors. No one patrolled the corridor outside his cell. Opposite was a solid wall. No use in prisoners being able to see each other. Laughter filtered through to him, and he sharpened his hearing. Two soldiers chatting and sharing a joke. Two souls so very close. Neither of them Galen's. The glass wouldn't be hard to shatter. He could kill them before they even heard it break. But he wasn't there to cause a scene.

He beamed into Nimue's head. She let him in, open enough so the tips of thorns scraped against his mind. *Are you alone?*

They've set someone outside to watch me while I cry. He keeps looking away. It makes him uncomfortable. This is almost fun.

You seem to have calmed down.

I was always calm, Emrys.

He left the comment alone. He told her about his fears they'd dig something up, but she dismissed them as irrelevant, like they were the fanciful worries of a child. He was still older than her in years, even if her opinion of the world was as sour as a hag's four times his age.

He told her about his plan to join their militia, which she agreed would be useful, but disinterest tinged her thoughts. Years of playing the child awaited her. She tried hard to ignore the body she was stuck with, her mind sharper than any adult's, her thoughts as crystalline as a cut diamond, that being reminded she must once again fill a role she detested while he got to play with the big kids made her touchy. She'd be relegated to work with the children, if they worked, or sent to school to relearn all the things she'd known for centuries. How boring. She'd be stuck being a kid for a few years and age a little, but she was too much a child, too underdeveloped, that even with their ability to alter aspects of their features, she would never look quite right.

Food and water were brought in on a tray under the watchful eye of two soldiers and put on the table. He was served a gruel without shape or color, but it no doubt offered sustenance. He ate to keep up the illusion. Once it entered his stomach, it was nothing, obliterated by the magic that kept him alive. Only one thing would fill his hunger, and he needed it soon.

He considered all the possibilities and wondered how he could do away with Brink without too much fuss. If he could get close to him, he could work the symbol fast, and it would look like he'd suffered a heart attack. But when it came to Brink, quick wasn't what he wanted.

Did you eat? Nimue asked.

Yes. Didn't you?

I pretended to be too upset. From the looks of it, I'm not missing out on much.

If you don't eat, they might force you.

Let them try. She laughed inside his head.

He continued tracing the infinity pattern on the table, around and around, but never taking his eyes off the glass. The soldiers returned and took the tray. He demanded answers but they ignored him. He went back to his chair, went back to circling, on and on. He walked to the glass, peered left then right down the hall, saw little. He paced, uncertain if he did it for show or out of frustration. Had the walls moved? Had the air stopped circulating?

He banged on the glass, demanding to see his daughter. A soldier came from down the hall and assessed him. His gun hung across his body, aimed at the floor.

Emrys focused all his anger on this lackey. "Where is my daughter?" His voice rumbled like an avalanche.

Nothing.

"Did you hear me? Where is my daughter?"

Silence.

"If you won't tell me where she is, I want to talk to whoever's in charge."

The soldier walked away.

He sneered and sat on the floor of the cell in the far back corner. Knees bent, he rubbed his hands, counting the seconds, then the minutes. Wanting to feel something beneath his palms. How long had they been there? Long enough for them to run their tests, to search the database, to draw a conclusion.

Nimue hollered inside his head. *They're coming.*

Muted voices filtered down to him. He sprang to his feet.

Keep calm, Emrys.

Three men and one woman appeared in front of his cell with their faces uncovered. Galen was one of them, but he kept slightly behind. Not their equal.

"You don't exist," the tall man beside Galen said.

Whereas Galen was young and warm, this man was as cold as a tomb. His skin was a dusty off-white. His eyes were gray, his lips thin and downturned. The surety of old age and—if his attendance at this interrogation were any indication—his position within Providence gave him the authority to wear such disdain on his face. This was a man who'd survived the purge of the old world and adapted to a new one.

And when he looked at Emrys he must have seen a disaster that he'd fought his whole life to avoid.

He wore a white tunic stitched with the letter P in gold over his heart. The woman next to him wore the same. She was middle-aged, her skin a deep brown. Her long hair was pulled together into a thick braid that curled over her shoulder. Its ends brushed the top of her breast. Her hazelnut eyes met his without fear.

The last man was dressed in black, the same utilitarian cargo pants as Galen, but his shirt was smarter, a tunic with a red embroidered P. He was large, broad across the shoulders with thick arms. His body seemed on the verge of action. Not as tall as the old man, but about Galen's height. They had the same green eyes, though his burned with the fire of fanaticism, not compassion. There was no mistaking a connection. Even the nose was similar, though in the elder's it had been broken and healed crooked. Galen's father?

They watched him like he was a lion in a zoo.

"But I'm standing right here."

"The system. You don't exist in the system." He spat the words like he lectured an imbecile.

"I don't know what to tell you. I was born in Endurance. Records after the gates closed are patchy at best."

"We accessed Endurance's records a few decades ago, before you went dark, but you aren't in them. Explain."

He swore inside his head. The muscles in his face tightened. "I can't answer for the record-keepers. But I was born in Endurance, as was Nimue."

"You're lying."

"I'm not. We're from Endurance."

"We cannot find you in any of the records from any of the arks we can reach. Where do you come from?"

"Are you deaf? I'm from Endurance."

"That's impossible. It's months of travel to the west. There is no way you could have survived the journey."

"But we did. We scavenged through the empty ruins of every ark we discovered, and there were days when we thought we'd starve. But I swear to you, on my daughter's life, we are from Endurance."

The old man sneered. "If you won't tell us the truth, you shall be turned out. You will be escorted to the surface tomorrow at first light."

He searched Galen's face for any sign of an ally, but he held his tongue. The old man turned, and the others followed.

"Wait! Ask me anything. I can tell you everything you ever wanted to know about Endurance and everything you didn't," he shouted after them. "I can tell you how many floors, how many rooms, how many people entered, and how many remained when we set out. Please. There are survivors, and they have put their faith in me and my daughter to find them safe haven. Endurance is broken. It cannot sustain life for much longer. Turn me away, and you condemn them to death. Their blood will be on your hands!"

Galen was the first to stop. Then the others.

Emrys loosened his shoulders. He hadn't realized how tense he'd been.

"Galen says you put up no resistance when they found you in the city. Why?" the old man asked.

"We'd spotted your soldiers coming. We wanted to be found. We didn't fancy spending another night in the open, even if there was the city to keep us protected."

"So, you lay down, gave up?"

"Why would we fight? I'm a military man—I *was* a military man—in Endurance. If I'd shown any sign of being a threat, chances are I would have been shot and Nimue orphaned. It's not as if you really want another mouth to feed, am I right?"

Galen's cheek twitched, the woman's neck tensed, but the two older men remained passive. Emrys smelled the chance for mischief.

"Tell me, how many other survivors have sought entrance to Providence?"

"You and your daughter are the first."

"Do you mean we're the only ones to show up, or the only ones to make it in *alive?*"

"Watch your tone. We're not averse to sending you on your way. Your daughter, however, looks like she'll be fertile in a year or two. Maybe she already is." The old weasel's flaps pulled into a wicked grin.

Emrys banged his fist on the glass and it reverberated.

"Step away from the glass," the military man—Galen's father—said.

He sneered at all of them. But he did what they said, stalking away, pacing the cell.

"You say you're military?" the father said.

"I am."

"Then you don't show much discipline. No salute, no stand at attention. You look strong, but I wouldn't count on you in a fight."

He gave them a crooked smile. "If you want a performing monkey, ask one of the men who brought me in. I was military but not a soldier, and I served Endurance's council well. I brought order to our home without fuss. Our people didn't feel like they were caged in Endurance. They had me to thank for that."

"Yet you say it has fallen. I'd hardly call that a success."

"I served the council. Their decisions are what slit Endurance's throat. My conscience is clean."

"What are you saying? That you're…an assassin?" the woman asked. It was the first time she'd spoken. Though her voice was softer than he expected, it resonated like the murmuring of a beaten drum. She'd given him an opportunity to explain away his absence from the system.

"I'm saying I acted upon their wishes to keep Endurance safe as best I could. I can do the same for you here."

He let their minds muse on the possibilities. Silence stretched while they mulled it over before the old man scoffed. "These could be lies to coax us into letting you stay."

"Test me. Any way you wish. I'll withstand whatever trials you set."

"Arrogance seeps from your pores."

"It's not arrogance but experience. Give me a task. If I fail, we will leave."

"If you fail, *you* will leave. Your daughter will stay."

His lip curled, quivered on the verge of barking. "Fine. But I won't fail."

The two older men and the woman looked at each other, not-so-secret meanings passing between them. What problems did Providence have that an assassin could solve? Though he wanted to study the older men and the woman for the power they wielded, the cool intensity of Galen's gaze flushed heat up his throat.

He's studying me to see if I can be trusted. That's all.

"Galen, any infections?" his father asked.

"The tests are due back shortly."

"Very well," he said. "Provided you are free of disease and answer our questions to our satisfaction—"

"I will tell you everything you want to know," Emrys said.

"If that's so, you will be welcomed into Providence on a trial basis. You will fit in. You will live among us. And your daughter, too. She will go to school. You will be found a place in our security forces, and you will be watched. Galen will be your guide and your shadow, and when we demand it, you will prove your trustworthiness and your usefulness."

"I look forward to the day I can be of service and earn your respect."

As long as it was within the next four days.

Galen's father's lip curled. "Do not mention your profession to anyone but the four of us and be warned, Stone. If you step out of line or make us even the slightest bit suspicious, you will be cast out with nothing but your skin. And even that will be beaten raw."

Emrys bowed slowly, deliberately. A mockery. The bastard knew it.

They filed out one by one, Galen the last to leave, a furrow to his brow. Whether it was fear or concern, Emrys couldn't decide. Galen probably didn't know either.

Nimue, we're in.

When the blood work cleared Emrys for release and he was brought to Nimue, she dashed into his arms. He hugged her and stroked her hair, forgetting that he was pretending to be her father and she his daughter. Forgetting that she was not Sian, and they weren't five hundred years after her death. When Galen tapped him on the shoulder, he tightened his hold.

"Come on, Emrys," Galen said. "She's safe."

He slowly relinquished his grip, positioning his body between Galen and Nimue. The soldier stood stiff and tall. Galen had the height advantage and used it, but he couldn't hold Emrys's gaze for long. What did he see that he didn't like? Cold-blooded assassin? Doting father? An uncomfortable mix of the two?

When the world had fallen, many were forced to do things they never thought themselves capable of. Perhaps Galen was too young to know this and the privilege he enjoyed in Providence kept him ignorant.

With a nod, Galen dismissed the three soldiers who'd escorted them from their cells and took over their supervision. He led them down the central corridor of the prison complex. Other passageways branched off from it. Emrys couldn't tell how many cells there were and how deep they went into the earth. Providence had been built to hold a greater population than Endurance, but there hadn't been time to get there and get inside, so his group of ten Darisami had crammed into Endurance. It had been a mistake.

"We have quarters on level six suitable enough for you and Nimue." He herded them into an elevator.

They went up one floor and exited down a utilitarian corridor with little light and no decoration. Emrys looked back as the door slid closed behind them and melded seamlessly into the wall. Somewhere there would be a keypad or card slot to grant entry, but during that quick glimpse there was nothing to see.

They passed through another doorway into another corridor with other doors deviating off from it. There was nothing special about the door they'd left, nothing to distinguish it from the others, little to remember and use to trace back.

They entered the main hub of the city.

Providence had been built around a central column that rose through the multitude of floors, acting as a sentinel. From where they stood, they could take a walkway on their left or one on their right, into the column, but they could not get to it by walking straight from one corridor and onto the bridge. There were eight corridors and four bridges, and they didn't align. Emrys walked to the edge of the railing and looked up and down. The bridges were on every second floor. The column was covered in one-way glass.

"The council chambers are in there. We call it the Tower," Galen said. "A couple of floors up is where they sit, with enough space for half of the inhabitants to have a seat inside and watch or bring forward their petitions. You'll see it soon enough. Let's go."

The lights had been dimmed to give them some semblance of the cycles of the world that continued outside. The hallways and balconies were empty, but as they turned down one of the corridors, Emrys saw a face watching them from around a corner. He stared after them, frozen, eyes assessing, studying. Their arrival wouldn't remain quiet long.

The elevator doors opened, and they stepped in. "Did you see him?"

"Who?" Galen replied.

"That man in the hallway. He saw us."

"We're not trying to keep you a secret."

"I thought you'd want to keep us under wraps for a while."

Galen snorted. "I wouldn't count on our soldiers keeping quiet about this even if we ordered them to."

"If that's so, our disappearance would also be something that wouldn't stay secret for long."

"Then you'd better not disappear."

Providence had ten levels. They stopped on the sixth floor and room 6380 was theirs. Two small, separate rooms each held a single bed made with white sheets, ready to fall into. There was a table and two chairs, a sofa and coffee table—not that coffee had been around for a long time—and a large monitor on the wall in the sitting room. Through another doorway, a white bathroom with a shower, toilet, and sink. It was clinical and bare. There hadn't been so much white in Endurance, which had always felt unfinished and grimy, a basement they'd infested with all its innards showing. Providence was a five-star hotel. Emrys wasn't sure which he preferred.

Nimue picked a room, crawled onto the bed, and lay down.

"She must be exhausted, poor thing," Galen said. "Though the fact that she has a warm bed to rest in is down to you. Not all fathers would do the same."

"Then they don't deserve their children."

Galen's smile rose and fell rapidly. He turned away from Nimue's door. "Are you sure you know what you're doing, offering to help the council…in that way?"

"You said I should be of service."

"But I didn't mean for you to…offer something you can't deliver. It's going to make things difficult."

"What makes you think I'm not what I say I am?"

Galen's head cocked to the side, lines deepening across his brow. "A man who shows that much care for his daughter cannot be a cold-blooded killer."

Emrys closed the gap between him and Galen and lowered his voice. "You don't know what I've done in my life to keep Nimue safe."

Galen's eyes searched Emrys's. "Give me your hands."

"What?"

"Your hands. Give them to me. That's an order."

Emrys held them out. Galen took a hold of each and examined them. He exposed the palms. Emrys never felt more naked.

Galen studied them. "Your hands are relatively unmarked." He let his left hand go and cupped his right. His thumb dragged across the skin, the small nicks he'd earned from making jewelry before he was made Darisami. "They're not smooth, but they're not coarse either. You don't fight, that's too hands-on, but they're dexterous. You make things with these hands."

Galen rubbed the mound of Emrys's palm with his thumbs. His touch made heat and sparked old memories he'd rather not remember.

"Delicate things. I can tell." Galen coursed the lines that had never faded. Emrys's life line had an end that had long since passed. A heart line that was deep but fallow. A fate line that meant nothing.

Galen's fingers stroked memories of his wife Myfanwy and how she would stroke the back of his neck, tickled memories of Sian as her tiny fingers tickled his palms while they played a game, and coaxed memories of Lysander and the way he'd brought Emrys out of his mortal life and into one of immortality. That, of course, was not the only thing he'd coaxed, and that pleasure had damned him and thrown his child on a funeral pyre.

Emrys's tongue thickened and dried. He snatched his hand away. "They might be soft but they're strong. Enough to choke a man." His mind slammed shut the steel gate around those relics, and he forced the talons clutching his gut to relax.

Galen stilled. His brow furrowed, deepening the vertical lines above his nose. His green eyes held concern. "I hope you know what you've committed yourself to. I'd hate to see you get hurt." He opened the door. "I'll leave you to rest. We'll organize clothes for you tomorrow, and I'll be by to check on you in the morning."

"What if someone other than you comes in the meantime?"

"They won't be allowed in. An announcement will be made early so the people of Providence know survivors have made it through."

"And then what?"

"I'm not sure. You'll just have to take every day as it comes. Goodnight." Galen left the room before Emrys could ask more questions.

The door slid between them, and a red light flashed on the lintel. He tried the button, but it confirmed what he suspected: they wouldn't be doing anything without the council's permission.

He studied the room. The walls were smooth and unblemished with no visible surveillance, but that didn't mean someone wasn't watching. He went into Nimue's room and sat on the edge of her bed. He stroked her hair while she feigned sleep, her mouth slack and her breathing slow. He kissed her head before pulling off her boots and turning up the cover.

He stripped out of his clothes and showered in gloriously hot water. A month's grime washed away, exposing his hunger. He needed to feed. Soon. He dried himself and slipped beneath the covers of his own bed, sighing with heartfelt relief at being in comfort once more. His hand hit the button on the side table and the room went dark.

All except for the red light.

Nimue's presence buzzed inside his head.

I've told Ragnar and Clara what has happened, but they'd prefer to hear it from you.

His head ached with ice. If he'd been treated the same, he wouldn't have been able to hold back his curses. But she was different, and the realization was a chill that stole throughout his body.

If they won't hear it from you, then I'll be damned if I'll give them the time of day. If he'd expected some warm glow of gratitude sent his way, he was left unsatisfied. There would be no comforting her when she was like this, no way to help her thaw. She'd come good in her own time. *Tomorrow, we have to be prepared for a lot of questions.*

You'll do most of the talking, so I'll follow your lead, but keep the channel open in case something happens.

Do you think we're alone here?

Too early to tell. The last days before we had to sequester ourselves underground were such hell, it's possible some Darisami got through to Providence. But if they did, they're no friend of ours.

I doubt they're skulking in the shadows.

Doesn't matter if they're an unknown or the Big Cheese in Providence, we can't have another Darisami in here. Two is more than enough.

It was no use now discussing plans about what they would do when the Darisami from Endurance wanted to come over—not in the mood she was in. And not with greed sharpening his hunger. He'd protect his food from anyone or anything. He'd done the work and had earned that right. He bid her goodnight and sought the relief of sleep.

But he lay awake for hours in the dark, his thumb caressing back and forth over his palm and retracing the feel of Galen's touch. Emrys's hand differed from Galen's, but there wasn't much to tell the tender touch of Galen's hand from Lysander's.

❧ 14 ❧

THE LIGHTS CAME ON, AND EMRYS'S EYES SHUTTERED OPEN. The red light blinked off. Company.

He sat up, the sheet slipping down to expose him to the waist, and in marched Galen and the woman from the day before, both unconcerned about invading their privacy. He glimpsed the black uniforms of soldiers flanking the door before it closed.

"Good morning, Emrys." Galen smiled with all the hope of a reborn Christian. Today was a new day, a new opportunity.

Emrys was on guard. He nodded hello. "I didn't catch your name yesterday," he asked of the woman. Out from under the heavy influence of Galen's father and the old man, she seemed kinder, her jaw not so taut, her eyes not so hard.

"My name is Elaina. I'm one of Providence's five councilors."

Five? Who were the others?

And why hadn't they attended his interrogation?

"Pleasure to meet you formally."

"There's been a change of plan," she said. "We are here to escort you and Nimue to the Tower for a public meeting of the council. You will be asked questions about where you came from, what it is you want of us, and what you can offer our people."

"I assume you want me to lie?"

Her politician's smile ossified. "Be careful what you choose to impart. We value order in Providence. Without it, we cannot survive. Creating undue panic will get you nowhere and will be detrimental to your future. And your daughter's."

He marked her words. Not only for her threat but for their similarity to the ones the Darisami had chosen to live by in Endurance. He had no intention of causing alarm. Slipping into the everyday workings of Providence suited him fine, especially if it meant he could get something to eat.

"You have nothing to fear from us," he said. "All we want is a home. We will not cause unrest."

"See that you don't. We haven't much time. The murmurings are getting louder. Please dress. We need to be on our way."

Neither Galen nor Elaina moved. He sighed and threw off the sheet. If they wanted to see him naked, they were welcome to watch. It seemed privacy didn't count for much in this place, and prudence wasn't a trait anyone wanted in an assassin. Elaina remained expressionless, but Galen's lips parted, and his eyes tracked Emrys's movements. Looking for what? Scars? Injuries?

He pulled on his grimy trousers and slipped on his once-white shirt. The clothes had lasted the journey, but the tears had widened, and threads had loosened. He ripped them some more and Elaina smiled. Who didn't love a bit of pageantry?

Nimue came out of her room, having showered during the night, and stood in the doorway, brushing her fingers through her hair.

"No need to make yourself pretty, little one," Elaina said. "The council is more interested in your tale than your looks."

Her fingers paused halfway through brushing and gave Elaina a concrete-slab stare dropped from a great height.

"You look lovely, Nimue," he said. "A few knots won't hurt."

She retracted her fingers but didn't smile. He held out his hand to her and she took it, but her eyes didn't leave Elaina.

The councilor raised her eyebrows and gave an uneasy smile. "Shall we?"

Lose the look, he transmitted.

I doubt you would look much different if you had Ragnar and Clara banging away in your head for the better part of the night.

The door slid open, and they stepped between the four guards flanking the door.

Your refusal to talk to them made them frantic, she said. *I barely listened to what they said, but it was difficult to ignore completely. We can't all sleep like you.*

Anything I should worry about?

I'm handling it.

They met no one as they walked the corridor with Galen and Elaina in the lead and the guards behind. The corridors, balconies, and bridges were empty. Providence hummed with an electric murmuring like that of Endurance, but he felt little human presence. How many people still lived there? Had they made a grave error? Surely to support a militia, they had to have people to protect. Where the hell was everyone?

They were taken across one of the bridges to the central column and into a small chamber.

"I have to join the rest of the council," Elaina said. "Galen will escort you in at the appropriate moment. We shall talk again." She gave him a warm smile and a nod, but nothing for Nimue. She left.

"Who's on the council?" he asked.

"Apart from Elaina, there's Christos, the older of the two men you met yesterday, and Isaiah, the military man, and Laurence and Kira. They're known as the Five, and they divide the running of Providence between them, though with respect and deference to each other's opinions and suggestions."

"I'm sure." Emrys knew a party line when he heard one.

Galen stepped closer and lowered his voice in quiet counsel. "That kind of talk doesn't go down well in here. If you want to stay, you'd better be careful."

Though he spoke a warning, the warmth from his body made it all the more inviting, like sitting too close to a campfire. It had been a long time since Emrys had warmed himself with anyone, and the last time he got burned.

"Dissenters won't be tolerated?" The distance between them shrank further and Emrys's skin prickled.

"Exactly. And considering what you're being asked to do, I hope you're fine with that." Galen's eyes searched Emrys's. What was he looking for? Confirmation of the truth behind his story? Little did Galen know how many humans Emrys had brought a quiet death to. Yet standing beneath that appraisal, feeding was the last thing on his mind.

And that was a problem.

Emrys huffed a short awkward laugh and stepped back,

hoping the heat rising in his throat would cool. "You'll hear no complaints from me." He sat next to Nimue. "How do you think the Five will vote?"

"They'll let you stay. For the price you've agreed." Galen looked away, uneasy at speaking even circumspectly of their bargain. He was a soldier. He should have understood the need for discretion. There was no point in being squeamish about a secret killer. This was not the twenty-first century.

Or perhaps he was still unsure Emrys was who he said he was.

Not that he'd told any human the truth.

"And what about the other inhabitants? Will they accept us?"

Galen opened his mouth to answer, but two armed guards burst into the room. Emrys shot to his feet and shielded Nimue with his body.

"It's time." Galen gestured for them to walk with him down the corridor, flanked by the guards.

Nimue's hand slipped into his as they neared the threshold of the council chamber and the growing chatter of thousands of voices. The doors opened.

Providence was far from empty.

The hubbub died as all eyes zeroed in on them. A heaviness descended as the collective weight of held breath and tongues marked their arrival. Galen led them to a dais in the center of the circular room, then retreated.

Rows and rows and rows of seats crammed full of Providence's people loomed over them, gazes intent on the offering beneath them, their entertainment assured. In front of Emrys was a cleared section where the five council members sat behind a long desk, reminiscent of courts of old or the emperor's box in the Colosseum.

"You have appeared at our gates seeking refuge."

Christos stood, pressing his fingertips into the top of the bench and commanding the attention of the masses.

Positioned in the middle of the Five, he was flanked by Elaina and Laurence, all three in white robes. Kira wore green and stood at the far left. Isaiah donned black as before and occupied the seat on the far right.

"You are the first to do so in sixty-five years. Your arrival is a cause for celebration yet also of concern. We are not so inhumane as to turn you away into the cold wasteland that lies beyond the safety of Providence's walls, however, we ask you to tell your story. Has the world beyond crumbled further in the days since the Fall?"

The air turned to ice, and the calculating bastard sat.

Christos wanted to keep the people afraid, keep the people under control, keep the people inside. Emrys had the greatest chance of staying if he stuck to the same lines.

Emrys took his time beginning, letting the silence and the tension stretch. He kept his voice low, quiet, so they had to lean in to hear him. "We come from Endurance, far to the west. The technology failed us, and we feared the darkness coming and being sealed inside like a tomb. Most people had perished, but some of us held on. My daughter and I volunteered to undertake the journey in search of a new home, not knowing what we would find along the way or how soon we would die. Communication with the other cities stopped some years before, as I'm sure you are aware. We worried we were alone, that tragedy had befallen our lost brothers and sisters."

He lifted his head and made eye contact with each member of the council. Isaiah and Christos were unmoved.

He raised his voice. "We travelled from ark to ark, from Endurance to Fortitude, Liberty to Salvation, but all were empty. Abandoned long ago. There were days where I wanted to give up, when it all seemed hopeless."

He paused and dropped his gaze, dropped his volume, dropped his composure. He let tears fall.

"But I could not quit. Not until we were sure all was lost." He clenched his fist and faced the crowd. "Some of you may judge me harshly for bringing my daughter, Nimue, on such a mission, but what parent would leave their child behind? If I didn't bring her, what would have happened to her in Endurance?" He put his arm around her shoulder and hugged her to him. He looked at her wet eyes. "I made this trek for her sake. To find her a new home and a new hope for her future."

No one spoke. His voice carried far.

"I admit, shamefully, that after seeing so much of the world devoid of life, we walked with heavy footsteps weighed down by heavier hearts, unwilling to come across another failed city as we neared Providence. We stood in the ruins and saw your walls in the distance and hoped. We prayed. And your benevolence and compassion took us in. We saw that not only have you survived, but you thrived. I look around and see children. You have order. You have built a life out of the rubble."

He returned his gaze to the council.

"We throw ourselves on your mercy and beg to be allowed to stay. We are healthy. We are strong. We can contribute."

"And if we let you stay, what of the remaining inhabitants of Endurance?" Christos asked.

"We do not know if they will follow or make it this far, but if any do, I would ask that the mercy shown us be extended to them."

Christos's lips curled. Kindness to two humans was

tolerable. More might invite the same disease that befell Endurance.

"How many remain in Endurance?"

"I believe there may only be a handful left. The strongest."

Christos grunted. "Or the most devious. When a community fails, it is often the most wretched of society that fight its way to survival."

Is Providence any different? What sins will Christos's soul reveal?

"I cannot say who remains in Endurance or what they shall do," Emrys said. "It has been many months since we left, but I ask that pity be shown, not just for their sakes, but for that of Providence's and the human race. I am certain you have thought about what must happen one day, and how we must reclaim the Earth. The strongest and most adaptable will make the Earth their home once more."

Murmurs rippled around the chamber, and Christos narrowed his eyes. Talk of outside must be a touchy subject.

Laurence cut across the chatter. "Allow us to confer. You ask a lot of us, but we will consider your request for you and your daughter to remain, separate from permitting the arrival of more of Endurance's inhabitants inside Providence's walls. Please wait outside while we deliberate in private."

The Five stood and filed through a doorway behind Christos's chair. Nimue and Emrys were ushered back into the antechamber.

Typical humans with their warring tribes.

Galen kept them company, but conversation wasn't forthcoming. Emrys and Nimue feigned concern over others deciding their fate to justify their silence. Meanwhile his head buzzed.

Clara and Ragnar gobbled up Nimue's commentary, colored with a bleak brushstroke. They demanded they do more to ensure the surviving Darisami would be admitted. Clara and Ragnar argued against each other, both trying to champion their plan. The pressure intensified, and Emrys's skull felt like it was about to split.

Restrain yourselves! He slammed his mind into theirs, and their thoughts reverberated into silence. *They can't turn us away, too many have seen us for that. This is all a show. We'll be used as a lesson on the dangers of the outside world, and our request to bring Endurance here will be forgotten. But that will not be the end of it. Let us do our jobs and you focus on keeping Endurance from crumbling further. Have any more humans died?*

No, but they're a pathetic lot, Ragnar said. *Prone to weeping or spitting at us as we try to feed them. Ungrateful pigs. Some will starve, but we'll attempt to harvest before they perish.*

I hope you're burning the bodies.

We're not stupid, Emrys. No trace will remain.

Good, because if Providence comes snooping around, the last thing they need to see is a few thousand prisoners and a lot of corpses.

A greedy thought flashed through his mind. It was so strong he wondered if Clara and Ragnar had expressed it as one. If Providence marched on Endurance, there would be such a feast before they got there.

The door opened and a guard spoke to Galen. Emrys stood and shoved the Darisami out of his head.

"They've returned," Galen said.

Have you told them yet? Emrys thought to Nimue.

She leveled a look at him that made him feel about two

inches tall. Radioactive weeds could wither between her suffer-no-fools stare.

Next time include me.

You were busy. No one paid me any attention.

I can do more than one thing at a time.

Again, that stare.

The meeting had resumed, and they'd been granted leave to remain in Providence subject to their laws and customs. Someone would fill them in on exactly what those were at some point.

The chatter resumed the second the Five departed. The caged people of Providence had something to gossip about. Possibly the biggest news of their recent history.

Outsiders.

It was like the Second Coming.

Guards marched Emrys and Nimue from the chamber and returned them to their room.

"The Council has ordered you to stay confined, while they sort a few things out," Galen said. "People will be by. Clothes provided. You'll go to work, and Nimue will attend school."

She scrunched up her face, her features crumpling so fast it couldn't have been faked.

Galen chuckled. "School's not that bad."

Emrys jumped in, lest Nimue lose control and Galen end up dead. "Nimue didn't enjoy school very much in Endurance."

"I'm sorry to hear that, but those are the rules. She will attend school five days a week, six hours a day. We must train the next generation to solve the problems previous generations left us." Galen rattled off the words with practiced respect. Another line. Another tenet. Another lie.

"Why should I fix their mistakes?" Nimue stuck out her petite jaw in childish defiance and planted her small fists on her hips. She had the image of a petulant child down pat. But her eyes were something else. As if they caught and wrestled tigers.

Galen jerked back, but Emrys couldn't tell if it was from her defiance or Galen's surprise at having the doctrine questioned. He scratched the back of his neck, looking like he was the schoolboy and she the teacher. "Because that's the way of things." The inflection on the last word lifted slightly. "And you can hardly blame me, I was born inside too, but that doesn't mean we can't hope for something better. Wouldn't you like to walk beneath a blue sky and through green grass?" Galen said it with care, as if speaking the idea aloud would get him in trouble.

"I've already seen the outside, and those things no longer exist." She spun and went into the bathroom.

Galen blinked after her.

"Never mind her," Emrys said. "She's used to holding her own against adults." He'd have to talk to her once Galen left. The last thing they needed was for her to make enemies. There'd been plenty in Endurance.

"Oh, it wasn't that, it was—" Galen's hand touched his mouth, then waved away the words he hadn't spoken aloud. "It doesn't matter." He refused to meet Emrys's eye.

What had he been about to say? As much as he wanted to hear more, it was a problem for another time. Emrys needed to be allowed free access to Providence as soon as possible before he starved. He'd managed to suppress the greatest part of his need as they walked through the packed halls of Providence. Thousands and thousands of souls ripe for the picking. His mouth watered, and he had to swallow to stop himself from drooling.

"What about me? When will I be given my first assignment?"

Galen stilled. His brow furrowed, deepening the

vertical lines above his nose. "You should hope they never come."

"Why? This is what I promised them, and they seemed keen enough for it. Greedy even."

"You should be thinking of a way to get out of it."

"It's too late for that. The sooner I become indispensable to them, the more secure my position here."

"Or they'll use you and throw you away."

"What are you saying, Galen?"

He seemed on the verge of saying more but swept it aside, and a false smile brightened his face. "Nothing. I think you should be careful, that's all." He opened the door. "Enjoy your morning."

"Galen?"

The soldier stopped.

"Thank you for worrying about me. It's been a long time since anyone cared."

"Don't mention it." Galen left and sealed the door shut.

There was some story slumbering in Galen's ready assistance and warning, a hint that something was rotten in the ark of Providence. He could use Galen's kindness and indiscretion as leverage to secure his position, but the idea rot like rancid meat in his stomach. There had to be another way.

For a moment, Emrys was alone. Blessedly alone. The sound of the water in the shower was just audible through the door to the bathroom. Nimue liked the cascade of water, the hotter the better, and she'd sit there as long as she could.

But soon a chime at the door heralded the arrival of fresh clothes and the first official, and once Nimue was clean and dressed, they were overwhelmed with information. It was impossible for the Five to oversee everything, so that left room for minions to flourish.

Like weeds.

The official—a sliver of a man with a high nasal voice—intoned the laws of Providence for two hours, without breath and without reference to notes. The laws were based on the old laws with a few minor but meaningful additions.

Discussion of the outside world was to be kept to a minimum lest it create revolt. This was the first law to come out of the man's mouth. Deference was to be given to the Five, and as Providence's elected officials—democratic elections every four years—they had no need to refer to their subjects—sorry, citizens—on most matters.

Emrys asked how long the Five had remained the same group. The official glared at the interruption but relinquished the knowledge. Christos had served for forty years, Isaiah and Laurence about twenty, Elaina and Kira ten and six respectively. Providence enjoyed the status quo.

The man rambled on, the laws ranging from the common sense to the ridiculous. After Emrys was informed of the prohibition on hanging objects over the balconies, he held up his hand for a pause. "I think we get the general gist, don't we, Nimue?"

She had pretended to fall asleep in his lap.

He stroked her hair. "You don't mind if we catch up on the rest some other time, do you? My daughter and I have had a long journey."

The official huffed, but Emrys fixed him with a look that all men who'd ever come up against a father would recognize. It said, *My daughter is the only thing worth a damn in this world and you don't want to test my devotion.*

Emrys smiled as warmly as he could as the dry little man left the room.

Nimue bolted upright and slapped her palms on her thighs. "I thought he'd never stop!"

"They have to do something to keep themselves amused. Order. Restraint. Survival. That's how they've lasted so long."

"Don't repeat that stupid phrase to me. It's not survival. It's living death." The sneer on her face subsided like a cliff face disappearing down a crevasse. She replaced it with a jagged grin.

"Don't get any ideas. We're here to find a place to shore up supply, not bring down another city."

"You seem to think what happened in Endurance was our fault."

"No, not that." He paused. "At least not mine."

She hit him with a baleful look.

A teacher came next to assess Nimue, then a man to talk them through the forms they needed to fill out on the screens in their room, then a woman to tell them what Providence subsisted on, followed by a mix of people who had no real purpose but found a way through the guards to gawp at the new residents under the guise of offering official advice.

A few looked on the verge of asking something, their brows knit in consternation. They wanted to know more about life on the surface, but he'd be damned if he would voice it. Too risky. He needed to get out of the room and wander the halls to ease his paranoia, yet even there, he would not be able to escape someone's eyes, someone's ears, or someone's designs.

So instead of talking about it or giving them leave to speak, he smiled benignly and held innocence in his eyes. He traced the eternity symbol on the cushion and resisted morphing it into the one that would unlock their souls and fill his widening hunger. When they finally departed, everyone was left unsatisfied.

Galen returned when the screen's clock flashed 18:00 and took them to dinner. They'd been brought some food through the day, but this was their chance for a small tour of Providence's mundanity.

The inhabitants had the option of eating in the large communal dining halls on each floor or in their rooms. No one had their own kitchen, as in Endurance, so either way they had to collect their meals from the mess. Most chose to eat there as well to save the journey back. If they wanted something to drink, they had to get it from water fountains in the hallways or out of their bathroom faucets.

When they entered the mess, news of their arrival spread, and the swollen crowd stuttered. The official who'd given them the long stale breath of the law sneered, but when Emrys caught his eye, he couldn't hold it and his color drained. He turned back to his meal. A bit of fear was beneficial.

Chatter gradually resumed, and the three of them joined a queue, took a tray, and were given a plate with a meat substitute in the shape of what was probably meant to be a small steak but more closely resembled a human liver. As they moved down the line, they added solid balls of something consisting of the healthy stuff humans needed minus the fun. Galen took them to a table, and they sat.

Emrys's hands strangled the handles of his knife and fork. He didn't want the fodder in front of him. He wanted to suck the life out of every single person in that room. His stomach ached for sustenance, not the offering on his plate. Bodies pressing in around him, souls within his grasp. His cells cried out to be fed, each one fighting for survival and yearning to snatch a soul from some unwilling body. Just one. If only he could have just one.

"You're not hungry?" Galen sat opposite him. He was so close. He could reach out, touch his chest, feign that he was cleaning something off his shirt then—

But the spotlight of Galen's green eyes forced his hunger into retreat.

"Starving." Emrys pressed the blunt knife into the meat and separated it into chunks which he shoveled into his mouth. The food was dry and bland, but he'd get used to it. And before long, he and Nimue would skip the communal dining experience altogether. He had something to look forward to.

"What have people been saying about us since the meeting? Any trouble?"

Galen swallowed a mouthful and used his tongue to clear food from his teeth. Ordinarily, Emrys hated watching people eat, but there was something about the contortions of Galen's face that verged on endearing. Cute even.

He hadn't thought that word in centuries.

"Minor rumblings. Despite what the Five told the people at the meeting, there are a few who think you've brought disease into Providence or that you're saboteurs. But the majority are intrigued about your journey." Galen put down his cutlery and leaned closer. "As am I. The fact that you made it that far across the country is astounding."

"I'd be happy to tell you more about the journey sometime." He wanted to tell Galen everything, but he had to be smart. "Though maybe when we know our place here is secure."

"I wouldn't worry about that. The Five won't boot you out."

"We'll see. It all depends on how well I do with my missions, doesn't it?"

Galen's eyes darted left and right but no one was close enough to hear their conversation.

"When will I be summoned?" Because as nice as it was sitting there with Galen acting like an ordinary human, the need to feed crushed Emrys's bones. He had to harvest in the next two days, and he'd rather do that in service to Providence. If not, he'd find someone—anyone—and suck out their soul. He didn't go through all this to die so close to his goal.

Galen pulled back and frowned, and Emrys realized he'd been staring like a slavering dog eyeing off a sickly lamb. He blinked and wrestled his hunger into precarious submission.

"We shouldn't talk about this here." Galen turned his attention to his plate and ate in a steady, measured pace—stab, slice, eat, chew three times, swallow, repeat. His plate was clean in less than a minute. Emrys quickly followed suit and finished shortly after. Nimue pushed her food around her plate.

"We should go." Galen stood. "I can imagine it's been a long day for you." He didn't wait for them to respond and headed for the exit.

He and Nimue shared a quizzical glance but hurried after Galen back to their room. They'd been out for less than an hour, and his skin crawled at the thought of returning to their little cell, but Galen was not open to alternatives. He stood aside while they entered their room, but didn't come in.

Emrys stopped at the doorway. "I'm sorry if I've offended you."

"You're doing what you think is best."

"But you don't agree with it."

"It doesn't matter whether I agree or not, others have decided what is best, and I accept that."

"Try telling that to your face."

Galen's seriousness cracked, and Emrys basked in that small show of happiness. But the warmth faded.

"I will be by to get you at nine, but if I were you, I'd use tonight to come up with an excuse. Nimue, you start school the day after tomorrow. One of the teachers will come for you. Goodnight."

Galen's departure made Emrys uneasy. Did he disapprove of what Emrys was being asked to do or that he had so readily agreed to it? If being the Five's extrajudicial executioner was so unpalatable, would Galen one day find himself on Emrys's list? He knew he'd never go through with that, not even if Galen was the last soul on Earth.

"He's a soldier, right?" Nimue said once they were alone. "Why be so squeamish? He must have had to shoot someone before."

"Perhaps not."

"The less you have to do with him, the better."

"I don't know about that. He's the only one who's shown any interest in our wellbeing."

"I think he's showing a lot more than that." She raised her eyebrows at him.

"Don't be ridiculous. He's just concerned."

"And I'm the Cheshire Cat." Even more so with that wicked grin.

He rolled his eyes. "That is simply not an option."

It had been too long since Emrys had entertained any thoughts of affection, with human or immortal. Lysander had been the last great romantic mistake and Sian had died because of it. No, he had to focus on keeping him and Nimue safe in Providence. There was no time for anything else.

＃ 15 ＃

"His name's Jared. He lives on level four, room 4514." With a press of his finger, Isaiah summoned an image of the marked man to the large screen.

He had brown hair and looked to be in his late twenties, an ordinary human being if not for the animation in his eyes. They drew Emrys in. What was it about them? Curiosity? Defiance? Whatever it was, it gave Isaiah a reason to want him dead.

Isaiah waited a few seconds while Emrys studied the picture, then a black screen replaced the image. "There are no cameras in the rooms, just in the hallways pointing to the elevators. We try to give our citizens a little privacy."

"I understand. Surveillance is for their safety as much as that of Providence's, but it wouldn't do for them to feel like they're living in a prison."

Isaiah leaned back in his chair and tapped the armrest with his finger. "Indeed."

They were alone in the room, and despite the clandestine nature of the meeting and the importance of what they were about to do, Emrys searched Isaiah for commonalities between him and his son. Given time to assess him, the shared eye color and nose were even more obvious, but the mouth was different. Isaiah's lips were losing collagen while Galen's remained thick and full. Isaiah also had none of Galen's warmth and he would not have flinched if Emrys slaughtered men, women, children, or puppies.

Emrys's fingers itched to pluck the soul out of Isaiah's chest. He could do it. Do it right then. Do it fast. He was desperate enough for it, and no one would know how it had happened. Then perhaps his little deal would be over. Galen's anxiety when he'd collected Emrys that morning had got under his skin, but the fact was he had to kill to live, and being a secret assassin was the best option. Isaiah would live until another day, when suspicion wouldn't so easily fall on Emrys. He traced a safer symbol on the glass-topped table.

"So, you want me to demonstrate my skills on Jared?"

"Correct."

"When?"

Isaiah's tapping stopped. "What?"

"When do you want this done?"

"You have two days."

More than enough.

"Very well." He stood and headed to the door, Isaiah's flinch filling him with a small dose of satisfaction.

"You didn't ask why."

He stopped and turned. "Is there any point?"

Isaiah's lips twitched. He understood as one soldier to another. Orders were orders.

"And Stone. Don't mention this to anyone, understand? No one."

He nodded and exited the room. He disturbed Galen leaning against the wall, his fingers at his mouth. He dropped his hand and hid it behind his back. "How'd it go?"

"I've been given my orders."

Galen's skin paled. "Are you…are you sure you want to go through with this?"

"I have no choice."

The soldier didn't respond with any inspirational bull-shit about everyone having a choice, but the silence labored. It weighed on the back of Emrys's neck, like an axe lining up for the chop.

"How does it feel to be the son of perhaps the most powerful man in Providence?"

"I try not to think about it."

They walked down the deserted hallways of the mili-tary quarter. Doors led off to who knew where, forgotten rooms out of the way that ordinary citizens had no idea existed. Rooms that were most likely filled with innocuous things but nevertheless served darker purposes than they could imagine. Life continued because of what was done in these hallways. Whatever was done there was done for the good of the society on which it preyed.

And on which he and Nimue hoped to grow fat.

"Whether you think about it or not, it's a fact."

Galen didn't respond.

He took hold of Galen's arm and forced him to stop. "Galen, you can talk to me." He should be pleased he'd found a weakness he could exploit, but Galen's discomfort came with no joy.

"And say what? I have a cursed position here, Emrys. I'm privileged, but I'm trapped. There. That's the situation."

"I didn't mean to upset you. I'm trying to understand how this place works."

"You do what they tell you to do, and everything works

out fine. And if you don't, you suffer the consequences. That's all you need to understand. That's all anyone here needs to understand."

But the shimmer in Galen's eye told him there was more to it. Emrys opened his mouth to ask a tentative question, but the door beside them opened, and Brink appeared. Galen stepped back faster than Emrys could blink.

Brink's lip curled up into a fierce sneer. "What's going on here?"

"Watch yourself, Brink," Galen said. "This is nothing to do with you."

"Seeing my *captain* and a dangerous outsider together is definitely something to do with me. I want to make sure my *captain* is doing the right thing by Providence."

Galen's right eye twitched, but though he had every right to dress down his subordinate, the reprimand didn't come.

Emrys stepped in. "Is that any way to speak to your superior?"

"Who the fuck are you to tell me what to do?"

Emrys's hunger surged out of its stasis, and his fist grabbed hold of Brink's shirt. The symbol blazed at the forefront of his mind. One soul. One tiny soul. One tiny dirty soul.

Mine. Mine. Mine.

"That's enough!" Galen pushed in between the two of them. "Emrys, let him go."

Air streamed through Emrys's nostrils as the snarling jaws of his need snapped at being denied. He'd been so close to ripping Brink's soul out of his body. The bastard would have died in his arms.

Right in front of Galen.

Emrys retreated, and Galen took over.

"I will not have my actions questioned by a soldier under my command."

"What about those who are above you? Like your dad? He's always interested in what you're up to—and who you're with."

"Then I'll answer to him, not you. Move on."

Brink didn't lose the attitude that tarred his face. He pushed between Galen and Emrys and stomped down the corridor.

Emrys waited until Brink had gone through the sliding doors. "He shouldn't talk to you that way."

"He's done worse." No emotion showed on Galen's face, leaving behind the blank surface of official business. "A lot worse." Galen started walking.

Emrys hung back. He shouldn't care what was going on with Galen and his soldiers, only insofar as any ruction would serve his and Nimue's aims. He could foment their feud until it frothed and bubbled over, find out what their exchange was really about and twist it to his advantage. He could take Brink's spot. Then Galen's. Beguile his way closer to the Five so he ensured his and Nimue's continued inhabitation in this cornucopia.

But he found he did care what was going on and why it hurt Galen so much. His hand buzzed with the remembered contact of Galen's fingers on his palm when they arrived, the way he'd traced the lines, a spot of calm while his stomach lurched like a boat on a wild ocean.

Was Nimue right? Was there the potential for more? Even if Galen was human?

No. It couldn't be allowed to continue. He was hungry, that was all. He'd suck out Jared's soul, and that would return him to equilibrium. He'd go on living his eternity.

He hurried after Galen and was informed he'd have until the next day to explore Providence before he started as a soldier. He had to have something useful and public to do, yet he wouldn't serve in Galen's unit. That was unwelcome news. Emrys would prefer to keep close to the councilor's son for more than one reason.

They stopped at the closed door at the end of the corridor.

"So, we won't be working together much?"

Galen's hand hovered over the button then clenched. "I'm still your go-between, but I can't oversee your training. As much as I'd like to."

Those green eyes… They disarmed him with their openness, their depth. Emrys wanted to fill them with his secrets.

"I'll just have to prove I'm worthy of being in your unit. I can already tell you I'm better than Brink."

Galen laughed. "That wouldn't be difficult."

They walked in silence through another series of corridors before Galen returned him to the public side of Providence. "I'll collect you at nine tomorrow and introduce you to your trainers. In the meantime…" Galen paused. "In the meantime, you should really think about what Isaiah's asked you to do." He held up his hand to stop Emrys's interjection. "I don't want to know anything about it, and I know you think you've got no choice, but what you do matters."

Some choice. If he didn't take Jared's soul, he wouldn't live long enough for Isaiah to banish him. And at least this death had been sanctioned.

"Galen, I appreciate what you're saying, but I'm committed to it. And I understand if you can't accept it, but I'd like to think, as one soldier to another, as one loyal citizen to another, you know I only do what has to be done."

Galen shook his head, a soft exhalation of breath like a

response to a bad joke puffing out of his lips. He gave him a quiet goodbye and slipped back inside the military warren. The door closed, and Emrys was left alone.

His stomach roiled. If Galen understood why he had to do this—it wouldn't make any difference. Either way, he needed to find Jared and feed.

Fast.

He rode the elevator up to the sixth floor. A few people gave him wary smiles but most avoided eye contact. That suited him. Right now, while he was so starved, any inter-action was difficult. He took the turns towards his quarters. He had until the morning to find Jared and—

He stopped. The soldiers who'd been posted outside his room were gone and, in their place, leaning against the wall, was…Jared? He straightened when he spotted Emrys.

"Hi, you're Emrys, right? Emrys Stone from Endurance?"

Emrys walked towards him slowly. Jared had grown a beard since the photo was taken. Not a long one, but more than stubble. Those eyes were the same, if a bit browner, like melted caramel. He stood straight, his shoulders not all that broad, but at least he wasn't stooped.

What kept Jared from buckling?

"Yeah. What can I do for you?"

"My name's Jared. Do you mind if I come in?"

Emrys looked around, half-expecting Isaiah and his soldiers to appear and say that this was all some ruse to have him kicked out so they could keep Nimue. But there was no one but him and Jared. He looked up at the ceiling but couldn't see any cameras.

"I see you don't trust them either," Jared said. "Let's get inside. We can talk freely in there."

He didn't share Jared's faith in the Five's respect for privacy but there wasn't anything to do but go along with it. His handprint unlocked the door, and Jared followed him inside. Nimue was out exploring.

Once inside with the door closed, Jared paced the room. "How are you liking Providence?"

"I like it just fine." He sat on a chair. Better to keep some distance. Killing Jared there would not work out well for anybody, least of all Jared.

"Better than Endurance?"

"Much."

"And the world outside?"

He hesitated. This was a test, but he wasn't sure where the results would lead. "You don't want to know what it's like out there."

"That's where you're wrong. Were you born in Endurance?"

"Yes."

"They tell me I was born in Providence, but they're lying. I remember the sun on my skin and a fresh breeze."

"I don't see how. You're not old enough."

"I don't believe the records they have on me. And I've spoken to people who lived in the world outside. They remember sunshine, they remember greenery. The time-lines don't match up."

"I think their minds have been distorted or they're choosing to remember better times. Trust me, the world is not what you think it is. Most of it is dead."

His words stirred a sadness he'd rather forget. Sharing his hopes with Jared of an eventual return to the world they'd lost would not make his job any easier.

"Maybe the parts you saw."

Emrys closed his hand into a fist. He understood why Isaiah wanted him dead, and though Emrys may wish that the surface was still inhabitable, now was not the time to upset Providence's stability.

"If you want to hear about my experiences, I'm happy to share them, but I'm not interested in talking with a man who has delusions about some earthly paradise beyond these walls. Providence is what keeps you alive. Step outside, and you'll be dead in a week. Two at most."

"Then how did you get here? Endurance is very far. Or so they say."

"We had lots of supplies."

"Now I definitely don't believe you." Jared narrowed his eyes. "Where did you come from really?"

"I've already told you—and ten thousand others—we came from Endurance."

"Yes, but you're lying. You're one of them, aren't you? You've been told to come down here and tell us your horror stories so we can be controlled. What are you hiding?" He pointed a finger at Emrys's face.

Emrys could have reached out and broken that finger before Jared realized the bone had snapped. He could have sucked out his soul five times over in the space it took to have this ridiculous conversation.

But he didn't.

As much as he wanted to.

Not yet.

"Listen, Jared, I'm not hiding anything. I came from Endurance. We travelled for many days to get here, and we have seen more of this country than anyone left alive. It is a wasteland."

"No one could travel that far and live, not if the world is the way you say it is. We're all living in an experiment designed by those on the surface."

Jared's ravings plucked at the tightly drawn tendons in the back of Emrys's neck. He stood to relieve the pinging tension. "You've been spending too much time in your own company."

"It's not just me. There are others. We don't believe the lies they tell us. There's no way the world is so damaged that we can't live freely on it."

"I'm telling you the truth. There is nothing out there for you." He rested his hand on Jared's shoulders to hold him still, but Jared broke free and stalked the room. Emrys sighed. "Talk to the soldiers who came and got us. The city is in ruins, the only people we've seen are those living in Providence. I don't hold much hope of anyone living out in the open for a very long time, if ever again."

"You're good. You're really good." Jared marched back and forth, scratching at the stubble on his chin. Back and forth.

"Believe what you want, but this conversation is over." Emrys went to open the door, but Jared grabbed his wrist in an iron clasp. These conversations were too dangerous. The longer he talked to Jared, the more claustrophobic he would feel. Emrys wanted to be on the surface, like all normal, right-thinking human beings, but he had to go where the food was. He'd just made it to Providence. He couldn't risk leaving it again.

"Wait! I'm sorry. I get carried away," Jared said. "You have no idea what it's like. You hold on to anything to believe there's a world beyond this one."

"Trust me, there isn't." He ripped his arm from Jared's grip and opened the door, then folded his arms and waited.

Jared skulked out and the door closed behind him once he crossed the threshold. Emrys laid down on his bed. Had Jared been marked for extermination because his rantings had stirred up trouble that could no longer be ignored? Or was this a mercy killing? The reasons shouldn't have mattered. Jared had been picked for slaughter and that soul was going to be put to good use. But even the prospect of a hearty meal didn't soothe his uneasiness and the remnants of Jared's frenetic energy buzzing in the room drove him out into the empty hallway. He sought Nimue.

Where are you?

I'm hunting Darisami. She giggled. *You should join me. I know you'd find it fun.*

Not without his golden knife.

I've started at the top. You should start at the bottom. I've met two people who were from the first intake, but so far none have reacted to me using the symbol.

His mind flinched. *You left them alive, didn't you?* The last thing they needed was a sudden spike in deaths to accompany their arrival.

I'm not an idiot, Emrys. I merely activated it to see if there was any recognition, but they remained unaware of what I was doing. That indicates to me that they're not Darisami. Are you going to help me, or do I have to do this all on my own?

He grudgingly committed to the task. She told him the story she'd been working with so he could corroborate, and he set off for the elevator to take him to the lowest level. Free from the confines of an official position within Providence for one more day, this was their best opportunity to find out if they were alone. It also gave them the chance to explore.

Most levels had living quarters and communal spaces, but some had workshops on them where they made clothes and machinery. The school was on level eight, food production on seven. Military occupied level five, but also a secret part of level four. Manufacturing was on three and medical wards on two.

The central column—the Tower—held the offices that kept everything running, sitting beneath the council chamber where citizens were free to petition the Five at sanctioned times.

He roamed Providence, cameras and sensors recording

his progress. Some residents avoided him, but others welcomed the chance to chat and directed him to the eldest inhabitants.

The first three he met had been born inside Providence, so the chances of them being Darisami were minimal. However, he let the symbol blaze bright and watched for any recognition. There was none. Not even a glimmer. Each time, it became harder and harder to snuff out the symbol. He could have taken one of them. His body strained with the need for a refill.

But he refrained. One of them, a woman with a hacking cough, would do for another month. She looked like she'd had enough of living.

He continued his search. Most people were at work, which left the elderly, who either could not work or had been permitted to retire, easier to find. From level one to level two then to three, he interrogated those he met, keeping the conversation light. He flattered them for their fine home, for their perseverance and survival, hoping to emulate them so he and Nimue could continue to live in peace and harmony.

There were moments he actually believed it.

He emerged onto level four.

"Emrys!"

He turned at the sound of Galen calling his name and marching towards him. He thought of walking in the other direction. He didn't want to answer a lot of questions about what he was doing or where he was going, but they probably had their own suspicions. The tension on Galen's face was all the confirmation he needed.

"Captain Rhodes. What can I do for you?" He straightened as a soldier would an officer.

Galen's brow furrowed at the formality. "I...I want to apologize for how I behaved this morning."

"It doesn't matter. You are my superior and can speak to me any way you wish."

The lines deepened. "Even so, I'm sorry. I haven't had much experience with...well, with someone of your talents, and I let that interfere with my professionalism."

"You're not a killer then."

Galen's eyes darted left and right. "I am a soldier, but no, I have not had to take anyone's life."

"Lucky for you I'm here."

He smiled but it failed to reach his eyes. "Lucky for some, unlucky for others."

"Indeed. Well, if there's nothing else, can I go? I'd like to explore my new home while I can."

"Do you mind if I tag along with you for a while? I can be your guide."

"I'd prefer to go alone."

"I think it would be better for you if I joined you. It would lead to fewer questions from those in charge."

"Have questions been asked already?"

Galen raised an eyebrow. "What do you think?"

More surveillance. He disliked being watched, but perhaps Galen could be of service. A question here and there to get the information he needed. It might save time.

"It appears I have little choice, so perhaps you can direct me to the eldest residents in Providence."

"What do you want with them?"

"It's a private matter."

"It'd be easier if you tell me what you're asking."

"I want their advice on surviving in Providence, what makes for a good citizen, the pitfalls to watch for, and how they differ from Endurance." He expelled a heavy breath. "I want to know we're safe."

Galen sucked at his bottom lip. "I know someone you

should talk to." He tilted his head to the space over Emrys's shoulder. He turned.

Christos was walking across one of the bridges from the central column.

"He was a young man when the Fall came. There's one woman who's older than him, but for sheer doggedness and loyalty, he's the one you want to talk to."

Emrys set off for the councilor. Christos would have little time for him, considering him less than human for the threat he brought into Providence. But seen through the prism of the Darisami, Christos met the requirements. He was youthful despite his apparent age, looked the conniving and cunning type to survive the apocalypse, and had a contempt of others that was borne of a bone-deep feeling of superiority.

"Councilor," Emrys called out.

Christos didn't stop when Emrys reached him, so Emrys had to keep after him.

"What do you want?" Christos said.

"I wanted to thank you for providing me and my daughter with a home. I hope you will not be disappointed by your decision."

Christos halted, forcing Emrys to stop short. "It is not a decision I agreed with so be warned that I will be watching for any excuse to see you expelled." Fury blazed in those eyes, and Emrys responded in kind with the symbol.

He made it as bright and as strong as he could, boring his gaze into Christos's and watching for any response.

Reveal yourself.

But there was no reaction.

"Is that clear?"

Emrys blinked, wrestling the symbol back into the darkness. He forced his hands into fists. He wanted Christos's soul, but Galen was by the councilor's side and it would not do to kill the old bastard out in the open. Another time, perhaps.

"Crystal. Thank you, councilor."

Christos turned up his nose, nodded at Galen, and continued his march through Providence.

"I don't think he likes me very much," he said once the councilor was out of earshot.

"Don't take it personally. He doesn't like many people. Despite all the time he spends with my father, I don't think they'd call each other friends."

"Allies, then."

"Just."

Emrys looked up at the six levels above him, each one home to thousands of souls. Any of them could house a Darisami. He had to keep searching.

"Maybe we'll have better luck with others. There are a couple of people on this level," Galen said.

"After you, Captain." Emrys bowed and swept his arm out, which earned him a smile that eased some of his frustration.

Galen led him down a corridor, towards quarters far from the center, and introduced him to a man and woman, both young when they'd entered Providence and both seeming to hold onto the terror and uncertainty of those final days. He asked his questions and waited for them to start to answer before forming the symbol.

There was no pause in anything they said, no stutter as if sensing it. They were not Darisami. He asked a few more questions, thanked them, then said goodbye.

"You didn't stay long," Galen said once they were in the corridor and walking towards the next meeting.

"I got what I came for. I wanted to see how they are faring. They say all the right things, but I wanted to see if they are living or merely surviving?"

"And?"

Better to give Galen a positive answer. "They're living, for the most part, as best they can."

They walked together in silence for a while.

"What was it like in Endurance? Were they living too?"

"We tried but there was always this sense of waiting for life to begin." *Or end.* "There was no sense of a future for any of us."

Galen introduced him to another old-timer, but they were human. He continued to the next. The hunger sawed on his nerves, and while Galen made introductions quicker, his continual presence meant Emrys never had a moment's solitude to calm his appetite. He covered it by asking questions about Providence's inhabitants, about how healthy everyone was and, in a roundabout way, finding out if there were often any unexplained deaths. As far as Galen knew, there weren't. Old age and cancer were the main causes, with a few accidents to keep things interesting.

"What happened to Nimue's mother? Was she your wife?" Galen asked after they visited another old and ailing human. He said it with such care and tenderness that Emrys's throat thickened.

Starvation had brought him to this point. He'd been using up his energy to counter the teasing and temptation so Galen's question caught him on the raw. He had rarely been asked about his family, and though Galen enquired about a fictional wife and a fictional mother to Nimue, his mind was in such a state as to replace both with Myfanwy.

When he didn't answer, Galen put his hand on his arm and stopped him. "I'm sorry, I didn't mean to upset you. It must be painful to talk about."

Emrys hung his head and hid his eyes. He tried to concoct a lie, but the fondness of Galen's touch made it hard to concentrate. "It's fine. I haven't spoken about her much with anyone other than Nimue. She…" He cleared his throat. "She was killed in a riot."

In truth, Myfanwy had died of consumption a few years before Lysander appeared at Emrys's workshop. He still felt her disappointment over his betrayal.

Galen swore. "A riot? What happened?"

"She wasn't involved, just got caught in the crossfires. She never wanted to hurt anyone, she was trying to calm the situation, but they wouldn't listen, and she was killed. That was the beginning of the end for Endurance."

"That's awful."

He looked into Galen's eyes, at the pity brimming within them. "It feels like a long time ago, but…look, I know I shouldn't be telling you this, but I'm asking these questions so I know Providence won't turn into another Endurance. I thought I helped Endurance, but I probably made things worse. Here, I need to know I'm making a difference for the better."

"I wish I could give you that assurance."

He gave one short, sharp laugh. "You should know how Providence stands. Your father is in charge."

"That doesn't mean I don't have doubts." The pity in Galen's eyes turned into something else, something hard, something vital and *alive* before he blinked, and the intensity faded. "You remind me of someone and the hard decisions we have to make to survive."

Regret coursed through Galen's words, and Emrys wanted to repay some of the kindness he'd been shown, but they arrived at another resident on level five and Galen's official façade returned.

Emrys asked his questions and unfurled the symbol. The human remained unmoved. Emrys's hunger itched. One scratch would turn into another and another and another until he was red and bleeding and howling. The symbol didn't fade easily. He gave a half-hearted thanks and beat a hasty retreat out of the room, gaining a few yards between him and Galen in which to gain control of himself. Even then it was hard won, and he snarled when Galen put his hand on Emrys's shoulder.

Galen stepped back. "Are you okay?"

Emrys heaved breath out of his constricted lungs. "I'm fine. I think I'm tired still and hearing about all their stories makes me wish for things that couldn't be in Endurance."

"Have you been reassured then?" Galen looked as if he wanted the answer to be no, but whatever his doubts, he would have to resolve them on his own.

"Yes, very much so. I don't think I need to meet anyone else."

Galen's mouth downturned. "Oh, right. I don't suppose—"

"I should get back and spend time with Nimue."

"How about I join you both for dinner tonight?"

The earnestness in Galen's question sounded off. Was he trying to delay him? Is that why Galen stayed by his side, so he wouldn't have the opportunity to kill?

If so, he needed to get away from Galen so he wouldn't be stuck alone with him and have no other soul to choose from.

"It'll be best if it's just the two of us. She's probably anxious about school tomorrow."

"Of course." Galen's face fell. "I should have thought of that. For what it's worth, I enjoyed spending time with you today, Emrys."

"Even if I am a killer?"

Galen's lips parted to answer but whatever he was about to say died on his breath.

Emrys waved away the awkward pause. "Forget I said it. I'll see you tomorrow?"

"Yes, you will."

Emrys retraced his steps through the corridors, the memory of Galen touching him or the concern in his eyes coming in fleeting moments. That was as infuriating as his hunger. He had enjoyed his time with Galen, much more than he should have, even more so if it came from a place of care. There was an ease to being in Galen's presence, and yet there was friction so delicious it had to be scratched. But the last time he'd scratched such an itch, he'd ended up as a Darisami and losing his child.

He had fallen for Lysander's charms, and though he had deluded himself into believing he had been tricked, he knew deep down to the marrow he had done it for his own selfish ends. He wanted Lysander, not just for his power but for his body, and he had tripped gaily down that dreaded path.

But things with Galen felt different. Or maybe Emrys hoped they would be. That was a theory he did not want to test, especially not while he hungered.

And after he fed and proved he was a killer, Galen would not want him.

Problem solved.

Right?

He cracked his neck, frustration and need rising within him, the symbol flickering in and out as it demanded attention. It had been wielded too often and put away unsatisfied. He needed to find Jared.

He descended to level four alone. The doors opened to reveal a white woman with auburn hair and a curvaceous frame. She was about thirty, her skin smooth and clear. If she spent time in the sun, she'd freckle. Like Myfanwy had. Guilt congealed in his stomach, smothering the symbol.

"Uhh, hello. Excuse me." He stepped out of her way and into the corridor so she could get into the elevator.

"You're the new one, aren't you? The guy with the daughter?" Her voice was strong and steady, to match her gaze.

"Yes. I'm Emrys." He held out his hand. "And you are?"

"Unimpressed." She didn't shake his hand. Instead she pressed the button for another floor, and she was gone.

Making friends in Providence was going to be hard work if he couldn't even make acquaintances.

The door to room 4515 was open. Jared sat on the edge of his single bed with his head resting in his hands. His back was bowed, and his hair spiked where he'd raked his fingers through it. He muttered under his breath.

"Hello, Jared."

His head snapped up. "What are you doing here?"

"I came to see how you were after our talk this morning." He stepped into the room, its walls marked and grubby. He closed the door behind him. "I was worried about you."

"Worried I wasn't believing your lies?"

"They're not lies. There really isn't anything on the surface worth risking your life and sanity for."

Jared stood and paced the room. Emrys tracked his movements before his eye caught on the scratchings on the white walls. Words had been carved into them. Mostly dates with a word here and there but whole paragraphs had been gouged into the surface too. Pens and markers were a luxury that the new era couldn't afford, but Jared had found a way to free his conspiracies. He'd covered the walls, and what Emrys had disregarded as the grubbiness of an unclean cell were Jared's attempts at escape.

"My friend Juliet was here. We think it must be torture for you to have to pretend there's nothing outside these walls."

Was that the woman at the elevator? That could complicate matters. Put him at the scene of the crime.

"You've had quite a while to work on these theories?" He found the date when Providence received its influx of survivors. Radiating out from it were questions and contradictions and conspiracies.

Records?

As if anyone had the presence of mind to think about recording humanity's desperation while they were fighting for survival.

Jared's eyelids closed to narrow, dangerous slits. "They're the truth, not theories. And you can cut the charade with me, all right? I know what's going on."

"I don't think you do." Emrys sat in the chair and leaned back, watching the insanity play out in front of him. Is this what had happened to Absolon? Had the other arks suffered the same fate?

"So, you admit there's something going on. You see? I can penetrate your lies. I can tell you want to help me but something's stopping you. Isn't that right? Otherwise, why would you come? Why would you chance it?"

"Jared, please, sit and I'll explain."

"Oh no, no more lies. That's all you're planning to feed me. More lies 'til I'm sick of them and vomit them onto their military compound floor. Well, I'll tell you what I know of the truth."

His ranting continued. Why hadn't Jared been treated already? These ideas had been breaking his mind for a while, but perhaps the appearance of two 'outsiders' had given him the kick he needed to topple into complete psychosis. It would be wonderful to give him something to believe, or to make him see that the world wasn't as he imagined, but the rot had dissolved his reason.

Emrys understood the desperate need to get out and

feel the earth, however barren, and the breeze, however scorched. Jared wasn't going to quieten anytime soon. His constant barrage filled the room until it shrank to the size of a coffin.

He approached Jared. It took a moment for him to realize Emrys had come near. "What? What are you doing?"

There was no more time for words, just the deed. No sound came from outside the door, but the corridor could have been filled with people and still Emrys wouldn't have stopped. He put his hand on the center of Jared's chest and forced him up against the wall. The symbol flared inside his head. He was ready.

"What are you doing?"

He got close to Jared's ear. "You were right all along." He raised his hand to rest on the bare skin at the base of Jared's throat. The symbol shot out of his palm with the speed and ferocity of lightning, and Emrys leaned back to hold Jared at arm's length.

The triumph that had ignited in Jared's eyes stuttered as he jolted and Emrys excised his soul. The elation of having all his fantasies affirmed crumbled and turned to sadness. His mouth drooped, and he would have fallen had Emrys not taken him in his arms and held him close.

His damaged soul slipped into Emrys's body, dragging with it the bittersweet glory of a pure, transcendental life force painted with Jared's life story—of a father desperate to get out and dying in the process, of a mother too scared to love him, of years of trying to fit in and hiding the ache that gnawed at him. He spied faces he'd seen—Juliet, Galen, Brink, Isaiah—and many he hadn't.

And he saw himself and Nimue and felt Jared's hope that he could escape.

Emrys closed his eyes. His body recharged with Jared's

soul but also filled with a pity that jammed his throat. He held Jared after he'd been devoured. He swayed with him, danced with him, hugged him as if he could make it all better.

The body grew cold in his arms, and Emrys lay Jared down on his bed. He positioned one hand on his chest, the other by his side and tilted his head. Jared looked as if he slept. Emrys wiped him of fingerprints and shook off the grief that clung to him. He reveled in his revitalized strength. The hunger had abated. He had been granted a stay of execution.

❧ 16 ❧

A TEACHER CAME FOR NIMUE AT EIGHT THE NEXT morning. Neither of them looked like they enjoyed the prospect of spending time with each other. Emrys was prepared to give a stellar performance, hamming up the emotion of a parent seeing their child off on their first day of school, but Nimue was on edge. This close to her harvest day, the teacher was likely to end up dead.

She had struggled the day before, as he had, with the lighting and extinguishing of the symbol during her search. She had found no one she considered a possible candidate for Darisami. They concluded that it was unlikely but not impossible they shared the ark with another immortal, but they had no proof. Time would tell, and they would remain alert.

At half past eight, Galen appeared at his door, but the previous day's familiarity had been replaced with anxious authority. Instead of collecting him for work, Galen herded Emrys back into his quarters and sealed them in together. Even after the door was closed, it took him a long time to speak. His lips fluttered, he blinked, the muscles in his brow pulsed, all these tiny movements without saying anything. Then everything stopped, like a decision had been made.

"Was it you?" Voice flat, barely a question.

Tension rasped in Emrys's throat. "Was what me?"

"One of the citizens was found dead last night. Was it you?"

Emrys opened his mouth to refute it but he shouldn't have had to hide the truth. Not from a soldier whose father had given the order. That didn't stop a heaviness swathing his body. "What would you like me to say? I was given a job and I did it."

"What was their name?"

"Excuse me?"

"The dead person's name. Tell me what it was."

There was no avoiding it. "Jared."

Galen covered his face with his hands and let out a long breath that blew away all those foolish fantasies Emrys had entertained of him and Galen.

"I told you this is what I am. You can't say I didn't warn you."

But he hadn't told Galen killing was more than a profession, more than a hobby, more than breathing. He had to kill to live. No one but a Darisami understood that but he'd long ago given up the hope of loving a Darisami.

Galen dragged his hands down his face, his skin stretching, then slid his fingers up to press against his temples. "I know. I just didn't want to believe you'd killed Jared."

The sorrow in Galen's voice disarmed Emrys.

"Did you know him?"

"Yeah, he was a friend. *Used to* be a friend. Long before you came along."

"Galen, I'm sorry. I had no idea." And it shouldn't

have made a difference. He was given an order to kill Jared as the price of admittance to Providence. But his heart burned with the pain he'd inflicted on Galen, then incinerated in rage. Why would Isaiah do this to his son?

Galen walked away from his apology, circled the room, and stopped behind the couch. Another barrier between them. "What did my father tell you about him?"

"Nothing. Just that they wanted him taken out."

"And you did it?"

Emrys shrugged off the accusation but the guilt remained. "Wouldn't you? As a soldier, I thought you'd understand."

Galen tapped his fist into the top of the couch cushion. The muscles in his forehead rippled. The space above his top lip stretched and strained until he clamped his teeth over his bottom lip.

"Were you close?"

Galen shook his head, a violent flick of his head. "Not for years, but…but I didn't want this to happen to him."

"You knew he wasn't well, right?"

"He had some strange ideas, but he didn't deserve to die for them."

"They weren't just strange, they were dangerous. You can't have someone like that running around saying this is an experiment." His words came out fast, flustered, fractious. They propelled him closer to Galen, but there was still too much in the way. Furniture, space, mistrust. "If it helps, I can tell you he died peacefully."

"Unfortunately, I don't think that's what Isaiah wanted."

"What do you mean?"

"He really didn't say who Jared was, did he?"

"Who was he, Galen?"

The length of time between heart beats stretched.

"Jared is Laurence's nephew."

"Laurence? As in the councilor?"

Galen nodded.

Heat rose up the sides of Emrys's face. "You are kidding, aren't you?"

"I wish I was."

"Why would your father order me to take out a member of the Five's family?"

Galen bit his thumbnail. "Presumably for the good of Providence."

Emrys took a few breaths, but they did little to ease his unsettled heart. "Why did Isaiah want Jared dead?" He crossed to the table and perched on its edge.

Galen sank onto the couch and rubbed at his jaw with his knuckles. "Sometimes people think they know best when they don't. Laurence believes we should make more of an effort to return to the surface. Jared took those views to the extreme and was making it difficult for the Five. Isaiah, Christos, and Elaina wanted Jared sectioned, but Laurence and Kira refused."

"So? That's three against two. What's the problem?"

"Kira controls the Scientists and Laurence the Workers, both significant factions. They made veiled threats of strikes that could have crippled Providence, so everyone agreed not to incarcerate Jared as long as Laurence did something about him."

"And he did nothing?" Emrys rocked on the table's edge.

"He talked to Jared but that made it worse."

"You didn't think to take him to the surface and show him?"

"I offered but he refused to go, saying we were going to kill him and dump his body. That was the last time we spoke. Believe me, I…I wanted to help him." Galen hung his head.

"It's not your fault, Galen. None of this is your fault. It's mine and Isaiah's. Why did he want him dealt with now? Surely killing him so soon after my arrival would raise suspicion."

Galen raised his head and snared his gaze. "I think it was meant to."

A bony finger carved its way down Emrys's spine, deep enough to sever nerves and stop a shiver. "What do you mean?"

"Isaiah wants suspicion raised—but not of him or Christos."

"Why?"

"They'll blame you so they can justify never letting anyone in or out. They'll say you were a menace who should never have been admitted, and the world is far too dangerous to ever step foot in again."

"And you're here to take me to cell, I suppose."

"No, Isaiah's hushing up your involvement. He didn't think you'd be so…clean."

"Excuse me?"

"With Jared. There's…there's no mark on him, no poison in his system, no broken bones, nothing. It looks like he died of natural causes."

Thank God for the mercy of the Darisami. "But why would that stop him from sticking me with the blame?"

"He was impressed. He thinks you'll be useful. And now you've done it, he figures you'll do it again." Isaiah might have been impressed, but Galen looked anything but. That was a good thing.

"Surely there will be an investigation. What about surveillance? Access points? There was a woman, a friend of his. Juliet? She might put me at the scene."

Galen wrinkled his nose. "She might stir trouble, but the rest can be denied. Jared sought you out, you talked to him, he left, then later you found him and did the same. No one knows what happened in that room."

"So that's it? I kill a man, and everything continues as normal?" He didn't know whether to be relieved or horrified.

Galen leaned back and pressed his palms together. "Pretty much, but Isaiah has changed his mind about where you will work. He doesn't want you in the military, so you're being assigned to the Workers. I think he wants you where you can spy on his behalf and do the most damage when called upon."

"I don't like this, Galen."

"Neither do I, but this is the choice you made. He owns you now." Something flickered across Galen's face, something that hinted at an intimate empathy, but it was too fast to catch and then Galen was standing. "You're reassigned to resource recovery."

Emrys snorted. Something he could do to keep his hands busy and far from Galen. That should be for the best, considering what he'd done to destroy Galen's impression of him. He shouldn't need his kindness and concern, shouldn't want it. He had a room to sleep in and enough souls to feed on. That was ample for a Darisami at the end of the world.

So why did he want more? And why did he want it from Galen?

He had to satisfy himself that this would not be forever. He may yet win back Galen's regard.

"If that's how it is, then so be it. As long as it's not picking through the garbage."

"No, you'll pull apart old bits of junk for its metal and

sorting it for recycling. They're expecting you now, so head to the Factory on level three."

Galen headed for the door, and his official tone and impending departure tugged at the knot inside Emrys's chest. "Why did you come to talk to me? You could have sent some junior with a message of my reassignment."

"I wanted to know for certain that what Isaiah told me was true. I couldn't talk to anyone else about Jared and…" His eyes slid from Emrys's and landed on the flat surface of the door. "You're right. I shouldn't have come."

"I'm glad you did."

Galen's lips parted, and his green eyes flicked back long enough for Emrys to hear his own blood pumping.

This couldn't become anything. He'd avoided falling for anyone ever since Lysander had made him into a Darisami. Five hundred years without love. His heart should have fossilized. And yet he felt a connection with Galen, a connection stronger and more welcome than the one he had with Lysander. He shouldn't encourage it. After all, Lysander had ruined him.

But Galen wasn't Lysander.

"Goodbye, Emrys."

"You mean 'see you later.'"

Galen paused on the threshold but didn't stop for long before he was gone.

EMRYS JOINED THE HUSTLE AND BUSTLE OF PROVIDENCE AS the populace hurried to their work. The elevators filled, and he slipped in among the crowd. He caught the eye of a few people but, on the whole, he was forgotten, if not actively ignored. The cameras, however, would track his movements, and the eyes behind them would be waiting for an opportunity to put him to use beyond collecting scrap on the factory floor.

The elevator stopped on level three, and he exited with six other workers who all led him to a sensor-locked door. One by one they placed their thumbs on the reader and entered single file. He was the last of his cohort, but soon a second group of workers formed a line behind him. When it was his turn, he followed the other's lead, but the light flashed red and refused to allow him entry.

A speaker squawked. "Please step to the side. A manager will be with you shortly."

Sighs and tuts popped at his back. He closed his hand into a fist and moved over. The line moved quickly, and he was left alone.

The door opened and out stepped Juliet, the woman he'd seen at the elevator when he'd gone to find Jared. Her eyes were red and puffy, her auburn hank lank and disheveled. She knew Jared was dead. Had she been the one to find his body?

When she saw Emrys, her hand tensed where she held onto the door. "What are you doing here?" she said.

"This is where I was assigned to work."

She frowned. "I…oh, I…yes, sure. I remember now." She stood aside to let him in. "My name is Juliet."

"I'm Emrys. Are you…are you okay?"

"Not really. My friend died overnight. You met him yesterday."

Isaiah and Galen must have known this would happen. How was he meant to play this? He tried for surprised. "Jared? What do you mean dead?"

"Just dead." Her bottom lip quivered, and he gave her time to regain her composure. "He wasn't ill or anything, but they say he had a heart attack."

"That's awful." He'd rarely been confronted with his

crimes. If this were the old world, he would have saved her the pain and taken her soul too, but he found he didn't have the appetite for it. Something about her hair and the pallor of her skin being so like Myfanwy's. "He looked fine when I left him yesterday."

"Left him?" Her tone hardened. "I saw you on his floor in the evening. You went and visited him again?"

"I did. He was upset after our first meeting. I went to check he was all right. That was when I saw you. He was still a bit agitated, so I didn't stay long. Maybe his heart couldn't take it."

"What did you talk about?"

"You were his friend, you must know. It looked like he talked about nothing other than the surface and getting out."

"True. And now he's dead." Her accusation stuck like a needle through his heart.

"You think the two are connected?"

She studied him for what felt like ten minutes, and his scalp tingled.

"I'm not sure, but I intend to find out," she said. "And if I were you, I'd be careful what you say to people in future."

"I really am sorry about his passing."

"Thank you." Her body stiffened, and her jaw set, but her eyes wavered.

"Are you sure you should be at work today? I can't imagine anyone would complain if you took some time off to grieve."

"Jared would not want me to wallow in self-pity." She sighed. "And I feel safer here."

Despite her grief, she summoned the strength to do her job and processed him so the next day he could gain entry to the Factory without requiring assistance. She showed him through the various workshops before depositing him in resource recovery.

He'd work an eight-hour shift with one hour for lunch, six days a week. The work consisted of breaking apart old electronics, stripping out the wiring and other metals, and salvaging everything that could be salvaged. It was simple work, but that suited him. It'd keep his hands busy.

The room he was sent to was stacked high with old equipment. Four other workers hunched over their desks wearing goggles and gloves, extracting scraps with picks and pincers. She pointed him to a workbench and told him where to collect tools before exhaustion poured down her face and she excused herself.

He'd done that. He'd hurt her. But she could never know the truth.

With Juliet out of the room, the other workers lifted their heads. He introduced himself, their hands wary of touching his, even with protective gloves. He almost laughed. He grabbed his tools and, once suitably attired, sat at his desk and picked up the first piece of equipment.

Chips, wires, plastics, metals...he stripped the carcass clean, apportioning everything into tubs he would empty later elsewhere. Larger pieces were dumped according to their materials for recycling. Everything could be used again. Such was the way of Providence, where new materials were near impossible to come by. The military may have collected things on their forays to the surface but, like Endurance, they had to make do with what they had. Sixty-five years of thrift.

He worked through lunch. The others might have assumed he wanted to make a good impression on his first day, and he was happy to let them think it. Avoiding lunch meant he didn't have to go through the effort of eating when he didn't need to. He could hide from anyone wanting to judge him. For the time being, the best thing for him and Nimue was to slip into the background, and Providence had enough people for that to be achievable.

While the others ate, the solitude afforded him the opportunity to work on something of his own. Stripped of gloves, his hands twisted and tinkered with colored wires, fashioning a small silver circle containing two interlocked Js —one red, the other green. It wasn't his best effort, but his muscles warmed with the memories of finer work. He clipped the last piece of wire in place as the workers returned, and he slipped the trinket into his pocket.

The pile of recovered materials grew through the afternoon, and his back stiffened from bending over the workbench, an ache that took him back to his old workshop, his eyes straining in dim light while mixing metals and setting stones. Myfanwy would come stroke his back and entice him into putting down his tools. There would be Sian to play with. There would be his wife to love. There would be a life to live.

Then Myfanwy was no longer there, and Lysander found him. It was his scent that had lifted Emrys's head from his work, lilac and sandalwood that even now filled his nose when both were probably extinct. His smile had caught him next, a hungry and appraising grin, then eyes of deep purple that seemed to glow and sparkle like rough-cut amethysts.

His gaze, presence, scent, charisma, and potency were the claw-like prongs that Emrys later understood Lysander had used to trap him, but at the time he'd only known Lysander was no ordinary customer, no ordinary man dressed in smart and clean clothes who smelled and looked divine. He hadn't known at the time how caught he was.

Emrys hissed and dropped the motherboard he'd been touching with his bare hands. Lysander's scent dissipated, dumping Emrys back in Providence. His fingers tingled from where they'd been touching the wires and microprocessors. He held it by the plastic edges and brought it closer, then with a wary hand, traced over the components until his skin sang with the burn of gold. It was miniscule but could be salvaged. He picked apart the pieces. The gold intertwined with copper and aluminum. The metals would be melted down and separated later, but every little piece of gold he could gather was a gift. Providence needed it, but he needed it more.

He pried it loose and tucked it away in a compartment on his bench that he hoped wouldn't be raided or emptied. He'd gather as much as he could and, over time, melt it down into a weapon. He needed a new knife. He preferred his old one fashioned of Welsh gold, but there was little likelihood of ever getting it back.

How many specks of gold had he given away prior to taking off his gloves to make Juliet's gift? He couldn't go back and check, but he'd work without gloves from then on.

By the time his shift ended, he'd collected another two chips of gold. One of the workers, a woman, tapped him on the shoulder and said it was quitting time and if he stayed any longer, he'd make the rest of them look bad. It was a grudging attempt at camaraderie. There was some hope for a good life in Providence—if he didn't get kicked out first.

He trailed them down the corridor, other workers filing in to pass back out to the public areas and off to eat, to sleep, to fuck, to get on with their existence. He hung back, conscious of the trinket in his pocket. Juliet appeared at one door and fought against the flow of people to reach another.

He followed. The door wasn't locked so he entered

after her and into a room with desks and monitors, empty of everybody except her. She was intent on the screen and didn't notice him until he was standing at her desk. Startled, she shot to her feet and backed away.

"Oh, Emrys. What is it?"

He opened his mouth to speak but there was something in her eyes that kept him silent. Did she suspect he was Jared's killer? He fished the brooch out of his pocket and placed it on the desk, pushing it towards her. He gave a conciliatory smile and turned away. He didn't expect the brooch to make up for what he'd done, but he at least hoped it would ease some of her suffering.

Much of the crowd had thinned when he returned to the corridor, but he still got caught in a jam leaving through the main exit. In the crush, as they spilled out of the Factory, he stumbled into Brink.

The soldier shoved him away. "Watch where you're going, Stone."

Emrys regained himself and glared. "If I didn't know better, I'd say you had a crush on me, Brink. Showing up at the most inconvenient moments."

"Don't flatter yourself."

"Then what are you doing here?"

"None of your business."

"You're right. I've got better things to do than waste my time with you." He pushed past, knocking Brink's shoulder hard out of the way. He could have gone harder, could have dislocated it with a little more force, but self-preservation stopped him. Brink took the impact.

"You don't belong here, Stone, and the sooner you're booted out the better."

"You should get used to the fact that I'll be here for a very long time. Much longer than you."

"Is that a threat?"

This was an annoyance. There he was, an immortal capable of killing this pathetic human within seconds, and he had to stay his hand.

"I wouldn't waste my time."

"Good." Brink grabbed hold of his shirt front and pulled him close, his breath hot on Emrys's face. But before he said anything else the door opened, and Brink released him.

Juliet emerged, stopping short as she took in the sight of them so close together.

Emrys stepped back but failed to smooth the tension out of his face. His lips didn't quite meet.

"What's going on?" She looked from Brink to Emrys. "You two know each other?"

Emrys shrugged. "Not really."

"Not at all." Brink put his arm around her shoulder and brought her in for a hard kiss. "How are you doing?"

"I've been better." She shrugged her way out from under Brink's heavy arm and flicked her look to Emrys.

Brink caught it. "Piss off, Stone."

Quick as a flash, he could have grabbed Brink.

Quick as a flash, he could have sucked out Brink's soul.

Quick as a flash, he'd be exiled from Providence.

He turned to walk away.

"See you tomorrow, Emrys," Juliet called.

He nodded and left the two of them behind.

What was Brink doing with Juliet? Apart from the obvious. Brink was military and must know that Juliet and Jared were friends. If she shared some of Jared's views, that would put her and Brink at odds. And did he know the part Emrys had played in killing Jared? Would he say something to her?

One thing was for certain. If he could go back in time, he wouldn't have killed Jared. Perhaps he'd do Juliet a service by disposing of Brink when the time was right, but his attempt at staying separate from the petty conflicts in Providence was doomed. Without realizing it, he'd gotten embroiled in the political struggles and paranoid fantasies of a caged people.

Welcome to Providence.

❧ 17 ❧

THE NEXT MORNING NIMUE WENT TO SCHOOL, AND HE went to the Factory. The task was tedious, but he relished the chance to use his hands. They kept his mind busy. Which was probably how Nimue launched her attack. He was unthreading a long string of colored wires when it came.

His head burned with the force of a hot poker, and he cried out. He put his finger between his teeth and bit down hard to keep from screaming, but even so his coworkers turned. He heard snatches of their alarm through the white noise in his ears. He gasped, trying to hold onto something as the fire incinerated the back of his brain.

Nimue! He fought against the assault. *What are you doing?*

"Are you okay?"

He didn't know who spoke. The black spots dancing in front of his eyes made it hard to discern anything real. Her attack lessened to a dull ache behind his eyes. He gathered what little strength he had to shore up his mind, but he was under no illusion that the pain abated because of her will.

The rod of burning metal retreated and left an oily slick that dripped all the way into his gut.

I'm bored.

I'm at work!

Lucky you. I'm learning pre-Fall history. Again.

Supplemented with some new skills, I see.

It wouldn't do to berate her. He wouldn't know how to protect himself if she tried again. She'd got to him through the soul shard, that was obvious, but he didn't know how such a thing was possible.

"I'm getting a doctor."

Leave me alone.

She vanished, and he was suddenly aware of the crowd around him. He called out to stop his coworker from getting medical help, forced himself to his feet, and smiled as if that would be enough to appease them.

"I'm fine, really. It was a migraine. I get them every now and then."

They eyed him. No one moved. What must they have thought of him, yelping like that? He brightened his smile, relaxed his shoulders.

"Thank you for worrying, but I really am fine."

They looked at one another, their wariness laced with a double-edged concern for him and for themselves. Who was this man, and what contagion had he brought with him? He couldn't stand their scrutiny, so he repeated his preference to get on with the work and returned to his bench. They eventually did the same and he was forgotten.

If only he could forget the fear Nimue's invasion brought. His mind was still raw where she'd gained access, like she'd peeled his skin. How had she done it? It couldn't have been from pure force alone. She had found a vulnerability that could be exploited, but why not keep it to herself?

Despite the month-long expiry date on their ingesting a soul for sustenance, soul-splitting afforded them extra time. He hadn't tested its limits but theorized it had to do with its purpose. A soul that fed a body used energy more quickly, but one that had been split for communication did not. Whatever the mechanism or the motive, they were stuck with each other until it faded. Plenty of time for her to launch another attack.

Or for Ragnar and Clara to do the same.

He needed to learn how to attack. Bending over his desk, he slowed his hands, giving the impression of working. He sought the little boy's soul shard and held back the rising gorge.

Concentrate!

He closed his eyes and circled through his head, sensing the other pieces and where they nestled. He refrained from making too strong a contact lest he draw their attention. Clara and Ragnar remained unaware, but Nimue's tensed and retracted. Her borders firmed. He didn't probe further; she would already be alert, expecting him to retaliate.

He delved into his shard, defined the jagged edges of it, and the way it jutted. He turned back to Ragnar's and Clara's. When he hovered a little closer, he found theirs had a rough and uneven shape which had been cloaked in a more uniform consciousness. Nimue's, however, was strong and solid, a smooth castle wall that resisted footholds.

Through the force of his mind and the strength of Jared's soul, he shaped his shard into a sphere. At first it was like molding mercury, but he gradually sculpted it like clay and fired it with his power. He made it defensible except for the access points which could not be removed. Though the soul shard worked by thinking of the other person, there was a connection that ran to the different parts of his brain and on to the other pieces of soul. He'd missed them before when the four pieces lacked definition but now he focused on the link connecting him to Nimue. It glowed bright, brighter than the piece of soul he had or that any of them had. This is the path she'd taken when launching her attack.

He opened his eyes, needing a moment to ground himself and slip out of an all-consuming headspace. No one paid him any attention. With any luck, they'd have no reason to. Despite his strength, Nimue had more experience in this. She would not treat him gently if she caught his approach.

He closed his eyes, sought the safety of his shard, and gathered his strength. He fashioned himself into a burning rod of metal that glowed white. Poised at his end of the line, he counted to three and launched towards her shard.

She braced, but he pushed on and sliced into her defenses, juddering like he'd hit a metal wall. She grappled with him, and they locked together in a brutal tension. Even near the end of her month, she was stronger than he'd anticipated. She screeched at him, and he allowed her to push him back, all while gathering more details about how she was able to withstand him. She slammed her soul shut.

He hailed her, but she ignored him. Either way, his reconnaissance mission had been a success, and satisfaction hummed through his body.

He shored up his defenses and explored Clara and Ragnar's shards while remaining unobserved. He learned that the more undefined the soul shard, the easier to breach its shields, but it couldn't be done without raising attention. Ragnar and Clara both responded to him as if he'd hailed them. He pretended he had and gave them a report on their progress.

In kind, they told him that Endurance was growing stale, the humans difficult, and all five Darisami were restless. He urged them to bide their time, that he wasn't yet assured of his position in Providence, but he'd press their case soon. They seemed unconvinced but were unwilling to make the journey without certainty.

"Emrys?"

Juliet's voice brought him out of the conversation and beneath her concern. Her eyes were still red.

"Are you okay? The others said you weren't well."

"It was just a migraine, I'm fine. I'll get back to work."

"About that. We've received a message." Her features softened. "Your daughter has been taken to the hospital."

Talons sank into his heart's flesh and tore holes. What had he done to her?

"I need to go to her."

He surged to his feet but waited for Juliet to agree before leaving.

"Of course. It's on level two—"

He was out of the room before she finished. He rushed towards the hospital, his pace hampered by the slow elevator. When he burst into the reception, a nurse informed him that Nimue had been taken for scans, but a doctor would be out to speak to him. He was directed to wait beside her bed.

He played the worried father, pacing the floor in between two sickly patients, but inside his head he buzzed for her. She refused him but her petulance was a kind of comfort.

Twenty minutes later, she was wheeled into the ward on a bed and dressed in a hospital gown. She looked listless, her hair limp and scraggly. Had he got it wrong? Was she really sick?

"You're her father?" the woman in the white coat asked.

"Yes, I'm Emrys Stone. What's happened?"

"We're not sure. Nimue collapsed in class this afternoon complaining of a headache. The teacher didn't know what to do considering where you'd come from."

"We're not harboring a virus if that's what you're afraid of. *Your* doctors have already checked us out."

The doctor's lips pursed. "Either way, it's better to take precautions. Does she suffer from seizures? Migraines?"

"No, nothing like that."

"We'll give her some analgesia and keep her overnight for observation. She might still be recovering from the stress from her ordeal." The doctor gave him a bland look as if to question his fitness as a parent.

"I want her to come home with me, if that's all right."

"It's not."

"But I'm her father."

"And you're living in Providence. We don't take chances on these things. The school is unsettled, and if they're not reassured, panic might spread."

"Taking her home would be the best way to show everything is fine."

"Mr. Stone, your daughter will be spending the night in hospital. That's final. Now, I have to go check Nimue's scans." The doctor left.

He took Nimue's hand and squeezed it. "How are you feeling?"

She lifted heavy eyelids to him and blinked slowly before turning her head away. That small dismissal deepened the wounds in his heart. When they communicated soul to soul, she was his equal, but seeing how sick she looked and knowing that he'd attacked her, she was so much greater than him.

He kissed her forehead. "I'm sorry. Is there anything I can bring you?"

She gave a slight shake of her head and curled up on her side with her back to him.

"I'll check on you tomorrow." He nudged her mentally, but she ignored him there as well. He sighed and left the hospital.

She couldn't be mad at him for fighting fire with fire, but whatever she was upset about, he was the cause. Attacking her was wrong, but he'd done it anyway, sensing a weakness he'd try to exploit. He thought he could depend on her friendship, if not her loyalty, but how far would either of them go to survive?

He didn't return to work. The shift would end in an hour, and he didn't want to sit through their pity. He retreated to his quarters but had only been back a minute when Galen buzzed.

He was dressed in what passed for casual wear inside the ark: pale gray tunic and trousers. Emrys's heart rose at seeing the soldier, before nosediving on the realization that if Galen were there, he came not of his own volition. Social calls were not part of their arrangement.

"What do they want?"

"Who?"

"Isaiah? Christos? The plumber from level three?"

"I…look, can I come in?"

Though the muscles in his legs had turned to rock, he somehow managed to shift out of the way to allow the captain inside. Everything was telling him not to, that Galen being there would lead to trouble for both of them, but as he passed him, the scent of sandalwood, sun-warmed leather, and the endless possibilities of summer evenings brushed his nose and nestled in his stomach. He couldn't stop his hand from closing the door.

"How are you?" Galen massaged the back of his neck. His bicep bulged, straining the fabric and restricting the air supply to Emrys's brain. "And how's Nimue? What did the doctor say?"

Of course, he was just here for intel. Emrys stayed by the door. His visit wouldn't last long. "I don't know. I think she'll be fine, though. It's probably exhaustion."

"Okay, and how about you? Are you…coping?"

"Can we drop this, Galen? I know you're here to pump me for information. Tell them I'm fine. The Factory's fine. Everything's fine." He hated his tone, too rough, too raw, too ready to fight. Reporting to Isaiah every morning would be easier than this. No chance of liking Isaiah. No chance of loving Isaiah. No chance of wanting to reveal everything to Isaiah.

Galen frowned, but not the frown of a commanding officer's disappointment. It was a frown of a friend's confusion. "That's not why I'm here."

"You're sure? Because you've already made it clear that you find what I do unpalatable. I don't blame you. I know if I were in the same room as the person who'd killed my friend, no matter how gentle it was or what orders they were following, I wouldn't be able to stand it. I'd want revenge."

Galen sank onto the couch and interlocked his fingers. "I thought about it." He cracked his knuckles. "I thought about hitting you, and then I thought about exposing you, and then I thought about how none of it would make a difference. Jared would still be dead, you would still be a killer, and I would still be trapped."

The distress in Galen's voice dissolved some of Emrys's self-righteousness but not the stiffness in his muscles. He no longer expected a fight, but he still expected to get hurt. He forced himself to sit on the chair opposite Galen.

"We're all trapped."

"You escaped," Galen said. "You escaped Endurance."

He chuckled. "And ran straight into another ark." *And straight into you.*

"But you still escaped. You got out. It's more than any of us will ever accomplish, no matter how much we wish we were free."

"What are you saying? Are you…like Jared?"

"No. I didn't share his delusions, and I didn't share his courage to question those above me, even when it mattered most. I'm not like him. I'm weak."

"Survival takes strength. Jared broke, but you haven't. Despite knowing what you know, despite feeling what you feel, you continue regardless."

"But I don't change anything. I'm not like you, or Jared, or Tristan." Galen blinked and a jolt fired through his body. He bolted to his feet, unable to meet Emrys's eye. "I should go. I just came to check that you were all right."

"Wait, please." He grabbed Galen's hand as he passed. "Don't go. I hate to see you upset. Stay."

Galen chewed his bottom lip and for one eternally long moment, he looked on the verge of leaving. Emrys would have done anything to stop that from happening. When Galen nodded and returned to his seat, Emrys breathed again.

"Who's Tristan?"

"I knew you were going to ask that." He leaned his head back and stared up at the ceiling. "Tristan. Tristan was a soldier, and he wanted to escape too." He straightened his neck and stared at Emrys as if to make sure he was listening. "No, not escape. Explore. He wanted to explore. To discover. There wasn't one part of Providence that he didn't know, and sometimes I think there wasn't one person in Providence that he didn't know either." He swallowed, his Adam's apple bobbing. "It was infectious, that hunger for the quest. I loved him for it. Loved him for a lot of things. And I think he loved me too, but it didn't matter in the end. It wasn't enough to keep him safe. *I* couldn't keep him safe."

"What happened?" Emrys asked.

"He agitated, he stirred. Always digging. Always exposing. But not too much—at least I didn't think it was too much, but what do I know? I was young, a new recruit. It was obvious I'd join the military because that's what Isaiah said was best for me, but I joined willingly so I could be closer to Tristan."

"That sounds beautiful."

Galen smiled a gentle smile that reminded Emrys of mornings when the light was soft and the day was full of promise and innocence. Galen winced and the smile flattened. "It was. And I thought nothing was wrong. I was happy. Sure, we talked about what it would be like to leave Providence, and then to go beyond the city once we started our missions to the surface, but I thought they were just fantasies. Not plans, never plans. Every time it got harder and harder to bring him back inside, staying out longer and pushing the boundaries. And then he was taken."

Galen paused. Emrys didn't breathe.

"Isaiah said he was a traitor who'd been plotting to overthrow the Five. He showed me proof and said it would be best for everyone, me included, if I didn't make a fuss, if I stopped trying to see him, if I turned my back on him." Galen stared at Emrys, but not into his eyes. Instead he stared at Emrys's chest, a long-distance stare into the past. "And I agreed because they know best. I followed their orders. I kept my mouth shut. And I never saw him again. He was executed, and all my sins were forgiven, but never forgotten."

The harvest symbol appeared in Emrys's mind, summoned not by thought but by white rage. "I can't believe Isaiah did that to you." He couldn't say much else. He had to remain still, or else he'd sprint from the room to hunt Isaiah.

Galen, however, appeared resigned, as if bothered by a mild chronic pain he had grown used to. "He could have done a lot worse, but that was part of the punishment, living with how I'd abandoned Tristan. I told them I didn't believe any of what Tristan said." He lowered his voice. "But I did. And I gave Tristan everything I could to help his cause without realizing. I told him about Isaiah's weaknesses and his dealings. I knew enough about Christos to make his situation untenable. I could see our exodus happening with the information I gave him, but I was never strong enough to be the one to lead, not even strong enough to follow. But I did it anyway. It's because of me Tristan is dead."

Emrys edged forward on his seat, closer to Galen. "You didn't kill him."

"I did. I could have stopped him before it got out of hand. I could have defended him. But I was a coward and part of me was glad they took him. Glad he died. I hate myself for thinking that." He lifted his eyes to Emrys. "But once he was gone, I felt like I could believe in Providence and the Five again. After all, they're in charge. They should know better than me."

"In my experience it doesn't always work out like that. How long ago did this happen?"

"Five years. Feels like more."

"That's a long time to hold onto that guilt."

"I had to, in case I hurt anyone else. That's why I

stopped seeing Jared and the others."

"The others?"

"Juliet and Brink."

"You were friends with them?"

He nodded. "That's how I met Tristan. He was Brink's brother."

"Is that why Brink is so antagonistic towards you? He blames you for Tristan's death."

Galen laughed, and there was never a sadder sound. "If only. That I could bear. I fell in love with the wrong brother, and Brink has never forgiven me for it."

"But he's dating Juliet."

"To drive a wedge between me and her. She'd always had a crush on him. With Tristan dead she could be the sympathetic ear to Brink's many complaints. And by going out with her, Brink isolated me further as punishment for not choosing him."

"Surely she understands that she's being used."

He shrugged. "Perhaps she's using him, too. All I know is I'm better off alone."

"And yet you still see Brink every day. That must be hard."

"That's part of Isaiah's punishment for the two of us. Brink has to stay under my command and never gets promoted. Meanwhile, I have a reminder of what I did wrong."

"That's cruel."

"The alternative was death, though some days the doubts and the rage are so bad I'm not sure that wouldn't be the better alternative. And then there's you."

Galen's eyes were on him. Not soft. Not weak. Not slipping away. Pleasantly unpleasant. Unwelcomely welcome. "What about me?"

"You're a lot like Tristan—forthright, self-assured,

brave. You've got a worldliness to you I've never seen. Some would say it's because of your journey, but it's more than that. It runs through you like it's been there since birth. While we're all focused on what's happening in our tiny city, you're someone who thinks bigger. It's a lot like Tristan used to be—or would have liked to be." His smile sputtered and died.

"That doesn't bode well for me then, does it?" He said it lightly.

"Perhaps. Perhaps you'll get it right."

"I don't know about that, but I can promise you that like Tristan, I'll never harm you."

Because Tristan had protected Galen. That was evident. No matter what deal Galen thought he made, it would have done nothing if Tristan had named Galen as his accomplice.

"Don't." Galen closed his eyes. "Don't promise." He opened his eyes, but the pain remained. "You don't know what we might be forced to do."

"I promise it anyway. As one survivor to another."

The tension in Galen's face eased, replaced with the beginnings of a smile that Emrys wanted to see grow more than anything else on the planet. But it was fragile, and whatever thought passed through Galen's mind next was strong enough to make it wither.

"I should go. I've burdened you enough with my self-pity." He made for the door.

"You don't have to leave. Nimue's in the hospital, and I enjoy your company." Enjoyed more than his company.

"Maybe another time." He opened the door and crossed the threshold, then paused. He looked back and life sparked in his weary eyes. "I'm glad you're here."

He was gone before Emrys could tell him he felt the same.

$\maltese$ 18 $\maltese$

The blaze of a thousand dying suns incinerated Emrys's dreams and he woke howling. Even when he opened his eyes to his dark room, searing white pain blinded him, and he clutched his head to keep it from exploding. Jaws clenched and teeth grinding against each other, he had nowhere else to go but into the assault that Nimue had launched on his mind. Forcing his way back into the fire, the soul shard scalding to touch, he struggled to fashion a shield strong enough to—

The attack stopped as suddenly as it had appeared.

Good morning! Nimue's thoughts glowed inside his aching head. Her unwelcome foray into his mind smarted, and he growled aloud.

What the fuck are you playing at? He reformed the defenses he thought he'd built strong enough to keep her out. More fool him.

Don't be angry with me, Emrys.
That's twice you've attacked me. Why?
So you can be prepared.
For what? You're the only one doing this.

That you're aware of. Your defenses have been far too open, Emrys, and that can be exploited.

By whom? Ragnar and Clara haven't attacked me. They've left me alone.

That's because they think you're one of them.

What are you saying? Have they done to you what you're doing to me?

Not yet. But I can feel them trying. And if they're doing it to me, it won't be long before they do it to you.

Nimue's thoughts—and their implications—crystalized in his chest.

You do this for my benefit? A warning would have been nice.

They won't give you any warning. You need to be ready.

You know what I mean, Nimue. You and I are meant to be on the same side. We're in this together. Do not attack me again.

The sooner the soul shards lost their power the better. Until then, he'd have to follow her advice and build stronger walls. If only to get a proper night's sleep.

I apologize. But we need to practice. I do not trust Ragnar and Clara.

Do you think they will use it?

I think they will do everything they can to ensure we do not forget them.

His thoughts stilled. *How long do you think we have before they grow impatient?*

Not long. It's been a month, and they are already worried the soul shards will fade before they get here.

For now, the pieces held their strength.

Wait…how is it that you're so strong?

Amusement hummed through her silence.

You've fed, haven't you? Nimue…

They were going to die anyway.

They? How many?

Two.

He froze. *You planned it all along, didn't you? That perfor-mance in the hospital bed? You just wanted to feed. I thought you were upset with me.*

As if I could be upset with you, Emrys. Her smugness riled him.

Well, you can damn well get yourself out of hospital. I've got to go to work.

At least he assumed he did. He hadn't checked the time, and the room was still dark.

She asked what had happened the night before while she'd subjected him to the silent treatment, and he filled her in on part of his conversation with Galen. He fumbled for the lights and the screen woke, flashing the time. He had an hour before he needed to be at the Factory. He showered.

What should we tell Ragnar and Clara? he said.

The truth. Providence is unstable which makes our situation unstable, which means they'll be less keen to leave Endurance's supplies behind.

We're playing a dangerous game. They won't like being shut out.

Separation anxiety will do them good. We were all becoming too co-dependent in Endurance.

He agreed. He could do with some peace.

He bid farewell, and she vanished. Despite the recommitment to their alliance, he doubled his mental fortifications.

❧ 19 ❧

FOUR DAYS OF TRAINING WITH NIMUE AND A BARRAGE OF nagging thoughts from Ragnar and Clara made Emrys's head about as peaceful as a herd of elephants pirouetting across a minefield. Emrys extracted metal wires and widgets, and every jerk and tug reverberated through his skull.

Meanwhile, he'd been more or less accepted by his fellow workers. They insisted he join them for lunch on his seventh day. He suspected the silence in the workshop had grown too oppressive. And so, when lunch was called, he got up from his desk to join them.

Only to find Juliet blocking the door. "Emrys, could you stay behind?"

He had no choice and the others left.

"What's this about?"

"Someone wants to meet you. He'll be here in a minute. Stay put." She left the room.

He returned to his bench to wait, picking carefully through the pieces of gold he'd collected, his fingertips itching from the contact and the need for more. Over the past few days, he'd explored more of the Factory's maze and discovered a metalworking room. Machines separated metals and fashioned them into ingots for later use. He'd need about an hour, maybe two, if he wanted to forge the pieces he'd collected into a weapon. Maybe a gold-tipped metal rod, long enough to hold, with a hilt for grip. He'd never get enough gold to create a whole knife but, luckily for him, and unluckily for the Darisami, he didn't need much.

"Mr. Stone."

He turned at the resonant baritone voice behind him. Laurence, Jared's uncle and one of the Five, stood at the door, his black-and-white speckled hair combed back and styled, his white councilor robes replaced with utilitarian gray tunic and trousers. An embroidered white P sat over his left breast. He leaned on a cane. "I'm glad we could meet in private."

Juliet stood a little behind him.

"Councilor." He nodded which was as close to a bow as he was going to get. "What is this about?"

"I came to talk to you about my nephew, Jared."

No accusation sharpened Laurence's words, but Emrys's chest and stomach hardened in defense. "My condolences on your loss. Juliet said his death was unexpected. It must have been a shock."

"Indeed. Healthy people don't often drop dead."

Again, no accusation. At best his tone could be described as good-humored curiosity. Emrys's shoulders stiffened. He looked to Juliet and back to Laurence. "Is there something I'm missing?"

"There are some of us who don't think it a coincidence that you talk to him and he dies the same day." He lowered onto a stool. The cane stayed in front of him.

"You don't think I had something to do with his death, do you?"

Laurence laughed an easy laugh. "No, no, not you. I examined his body myself and grilled Elaina's doctors, but none of them could provide any evidence of foul play. Don't think me rude, but whoever did it was incredibly sophisticated in their attack."

"Have you considered Brink?" Not that Brink could ever be described as sophisticated.

Juliet's eyes widened, and Laurence straightened, one hand rising off his cane as if to hold Juliet's tongue.

"Why would you think Brink had anything to do with it?" he said.

"He's had it in for me the second he put a gun to my head. He didn't want me getting in, so I'm sure he wouldn't want anyone else getting out."

Juliet brushed aside Laurence's reprimand. "They were friends. He never would have hurt Jared. Never!"

Emrys shrank from her outburst. As much as he didn't like Brink, he didn't want to hurt Juliet. "I'm sorry. I don't yet know who's allied with who. I apologize, Juliet."

She didn't seem placated, but she retreated to the back of the room.

Laurence's hand massaged the top of his cane. "Brink is…an interesting choice. But the expertise required to make Jared's death look so innocuous would be beyond the talents of one man, you *or* Brink. What did you and my nephew discuss?"

"He wanted to know about the surface. He believed Providence was an experiment and the world outside wasn't as ruined as everyone was told."

Nothing changed in Laurence's face, body, or voice. "And what did you say in response?"

"The truth. That the surface is, for the time being,

uninhabitable, and Providence provides everything he could ever need." Though perhaps not all he could want.

Laurence tapped his cane on the floor. "And yet, you survived a journey of thousands of miles, you and your daughter. I'm not saying you are part of an experiment—I have been to the surface during my tenure—but the world beyond Providence must have regenerated for you to make it all that way."

"We were lucky, and we almost starved."

"Come now, don't be so circumspect. I am not as narrow-minded as Isaiah and Christos. Providence cannot keep us forever, yet most of the Five do not wish to look for alternatives."

"And you think we should be looking for a way out?"

"Don't you? You have seen so much of this country. You have seen the sun rise and fall—something many in Providence have never experienced. Are you happy to spend the remainder of your years in the bowels of the earth? Do you want that? Do you want that for your daughter?"

If it were possible, Emrys would choose the surface to this cage, but they were not apples and apples. They were apples and hand grenades.

"The surface cannot support us." Humans or Darisami.

"Not yet. Not without planning and work. Yet the Five, as a whole, do not want to consider it a possibility. They believe to entertain the idea is to bring about our destruction, when all it will do is put an end to Isaiah and Christos's control. It's harder to oversee the lives of every man, woman, and child if they aren't all in one place."

Emrys grimaced. "People have tried before."

"And failed. Which is why we're in this mess. Too busy

looking in and down, when we should be looking out and up."

Had Galen spoken to Laurence about him? He trusted Galen with his own desire for a return to the surface, but no one else. Especially not a member of the Five.

"These are all nice sentiments, Laurence, but they do not change the reality that the surface is desolate."

"At the moment, perhaps, but maybe not in the future, and Providence is best placed to explore that if we act now. From what you have said of the world, we may be its last hope."

He understood the danger in Laurence's proposal, not just in that it put him contrary to the wishes of the majority of the Five, but for the hope that it gave. His heart reached towards the possibilities that Laurence conjured out of recycled air. It would be better to do nothing, to ensure Providence remained functional below ground.

And yet...

"What do you want of me? I am nobody. I can change nothing," Emrys said.

"You matter more than you know. Your presence has brought an opportunity."

He had to be careful and not appear too eager. "I would have thought I brought despair. And if your theory is to be trusted, that Jared was murdered, perhaps I bring more trouble than it's worth. There is nothing out there. If Nimue and I could have survived longer in the wild, we would have, but I saw very little that could support a large population."

"You survived. That's what matters."

Laurence's words hung in the room between them. Juliet remained still but tense, and Emrys tried not to fidget beneath Laurence's gaze. He was caught and how he chose to act would determine what kind of life he and Nimue had in Providence.

But it wasn't just his life he was gambling with. It was Galen's too. And his future.

"What do you want me to do?"

A genuine smile broadened across Laurence's lined face. "Nothing yet. I just wanted to chat. I would never presume to force you to anything, though I hope that when the time comes, you will support me in my endeavors."

"I'm keen, but how I act will depend on what you plan to do. Nimue and I have a safe home here. I would need to be certain what you ask me to do would be worth the risk."

Laurence rose out of his seat without using the cane as support. An affectation? "It will be. A man who risks everything for his daughter as you have done would not be satisfied locking her away in this prison. You want more for her, just as I want more for our people." He held out his hand for Emrys to shake. Light glinted off the gold band on his middle finger.

Free of discoloration, there was a strong likelihood that it was real gold. One touch would be enough to confirm it, but either way, Emrys wanted it.

"Your ring. I want it as a sign of faith."

Laurence closed his hand into a fist and pulled it back. "I don't pay for my loyalty."

"You'll pay for mine."

Laurence looked to Juliet, touched the ring for a second, then slipped it off, holding it in his palm. Emrys shook Laurence's hand. His palm stung, taking the edge off his worry about what he'd agreed to. He collected the band and put it into his pocket.

"What was it you did in Endurance?"

The story he'd told Isaiah, Christos, and Elaina about him being in the military wouldn't work here, and he had to take the risk that it hadn't been passed onto the rest of the council. "I was a metal worker, which is why I was assigned to the Factory. To tell the truth, I wouldn't mind being reassigned to something similar. I'm sure it's within your power, or Juliet's."

Laurence's eyes studied him, but he wouldn't see anything but a humble worker.

"The decision is Juliet's. And now, I think, our business is concluded. I look forward to the next time we meet."

Laurence returned to the charade of using his cane as his back hunched, his right foot shuffled, and his arm strained on the end of the stick. For all that he cloaked himself in falsehood, Emrys believed he was authentic in his belief and in his hope to do more for Providence. A marked contrast to Isaiah and Christos's naked ego and ambition.

Laurence and Juliet left, and Emrys returned to his bench to continue with his work.

Juliet returned a few moments later. "That ring was his grandfather's."

"And now it's mine." He broke another piece of metal free and sorted it into components.

"Is that it? You'd help him for some trinket?"

He kept his tone light, soft, like they were having an ordinary conversation. "I wanted to see what he was willing to give me in return. People seem to only want things from me."

"But he's just lost his nephew." Her hand went to the double-J brooch on her belt.

"And I'm sorry about that, but it doesn't change the fact that by talking with him, I've put my life—and the life of my daughter—in jeopardy. If I said no, what then? What petty retribution would he bring down on me?"

She folded her arms. "He's not like that."

"I've only just met him, and I need something more than his word. I need commitment." He dropped his pitch. "I was serious about changing jobs."

She pursed her lips. "I'll think about it." She left the room without another word.

He shook out his arms and hands, trying to dispel the syrupy feeling of having lied to her, but he was confident he'd be moved by the end of the week. He returned to his work, hopeful of finding more gold.

The rest of his shift dragged, and the skin between his shoulder blades twitched in anticipation of another councilor coming to demand his aid. He could feel threads of intrigue running throughout Providence, but he hadn't been there long enough or talked to enough people to find out where they all led and who was connected to whom.

When he got back to his quarters that evening, Nimue was absent and her mind closed. Though he reached for her, she ignored him. He considered trying one of the tricks they'd been working on and sneak into her soul shard, but he preferred to rely on their trust. If she needed to tell him anything, she would.

He hailed Ragnar and the Darisami's mind was gruff and built with hair triggers. When Emrys brushed them, Ragnar launched, but he'd already backed out of the way.

Easy, Ragnar.

You and Nimue have been testing my patience.

And his defenses.

You seem tired. What's been happening in Endurance?

I'm more intrigued by what's happening between Clara and Nimue. Those two have been in solitary communication for some time.

How do you know this?

I have my ways.

Nimue had warned him Clara and Ragnar would not let the connection between them go without using it to their full advantage. He was surprised they had not yet invaded his mind.

What of it? They are sharing information.

They are plotting, and you know it.

We are both preparing for your arrival.

When? When is this so-called arrival?

It will be soon, Ragnar. There are complications. All is not well within Providence, and the alliances that keep this place together are being tested. Our presence hasn't been welcomed by all, and if you and the others show up, Providence may break further.

Ragnar snarled and struggled to regain control. Even when he did, he bristled. What had been going on in Endurance to unsettle Ragnar so much? Or perhaps it was the loss of Absolon that made him so irascible.

I will not stay here much longer, Emrys. Wyatt and I will make the journey, whether you are ready or not.

Patience, brother.

Do not counsel me! I will do what I think is right, and you do not have long before we march on Providence.

It's unwise to threaten me or Nimue. We are doing our best to secure your welcome but—

How have you been doing this? I have heard of no such effort, from you or Nimue. You work in a factory, Emrys. That's hardly useful.

That's because you lack subtlety. I must show that I have no designs on power, no wish to do anything beyond serve Providence. Meanwhile, I have the Five fighting over me, so everything must be handled with care. One faction wants me gone, the other wants me to act as a lightning rod for change. When you show up at our gates, you will want them to open, and that takes effort.

See that you're putting it in.

You don't have to question my loyalty, Ragnar. I wonder, however, if you are going to be fit to confine yourself inside Providence's walls.

You have been lord of Endurance for so long I don't think you know what it means to be a servant.

Providence will be a welcome tonic to what we are enduring. We're all fading. The halls echo with screams and wailing. I can go days without seeing the others, and Wyatt has gone almost mute. We need to get out.

But you cannot come if you cannot gain entry. Please, Ragnar, hold. Hold for me. Hold for Absolon. It will do no one any good if you perish outside Providence's gates.

Ragnar's mind sighed, the spikes of his tension retreating in response to Emrys's soothing tones. He filled his mind with hope, with peace, and sent that through the connection to his soul-brother. Only his shame and artifice did he restrain.

Do you know the thing I'm looking forward to most when we reach Providence, Emrys?

Tell me.

The company. Ragnar retreated and the connection ended.

Emrys released a long breath and sank back into his bed.

I never pegged Ragnar as a sentimentalist, Nimue's voice whispered inside his head. *I haven't felt that nauseated since I had cholera.*

You heard all that? How?

Through your mind and his.

Cockroach legs scuttled beneath the surface of his skin. *What are you playing at, Nimue?*

Ensuring the odds are stacked in our favor. Do not worry. All will be well.

She vanished before he could ask her what she meant or where she was.

The machinations of Providence and Endurance wore out his patience so that when the door chimed, he not only considered ignoring it but also wondered if he was even able to stand. Eventually whoever it was would leave, and he would not have to move. If he stayed still long enough, the whole world would pass him by without him having to do anything. But he brushed aside his self-pity, heaved himself off the bed, and opened the door.

Galen.

A smile broke across Emrys's face as he took in the casually dressed soldier.

"It's good to see you," Emrys said.

"You might not feel the same way after my visit."

Galen's words hardened Emrys's stomach like molten metal starting to cool. Emrys tried to keep the heat on, keep it soft and malleable. He stepped aside to allow Galen in. "What's this about?"

"What did you tell Laurence?"

The loose control he had on his gut slipped and it plunged into a cold bucket of water. Instantly hard. Instantly stuck. Was nothing a secret in here? He forced himself to take a seat on the sofa while Galen remained standing. He looked every bit the man in charge, the man who was used to giving orders. It was sexy in a domineering kind of way. A distraction Emrys needed from the hot water he'd boiled for himself.

"I was worried when I hadn't seen you for a few days, but it appears you've been keeping tabs on me anyway."

"I needed some time to think through what I told you. I was scared I'd put you in a dangerous position and…and I needed to see what you'd do."

He pitched back and crossed his arms. "And you think I told Laurence? Thanks for thinking so little of me."

Galen took the seat opposite him. "But that's it. What am I meant to think? I trust you, but I've trusted people before, and it's been to my detriment."

"I am not Isaiah. I am not Brink." *I am not Tristan.*

"I know." Galen rubbed his palm. "Or at least that's what I want to believe."

"Know this. I did not talk to Laurence about you at all. He sought me out, not the other way around. Wait…if you know this, does that mean Isaiah does too?"

"Probably. I haven't told him, but I'll have to, once I know what the right thing to do is."

"You're asking the wrong person. I'm an outsider, remember?"

"Which means you'll have more clarity than me." Galen let out a long breath that blew out his lips. He was on the verge of defeat, and Emrys didn't want him to fall.

"Tell Isaiah."

Galen's head snapped up. "Why?"

"Because it will put you in his favor. You can't keep things from him. It's too risky for both of us."

"And what do I say?"

"Say that Laurence asked about Jared. He suspects he was murdered but doesn't suspect me. He knows Jared and I spoke about the surface."

"Was that all?"

He'd have to trust Galen knew what to say and what to hold onto. "It can't come as a shock to anyone that Laurence believes Providence should make plans to return to the surface. He wanted my opinion on it. Tell Isaiah I expressed nothing but doubts."

"And is that true?"

He sealed his lips and let them curve upwards.

"Be careful, Emrys. Laurence always has a lot of pretty words, but I don't think he can protect you if things go badly."

"Did Tristan put his faith in Laurence?"

"No. He was naïve like that, thought everyone could be

changed all at once. He didn't want to play games, but that didn't stop anyone else." Galen mashed his palms together. "If I tell Isaiah this, it's going to increase the pressure on you. Can you handle it?"

"I've been living underground for a very long time. I'm used to pressure."

Galen laughed and joy sparked in his green-fire eyes. "Well, if you can withstand it, so can I."

"Have you considered working with Laurence?"

"He would never trust me, and I don't trust him entirely either."

"What makes you say that?"

"Self-preservation. I could never guarantee he wouldn't try to blackmail me into sabotaging Isaiah. It's not how I want this to go. Tristan wouldn't have approved."

"And it doesn't have anything to do with Juliet being so close to him?"

Galen looked at him and thankfully took it as the jibe it was intended as. "I trust her more than I trust Laurence, but they're one and the same."

"It might help you to have an ally on the other side."

"It hasn't in the past. I can see why you think it would be a good idea, but I'm not about to align myself with another faction. Yes, I want to see us work towards returning to the surface, but I can do that by making sure you're safe."

"Don't put yourself in more danger than you're comfortable with. I don't want that on my conscience."

"This is my choice, Emrys. I'm aware of that. Always. And whatever happens, you can count on me to do right by you."

The irony of a human trying to protect a soul-eater tickled at Emrys like a chaff of wheat over his skin. He scratched his forearm. Could he let Galen be his crusader?

As much as he wanted it, as much as he needed a partner to navigate Providence's intrigues, could he allow Galen to put himself in peril? But the intensity of Galen's gaze, lit with revolutionary zeal, showed that choice was not his to make.

He held his hand out over the table, and Galen took it readily.

"And I with you."

20

Emrys emerged from the bathroom, fresh from his morning shower and drying his hair. "You look worried, Nimue. Algebra getting you down again?"

Nimue's head rested in her hand but her eyes darted up to fix his with a malign glare. She'd never taken kindly to mathematics.

Calculations, yes. Math, no.

Her faked death in Endurance happened to fall on the same day as her geometry exam. Ironically, she'd worked out the precise velocity and angle required for her drop from the fourth-floor balcony, and her death had gone perfectly.

"Luckily, they have not yet exposed us to that." She let her hand drop onto the table. "I've been talking to Clara most of the night."

His spine locked. "What are you doing?"

"It's best you don't know. Ragnar is already suspicious, and it serves us well that he be paranoid."

He tossed the towel back into the bathroom and pulled on his shirt. "Only if he stays where he is."

"He won't do that. He'll come, but not before we're ready for him." She winced and her eyes stayed screwed shut like she counted to six in the hope that would be long enough for the pain to pass.

He crouched beside her. "Are you okay?"

"I'm fine." She kept her eyes closed and breathed slowly. "Her chattering gets worse, but it'll all be worth it." She sounded like she was trying to convince herself rather than him. "It'll all be worth it."

"Let me help you."

"The time will come when I need your help, but right now, all I need you to do is not interfere. No matter what happens."

"You're scaring me, Nimue."

"Good. That'll help."

She passed him on the way to the bathroom, but he grabbed her arm. "I'm serious. I don't want anything to happen to you."

"I can take care of myself. I'm not Sian." Her words struck him and forced him to release her. She closed the door to the bathroom.

Sickness bubbled in the pit of his stomach. Nimue was not Sian. He forced himself to understand it, but even as the thought came, he tasted bile. She might not be Sian, but he didn't want to lose her either.

He waited for as long as he could, but she didn't return. He didn't reach out to her but called out a good-bye. She didn't answer.

When he opened the door, Galen was there, hand ready to ring the bell. Emrys's stomach twisted on itself, part desire, part apprehension. Galen at his door first thing in the morning was unlikely to mean good news.

"What are you doing here?"

"I told Isaiah about your meeting with Laurence. He's requested your presence."

"Requested? That doesn't sound like Isaiah."

He gave an off-kilter smile, powered by a rumble in his throat. "I may have tidied up the language."

Some of the tension dissolved. It was in those moments of shared humor—no matter how bleak—that he felt closest to Galen. It also emboldened him to go further to protect him and not act solely for his own immortal benefit.

"We'd better not keep him waiting." They started walking. "Don't look so concerned, Galen. It'll be fine."

"I'm impressed with how calm you are."

"He won't expel me today." Though he wouldn't put it past Isaiah to have him shot while his back was turned. It would be inconvenient but survivable. He'd rip out a soul or two. That would at least tide him over for another month. But it would mean life in Providence was finished. And standing in front of Galen, that thought was harder to brush aside.

The corridors thrummed with people on their way to serve Providence. Despite his outer bravado, Emrys wished he could join them.

When the elevator arrived, the doors opened, and he was forced to look into Juliet's face. Her hair had been tied back and not a strand hung free, but those eyes showed a conflict that was anything but still. He nodded hello and stepped in beside her, catching a glimpse of the brooch on her belt. She and Galen exchanged greetings, cool but not unfriendly.

The elevator stopped at each level, more people getting in and out, pushing him and Juliet and Galen together. Galen's hand brushed his, and his skin shivered at the touch. It was fleeting but the feeling sparked its way into his gut and latched on. Deliberate or not, he wanted more.

The elevator stopped on the military level, and he and Galen stepped out.

"You're not coming to work today?" Juliet asked.

"We need to ask him a few questions," Galen said. "He'll be back within the hour."

Her eyes flicked from Galen to Emrys, her mouth open but tense.

"It's okay, Juliet. I won't be long." He tried to sound reassuring, but when the doors closed, the lines on her forehead had deepened.

They passed through secret doors and along clinically quiet corridors. Galen looked back like he wanted to say something but thought better of it. Maybe he wanted to remember Emrys's face in case this was the last time he ever saw it.

Despite himself, despite knowing better, and despite hating himself for wanting it, he longed to reach out and take Galen's hand. He longed to hold it for his own comfort, to feel those thick, long fingers interlace with his own, to feel palm against palm. In case this was about to be taken away.

Galen stopped outside a door. "Are you ready?"

"I wish I knew what I was getting ready for." Galen was close, so close Emrys could smell the leather and sun coming off him, a scent that he wanted to dive into. But Isaiah was waiting and the last thing they needed was for him to open the door and find Emrys necking his son.

Though maybe that was a torment he could devise for another time when his position was secure.

Reassurance brimmed in Galen's eyes, and he gave a nod before unlocking the door.

Isaiah sat behind a table in a bland room, a screen on

the wall, a few chairs around the table, and a door on the other side of the room from where he'd entered. At least the room wasn't filled with guards, though they may be amassing outside the doors. Isaiah thrummed his fingers on the top of the table and glowered at them both.

"Next time I give an order to attend, you'd better be puffing for breath when you arrive." His gaze tracked Emrys's entrance before slashing across to Galen. "Out!"

"But—"

"I said out, Captain. This meeting is private."

Galen swallowed his objections, straightened as a soldier would before his commander, and exited without making eye contact with Emrys. The door sealed him in alone with Isaiah.

"You don't trust your son with what you're about to tell me? That's interesting."

"You should put your interest elsewhere. Sit."

Emrys settled into the chair opposite Isaiah and matched the councilor's pose. He rested his forearms on the table but instead of strumming his fingers, he traced a figure eight and tried not to imagine the harvest symbol.

"I wanted to talk to you about the unfortunate predicament you find yourself in."

"And what predicament would that be?"

Isaiah's smile stretched across tight lips. "Having to lie to Laurence about his nephew's death."

"I'm hardly likely to tell him the truth."

"I don't know. You might have thought there'd be something to gain."

"I said nothing to Laurence about my involvement."

"But you didn't disabuse him of the idea his nephew was murdered."

"And how would I know that with any certainty? He's

got access to more information than I do. If I said anything about it to him, it would increase his suspicions."

"Then what *did* you say to him?"

He stopped tracing the symbol. "Why do you want to know?"

"I'm a naturally curious person."

"Not curious enough to want to explore the surface. Or so I hear."

"I see Laurence has been spreading his usual delusions. I have seen the surface. Not as much as you, but enough to know there's nothing out there worth my time."

"And what is worth your time?"

Isaiah leaned closer, his eyes boring into Emrys for answers. "Making sure Providence keeps running."

"Then you and I are in agreement."

"I should hope so, considering what we have provided you with. A home, work, your daughter's safety." Isaiah leaned back. "How is she by the way? Recovered?"

"She's fine."

"I am glad." No, he wasn't. His smile was entirely faked. "Though of course we can never be too cautious. I'm sure you and I want what's best for her and her health."

"And the health of Providence."

"Exactly. Which is why I want to know what you talked about with Laurence."

He huffed out a breath. "Nothing of importance."

"I'll be the judge of that."

He chewed his tongue. What to keep back? What to leave out? "He wanted to know what I spoke to Jared about before he died."

"And you said…"

"We talked about the surface and whether it was livable. He asked about my journey, how I was settling into

Providence, what my favorite color was, and whether you're as evil as he suspects."

"It's unwise to mock me, Stone."

"Considering my skills, it's unwise to threaten me."

A fire lit inside Isaiah's eyes, obliterating any fear from Emrys's threat, if he'd felt any. "I was going to ask how you killed him so cleanly."

"That knowledge stays with me."

Isaiah peered over the desk at him with something bordering on admiration. "But there wasn't a mark on him. We tested him for everything we could. Seemingly healthy people don't just die."

"Would you rather a dagger sticking out of his back? For you I'd make an exception."

Isaiah's fists clenched and unclenched.

Emrys suppressed a smile.

"You may think you're valuable with your skills," his hand waved in the air, "or whatever you want to call them, but they're not enough to keep you from fulfilling your obligations. I own you, and you will do as I say. Which brings us to your next assignment."

The feather-light but steel-strong thread of Isaiah's web crawled across his skin. He had twenty-three days until he next had to harvest, but his appetite for political assassinations had soured. Perhaps he could stretch out the intervening period to make it work for his diet. "Who is it this time?"

A smile slithered across Isaiah's lips and poised ready to strike. "Laurence."

"You can't be serious."

"Deadly." His eyes flared as he said it.

"People will become suspicious. His followers will see a pattern."

"Then they'll know their place."

"I'm not doing it. I'm not here to take out your rivals. If I kill anyone, it's for the good of Providence, not to serve your ideology."

"Let me put it in terms you'll understand as the opportunistic scum you are. If you do not kill Laurence, your daughter will be seized and become our latest medical experiment. You won't even recognize her when we're done. Do you understand?"

Emrys had no fear for Nimue's life. She would fight her way out of anything, but they'd be banished, or Providence would fall around them. Then it was anyone's guess how many cycles of the moon they'd have left to live.

"You have thirteen days to kill Laurence."

"What happens in thirteen days?"

"The Five meets to discuss Laurence's newest proposal for repopulating the surface. We want his plan to die with him. Do I have your cooperation?"

He could stall. He had time. He could find a way free of the mire.

He glared at Isaiah, his jaw locking until the words slipped out. "I accept."

"Good." Isaiah rapped the table with his knuckles then pointed at Emrys. "Next time don't take so long to agree. Leave." He waved Emrys towards the door.

Emrys slid his hand off the table and stood.

"Oh, and Stone? We'll be watching you this time. Very closely."

"Isn't that risky? A record of my deeds. Or is that the intention?"

"It's a bargaining chip. To make sure you go through with it."

Nimue would be watched, too. Someone would never be far from her in case he fought the yoke that had been placed around his neck. But the glint in Isaiah's eyes showed more than glee at his blackmail. He wanted the knowledge of how Emrys could kill so quietly and cleanly. No amount of inducement could make Emrys reveal his secrets. Not unless they were the last thing Isaiah ever discovered.

"You won't get it on film. I guarantee it."

"We shall see."

"No, you won't." He opened the door and walked into the corridor. Galen was waiting and gestured for him to follow in silence. After a few turns, they entered a changing room. Shower cubicles down one side, lockers down the other. They were alone.

"They're watching me." Emrys kept his voice quiet. "This won't look good for you."

"They expect me to be close to you. If anyone asks, I'll say I was giving you extra orders."

He raised his eyebrows. "In the locker room?"

Galen missed the innuendo. He looked agitated enough to have missed a neon sign. "As good a place as any. I'm sorry I couldn't be in there with you."

"It's good that you didn't make a fuss. We don't want Isaiah to suspect anything."

Galen looked back at the door. He recognized that look, a longing for something that had always been there, a surety you could count on. Emrys would have worn that look after he'd walked away from his village, hoping Sian was still alive. It was a lonely look.

When Galen's gaze met his, the uncertainty remained. "What did he want?"

"He wants me to kill Laurence. He's threatened to torture Nimue if I don't."

Galen blinked. "That's bold, even for Isaiah."

"Bold? It won't be him who does the killing."

"And maybe you don't have to either. He can't expel you without good cause."

"That won't stop him. He has a whole apparatus set up to ensure compliance. If he doesn't get me for killing Laurence or Jared, he'll come up with some other reason. I'm useful until I'm not."

"How long do you have?"

"Thirteen days."

"We'll think of something, but in the meantime, keep Nimue safe. No more running off on her own."

"You've been tracking her too?"

Galen shrugged one shoulder. "Trying to. I've lost her more often than I care to admit."

"She was the same in Endurance. You could never find her if she didn't want you to. It was a pain then, but it might be what keeps her out of danger. What about you though? The more time you spend with me, the more suspicious they'll become about your involvement. Perhaps we shouldn't be seen around each other. We should use an intermediary."

"It might be safer…" Galen looked into Emrys's eyes. "But it's not what I want."

Desire tightened its velvet rope around Emrys's throat. "What do you want?"

They were already standing close, their voices a harsh whisper. "I want you."

Then Galen kissed him, and the world stopped. Not stopped in that apocalyptic way. Not stopped in that hopeless way. But stopped in that peaceful way, in that quiet yet intense way where nothing else mattered but Galen and his soft, full lips. Centuries had passed since Emrys had experienced a kiss like that, centuries in which he'd forgotten that lips could taste of happiness. Galen's tongue swiped against Emrys's and lit a fuse that raced down his throat, ignited his heart, and detonated.

This can't happen. Not now. Not ever. Galen could never know what he truly was, and without truth, how could there be love?

He stayed very still until the pressure of Galen's lips abated, but that fading of potential tore strips from his soul. Why deny himself such beauty and such pleasure and such purity? He could be dead within a month.

He grabbed Galen, his breathing heavy, his eyes searching for an answer. Emrys didn't want to stay separate any longer. He didn't want Galen to go.

Denial warred with desire. Could he allow this chance of something more than empty survival to wither? No! No matter the danger to them both, he couldn't let it go.

He *wouldn't.*

He pushed Galen against a locker and kissed him, hungry, insistent, primal. There was nothing chaste about the way he plundered Galen's mouth, nothing proper about the desperate moans reverberating in his throat. He slipped from Galen's mouth and kissed along his straining, lengthening neck, forcing short-breathed pants out of his throat. Galen's hands wound into Emrys's hair and pressed him closer, harder, making his scalp sing.

"More. Yes. More."

Memories of Lysander threatened to rise but melted in the heat of Emrys's desire for Galen. Lysander had no place there, and as that old hurt slipped away, he wanted Galen with a white-hot ferocity.

Tension gathered in Emrys's cock, filaments of energy drawing in like a vacuum and converging in his groin. He wanted to take Galen there and then. His hands slid up under his shirt to splay across his hard abdomen and push him harder into the locker, while his pelvis ground against Galen's thick erection. He had to have him before—

Nimue sliced through his consciousness with the care of a chainsaw. His cries contorted his face, but he made no sound. Her attack blinded him and obliterated his lust like dynamite blowing up a mountain. He collapsed on the ground and crushed his head with his hands.

Stop!

Galen put his hand on Emrys's back and said something, but Emrys couldn't make it out through the screaming in his skull.

WHAT ARE YOU DOING?

The pain eased slightly, and Nimue dragged him down the connection, her mind cloaking him, suffocating him, smuggling him in to peer through Clara's eyes.

Fires, the roar of alarms, the thundering of footsteps, the rattle of gunfire, the endless screaming. Armed with nothing but her harvest symbol, Clara fought a tide of people and harvested with extreme prejudice. Her heart rate rose but didn't falter. What had happened? He wanted to probe further, but Nimue dumped him back in his mind with an order to find her.

"Emrys!" Galen shouted again.

He blinked out of the fugue and tried to remember how to speak.

"Do you need a doctor?"

"No." He sat back, huffing oxygen into lungs rung out like rags. Energy drained from his body, his passion limp. "I'm fine."

Apart from the flush of Galen's skin and the heat reddening his ears like devil horns, concern had replaced his desire. He was still close enough to kiss.

A voice outside in the corridor made Galen retreat and look to the door. "We'd better go."

Emrys didn't want to and would have killed anyone who disturbed them, but Galen was unlikely to appreciate the gesture. He wiped the saliva from his mouth and followed Galen to the door.

"Are you sure you're all right?"

"A migraine. I get them sometimes." *More since getting here.*

"I thought that maybe you regretted it."

Did he? With the state Endurance was in he had to find Nimue and figure out what it meant for them. Indulging in an affair with Galen was a distraction that could end in disaster for the both of them.

His pause was too long, his refusal not quick enough. Galen turned away to open the door, but Emrys had seen his face fall. He put his hand on Galen's arm to turn him back, to explain, but the door opened from the outside.

Brink's crazed eyes took in the two of them and charged Emrys all within one beat. He shoved him in the chest before Emrys even noticed the soldier had attacked.

"Brink, stand down!" Galen ordered, but Brink kept coming and herded Emrys across the room a few yards before Emrys found his feet and hardened his stance. Then Brink struggled to move him an inch.

"You'd better calm down, Brink, or you'll regret it." The symbol bloomed at the front of Emrys's mind. All he had to do was send it, a slight brush against Brink's skin would be enough to embed it like a tick and suck out his life.

And he would have, if Galen wasn't there.

He scoured the symbol. His hands rendered benign, he put both on Brink's chest and pushed him away.

The soldier's eyes widened until white surrounded his irises. "You just threatened an officer."

"Like I give a shit," Emrys said.

"You will. Galen's a witness."

"I saw you attack an unarmed citizen," Galen said.

Brink's eyes narrowed as he turned to Galen. "He's not even one of us, and you'd choose him over us so you can get fucked."

"What are you talking about?" Galen said but not quick enough. Even Emrys spotted the pause.

"Check your ears." Brink sneered. "They're bright red. Only one thing does that to you, you fucking whore."

Rage rocketed through Emrys's body. He threw Brink off him, and while he stumbled back, Emrys charged and smashed his fist into Brink's stomach with enough force to throw him into a locker.

Stunned, Brink tumbled to the floor. He tried to stand but flailed. Emrys readied for a second attack.

"That's enough!" Galen got in between the two of them. "Brink, get out of here before I lock you in a cell."

"You and I both know you haven't got the authority to do that. Besides, what will you tell them?" Brink stopped trying to get up, labored breathing all he was capable of doing. "That you're fucking the stray?"

"Attack him again and it won't matter who I'm fucking. Come on, Emrys. You need to get to work."

Emrys knew better than to argue. Galen didn't talk as they walked out of the compound, and unlike before, he didn't turn to check Emrys followed. His hand was farther away, his lips, his body, everything was getting further away as his pace quickened. At the final door, Galen stopped and waited for Emrys to walk through and stand on the other side.

"I'm sorry for what I said. I'd never hurt—"

"I'll speak to you later." The door slid closed. Galen hadn't even been able to look him in the eye.

Emrys wanted to bang and holler on the door to be let

back in, but unfriendly eyes were watching. The little that he'd said would be incriminating enough, but what else could Galen do but act cold?

He hoped it was an act.

Nimue buzzed him, and though he was tempted to deny her while in this turmoil, they had important business to discuss.

What happened in Endurance? He tried to walk normally, knowing he was being tracked. What would Galen do? Was he still in charge of his surveillance? Had he gone to placate Brink?

Could you pay attention, please?

If you don't like it, get out of my head. What happened?

I'm still piecing it together but, from what I can gather, Yusef got into the control room and freed the humans.

Emrys stumbled. *Why would he do that?*

Clara told him to kill that woman he loved.

She did what?!

She wanted his loyalty. She'd been doubting it ever since we left.

He stopped walking, his head dizzy and lightheaded. He grabbed the banister. *This was your doing, wasn't it? You put those thoughts there.*

I didn't need to put them there.

But you encouraged them to grow.

It had to be done, Emrys.

So what of Endurance? What of Yusef?

Clara doesn't know. She's fighting for her survival.

Fuck. And Ragnar?

Same. A hint of glee sparkled in her thoughts. He kept walking, his heart rate ratcheting up too fast for him to stand still. He had to look like everything was all right. He had to get to the Factory and some normality.

What now?

We wait to see what happens and who survives.

The memory of Clara's battle flashed in his mind and brought to the fore the bodies strewn beneath her feet. She'd been standing near the armory.

You condemned thousands of people to death, Nimue.

They were going to die anyway. There was no hope for them, not after what Absolon did.

And what if any of the humans get out? What if they come here?

They won't make it out of Endurance alive. And if they do, they'll have no supplies, no map, no compass, no knowledge of where Providence is. They'll perish.

And Clara? She'll figure out this was your doing and want revenge. Or if not her, then the others.

Then we'll be ready for them.

How? If they show up, we can't stop Providence from letting them in.

Yes, we can. The Five will want you to verify who they are before they're allowed in. You can tell them anything to stop them.

And if Ragnar contacts me? Or Clara?

Sympathize. Or, better yet, tell them it was me. Then they might think twice about coming after us.

She vanished. It happened so suddenly it was like the earth gave way beneath his feet. He had a moment of weightlessness before the rush of gravity sent him crashing to the ground. The strength of her mind, the depth of her plans, and the callousness of her existence left him faint.

If she had engineered the final collapse of Endurance from Providence, what hope did he have of surviving her? She could invade his mind without him knowing, and no matter how much he tried to defend himself, she always found a way in.

He hurried to the Factory and buzzed in but didn't go straight to his station. He needed to find Juliet and demand an immediate transfer. He just hoped he'd accumulated enough gold to kill a Darisami.

❧ 2 1 ❧

THREE DAYS PASSED WITHOUT SIGHT OF GALEN AND without word from Ragnar and Clara. To compound Emrys's agitation, Juliet denied his request for a transfer. He could have traded the information about Laurence's impending assassination, but she would want to know how he'd received it. He waited and salvaged more gold. A piece here, a piece there, anticipation tricking his hands into feeling things that weren't real. Hope burned in his palms when he wished it were gold. By the time Ragnar reached out, his stockpile had grown by another twelve pieces.

Ragnar nudged him. *You wanted a meeting?*

I was concerned for your wellbeing.

I'm sure. While the two of you are enjoying your new lives, we're wading knee deep in blood. And that's not an exaggeration.

Ragnar's bitterness stripped Emrys's tongue. *How bad is it?*

Look through my eyes and I'll show you.

He was thankful Ragnar had not yet learned Nimue's

trick of seizing his mind and dragging him through against his will. But the sight he was shown dashed that relief.

Countless bodies lay scattered across the floor, twisted in and over themselves, agony frozen in death. Red stained his hands, and his trousers had darkened four shades. Smoke laced with burnt plastic and heated metal wafted through the air. Emergency system lights flashed, casting their orange light over the butchery. Most people had been gunned down.

A scream rang out somewhere far away before being cut short. Ragnar's head turned slowly towards the sound, but his heart rate did not rise. No fear stabbed his gut. He was numb.

Who's left alive?

Clara and Wyatt. Denari's dead.

He flinched. Of everyone, he expected Denari to have the greatest chance of surviving such carnage.

Yusef killed her with your knife, released a few captives to create chaos, then attempted to turn his woman into a Darisami. She refused and ran straight into Wyatt. He finished her and fought with Yusef. Wyatt would have died too if Yusef hadn't fallen and if Wyatt wasn't the better fighter.

How desperate had Yusef become that he'd risk so much?

So, it's just the three of you left in Endurance?

And a few hundred humans.

They're not all dead?

We had to kill most. Some breached the inner doorway to the tunnel but those that hadn't yet been freed are still in their cells.

About a thousand dead. Three Darisami remained. The void echoed. *Endurance is finished.*

It's been finished for a long time. What I don't understand is how it fell apart without us realizing?

Emrys kept his thoughts to himself. *How is Clara taking the loss of Denari?*

Like I give a fuck. Evil bitch. We should never have let her in in the first place.

The same could be said of a lot of us.

The edges of Ragnar's mind honed to a sword edge. *Is that supposed to be a hint about our coming to Providence? I swear to God if you two are trying to double-cross us, there will be nothing in this world to stop me from getting my revenge.*

The space inside Ragnar's mind shrank, and Emrys bolstered his mental defenses. He pulled back a little. *Easy, brother. We are still with you. Although the council is proving difficult. There are divisions that unsettle me.*

Then settle them.

I'm trying. But if I back the wrong side, it won't just be disastrous for me but for all of Providence.

What do they want you to do?

Emrys filled Ragnar in on his assignment. Ragnar's response was short and surgical.

Kill Laurence.

But the humans can't stay in Providence forever.

Don't be a fool. That kind of unrest will lead to a collapse. Let another generation sort it out. It is not yet time for change.

The metallic atmosphere of Ragnar's mind grew hot, scalding Emrys's resistance but he remained. *I disagree.* He wiped the sweat from the back of his neck.

That is because you had a taste of the outside. But Providence provides safety, not just for the humans, but for you as well. One moment in the moonlight, and you'll give rise to another generation of stories about angels. We do not need to draw attention to ourselves.

He needed no lecture on the power of people's stupid beliefs. He'd lost Sian because of them. But keeping hidden in Providence would only last for so long, and if they missed their chance to begin a new chapter in human history, Providence would fall, and humanity would be lost.

It's no use, Ragnar. The Five are not content to let me lead a life of anonymity.

You're not trying hard enough.

There isn't anywhere to hide. Both sides want to use me for their own causes.

Then kill the council and start again.

I think there's been enough death, don't you?

Ragnar looked down into the open dead eyes of an adolescent woman. Emrys knew her but couldn't recall her name.

Didn't want to.

Death brings life, Ragnar said. *As a Darisami, you know that. Whatever you choose, make sure it is for the greater good and for the most benefit.*

But whose?

The Darisami's. I must go. There may be a few escapees that need to be corralled.

Ragnar released Emrys, and he returned to his own mind.

Juliet shook his shoulder. "Emrys?"

He blinked and looked from the microprocessor in his hands to Juliet's creased brow. "Sorry?"

How long had she been standing there?

"One of the other workers was concerned. You've been staring at nothing."

He looked around but they were alone. "Where is everyone?"

"They've gone to lunch. Are you okay? You looked like you were daydreaming."

More like a waking nightmare.

He looked at her hand on his shoulder. She let it fall away.

"I'm fine, but if you're really worried about me, a transfer to metalworking will make everything better."

"Nice try." She made to leave.

"Why not?" He spun around on his stool.

She folded her arms across her chest. "Why metalwork? Why that area in particular?"

"I'm good with it, that's all."

"Then if that's all, you should be happy with the work you're doing now. You're here long enough. I don't think I've seen you take lunch more than once since you arrived." She cocked her head and raised her eyebrows in his direction, a fat and derisive smile on her lips. He'd love to say smug didn't suit her but with her fiery hair and dark eyes he'd be lying.

He leaned back. He wanted to play but he needed to remain loose. "I thought if I showed I was a hard and committed worker, I could be rewarded."

"You want rewards? Help Laurence."

"Sweeten the deal, and I will. Does he know you're blocking me on this?"

"I've told him my reservations."

"Maybe you can fill me in. I've done nothing to you, except talk to your dead friend."

His tone and words were hard, and she hardened in response. "Then why were you with Galen the other day?"

"I'm hardly likely to refuse a summons, am I?"

"What did you talk about? What did they want to know?" She came closer, used the fact that she was standing and he was sitting to press her point. He wanted to stay still, but he had to shift position. He wanted to believe it was the stool that made him uncomfortable. Nothing to do with what she wanted to know. He couldn't reveal the plot to kill Laurence without confessing to his involvement. Perhaps there was something else he could exchange.

"If I tell you, I want a promise I'll be moved."

She mulled it over, while her hand thumbed the brooch on her belt. "All right. Tell me what they wanted to know, and you can move to metalwork when there's a vacancy."

He sat upright. Playtime was over. "No, it has to be now."

"We're full."

"Then move someone. Give them a better position. I want to start in metalwork tomorrow morning."

"Why?" Her lips rounded around and stretched the word.

"The reason doesn't matter. Do we have a deal?"

"Not without telling me why. The more you push this, the more suspicious I become. The fact that they sent you to us is problematic enough, but now you're so desperate to get into that workshop, I'm starting to think conspiracy."

"I've promised Laurence I'll help him but, in the meantime, I want to do the work that suits me better."

"But why should you be treated any different? You're in Providence, you serve at the will of the Five for the good of all. And if I say salvaging is where you can best serve Providence, that's what you'll do." She glared at him.

He glared back, but he'd overreached.

The sight of all of Endurance's dead, Nimue circling his mind, the need to talk to Galen, all converged. He'd been in Providence for fourteen days. How would he survive the next ten years?

He reached for truth.

Or a shred of it.

"I used to make jewelry—trinkets and the like—for my wife. Nothing made of anything precious or rare, nothing that Endurance needed, but they were beautiful." He scratched the back of his hand. "Like that brooch I made for you, but better."

Myfanwy had liked the simple things best.

"When Nimue and I left Endurance, we left behind many things, but I brought mine and my wife's wedding bands. I intended to give them to Nimue if she ever found someone to make her happy enough. But I lost them on the journey. I wanted to search for them, but we had to keep going. Now that I'm here, I want to make a replacement for Nimue to commemorate our new life. There has been so much upheaval, but this is something I can do to give her some security, some sense of where she came from."

His shoulders had sagged under the weight of the lies, under the weight of memories, under the weight of never-would-be. He shrugged it off, buttressed his shoulders and his spine, and steeled his voice. Juliet had to give him what he wanted.

"That's why I want to be moved to metalwork. But if you think it's some plot, then forget it, and you can forget about me telling you why I was with Galen."

He turned back to his workbench, but when he might have once felt Myfanwy's hand stroking between his shoulder blades, he felt a chill. Part of him didn't want her to yield. He didn't deserve it. She'd been right about that.

"I swear if you're lying to me, I will make you regret it."

He refused to let triumph prematurely lift his lips. "Does that mean we've got a deal?"

She leaned against his bench. "After you tell me what Galen wanted."

If only he knew. Galen hadn't come to find him since their kiss. He was sure Galen watched from a distance but could not be certain who else tracked him.

"He took me to meet Isaiah. The councilor asked me about the surface and the arks we encountered."

"Surely he's asked you this before."

"He wanted more. Isaiah said Laurence has called a meeting to raise Providence's future, so I think he was looking for anything to justify it being hopeless."

"And is that the impression you gave?"

"I told him that with the right leadership and the proper plan, over time we could leave Providence and return to the surface."

She cocked an eyebrow. "And he didn't throw you in a cell?"

He laughed. "He wanted to. He definitely thinks I'm dangerous."

She combed her fingers through her hair, her hand's descent slowing as most of the threads fell until she held only a few final teased hairs. "He may try to remove you before the vote if they know those are your views."

"I am worried about that. He made threats. He wants to use Nimue to keep me silent."

She wavered, shifting her weight from her right foot to her left. "You can't be serious?"

She couldn't be so naive.

"Yep. I've seen his type before. He grew up with stories of before the Fall, surrounded by people with memories of the trauma of those final days and how hard they fought to survive. He will do almost anything to avoid returning. Christos is the same. You're not dealing with rational people." He snorted. "Though look who I'm talking to."

"What do you mean by that?"

"You're dating a psychopath."

"Brink's not a psycho." She pushed away from the bench and walked halfway across the room. "He's...complicated."

He wielded the motherboard he'd been ripping apart. "Microprocessors are complicated. Brink's a psycho. He should be locked up. And I doubt he thinks highly of your collaborating with Laurence."

"I don't tell him." She held his gaze and refused to buckle under the shame. She was a warrior. He liked her, but he'd fought and bested plenty of people he'd liked.

"Good basis for a relationship."

"What I do with Brink is none of your goddamn business." Her voice raised, steadied, boomed.

"I know about you four. I know about you and Jared and Brink and Galen. I know about Tristan."

"There's nothing to know. We were all friends and then we weren't. Tristan's dead, Jared's dead, and Galen skates through as smoothly as ever." Accusation shadowed her words.

"If you're looking for someone to blame, try Brink."

"I've told you, he'd never hurt Jared."

"Or Tristan?"

She flinched. "He was Brink's brother. Brink was destroyed when Tristan was killed."

"Then all the more reason to suspect him. From the little I've had the misfortune to do with him, I can tell he's not stable. A man that jealous can do terrible things."

She narrowed her eyes. "What do you mean? What jealousy?"

Either she didn't know about Brink's obsession with Galen or she was willfully obtuse. He could tell her the truth, but that would reveal how close he and Galen were getting. He had to retreat, regroup, redirect.

"I think he's jealous of anyone who gets close to you. And here I am working near you every day. Have you told him where you got that?" He pointed to the brooch on her belt.

She stroked the interlocking Js. "Brink might be difficult, but there's no way he would have harmed Jared. Galen on the other hand…"

"Galen's not beyond reproach, but Brink's the sort who looks after himself first and his friends—and lovers—second. If you're worried about a threat to yours and Laurence's plans, look at Brink."

She shook off his assertions, hair flashing red and redder. "He knows I'm keen for us to return to the surface, but he wouldn't hurt me because of it."

"Not even if he was aware how close you are to Laurence?"

He hated making her doubt herself, but Brink was a problem. If he really did love Juliet, that was all well and good, but his assault in the locker room had not been that of a man who was in love with the woman he was dating. And if Juliet was worrying about Brink, she wouldn't have time to worry about Emrys.

"He knows I'm loyal to Providence in my own way. His…brother had views similar to mine," she said.

"And look what happened to him."

Offence flashed in her eyes, her mouth opened to fire a retort, but as quickly as her anger came, it dissolved. "It's different this time. Brink wouldn't harm me."

"I'm happy to hear it."

"I'm sure."

"I'd be much happier if you told me I was going to be transferred. I've told you all I know, so will you honor your part of the deal?"

A muscle in her cheek twitched. "Fine." The word shot from her mouth like a blank from a starting pistol. "Report to metalwork tomorrow afternoon."

The afternoon would do. "Thank you."

"This is a trial. I'll supervise you to make sure you

know what you're doing and that you can be trusted. Restrict yourself to scraps after they've been approved by the supervisor. Understood?"

He gave her a mock salute and a click from his back teeth. "Perfectly. Thanks, Juliet. I mean that."

"You know you're wasted as a worker. You'd be better off on the council."

A breathy chuckle fluttered out of his nose. "I have no desire to ever sit on that council. I serve, that's all."

"So do they."

Juliet headed for the door but as she opened it, he called out to her to stop. Voices bubbled and burst in the corridor—workers returning from lunch.

"What?" she said.

"If I'm wrong about Brink, I'll happily make you something to apologize. Perhaps your wedding bands." The sarcasm in his voice earned him an eye roll worthy of Nimue.

"Yeah, you could *definitely* serve on council." She left, and he smiled.

One more day of collecting gold, and he'd be that much closer to forging a weapon. That would mean one problem sorted. If only he could solve all of them with a few hours at a forge.

❧ 2 2 ☙

THE DOOR TO THE APARTMENT OPENED FROM THE OUTSIDE while Emrys was lying on his bed. He surged to his feet to confront whatever military unit was about to storm his quarters, but Galen entered alone. Emrys remained standing, poised for a fight.

"Is Nimue here?"

"Shouldn't you know?"

Galen smiled sheepishly. "She got away from me. Again." He sealed them in together.

"Are you here to see her or me?"

The sheepish smile turned wolfish. "You."

But Emrys didn't hurry to pick up from the kiss they'd shared in the locker room. Four days had passed without a word. He didn't like this *feeling* in the middle of his chest. Like he'd lost a breastplate.

"Where have you been?" Emrys retreated behind the wall of ice in his voice.

"I thought it best if I stay away after what happened with Brink."

"Is that for my protection or his?"

Galen's mouth froze open.

"You're worried I'm going to kill him, aren't you? Would that really be a bad thing?"

Galen hugged himself, rubbed his bulging bicep like he was warming a chill. "I know I shouldn't care about him, but he reminds me of Tristan—not that Tristan was ever cruel. But then you came along, and there's something about you I can't resist. Perhaps it's the way you are with Nimue, or the confidence, or the worldliness, but whatever it is…from the moment we picked you up, I felt it." Wariness stalked his eyes. "And Brink sees it, too. So, after we kissed, I needed time to think whether this was worth the risk."

"Brink is safe from me. You should know that." Emrys breached the blockade between them and rested his hand on Galen's shoulder. "If you want him to live, he lives. I'll put up with his bullshit. End of story. Is that what you want?" He let his hand slide down, smoothing over the curve of his arm, and curled his fingers into Galen's.

Galen's grip tightened, and the secure sensation of it reached all the way to Emrys's sacrum.

"Yes, that's what I want. And a whole lot more. If that's what you want, too," Galen said.

"What if Brink says something to Isaiah?"

"Let him. Isaiah would be pleased to have another rope to bind you to your word, and he'd never suspect I'd actually do something to bring revolution to Providence. Meanwhile, Brink's jealousy will be his downfall."

Lysander had been jealous too and couldn't countenance Emrys's love of Sian. He had even been resentful of Myfanwy's memory and Emrys's devotion to it. At first, his blind lust for Emrys had stayed his hand from killing his daughter, but even that couldn't withstand his selfishness forever.

Emrys had been forced to choose when really there had been no choice. He'd tricked Lysander into meeting him, promising that he was leaving with the Darisami, and killed Lysander when he was placated. But it hadn't been enough to protect his child. He killed everything he touched and lost everyone he loved.

"I'm frightened for your safety, Galen."

"And I yours. And Nimue's. You have a duty to keep her safe. But none of us are ever safe. If you don't kill Laurence, they'll come for you, so isn't it worth having now in case we never get another chance?"

They were such tempting words—throw caution to the wind because it may not blow in your favor tomorrow.

Emrys wanted it…but he struggled to hold on to it. The years fell behind him in one long road, and with any luck, the path would lay ahead for centuries yet, but what future did Galen have? The only thing that awaited him was death. He would not make Galen into a Darisami, and he would not watch a lover grow old and die.

"Can we, though?" Emrys said.

"We have so much to hide from but this…what we could have with each other. I don't want to hide from it. I want to hold onto it while it lasts."

Emrys looked up and those green eyes weren't just looking at him but at a whole future. Emrys could almost see it too.

"Please, Emrys. I know you feel the same."

He was right. Hope and terror lived in the tightening of his skin and the churning in his stomach, in the boom of his heartbeat and the thrashing of his soul. It would be easy to say that this was as doomed as his relationship with

Lysander, but Galen was to Lysander what Heaven was to Hell.

But even so, he had misgivings. He wanted Myfanwy's ghost to stir and demand he retreat. He wanted Sian's screams to force his withdrawal. But they stayed silent. Even the Darisami voices that could invade his head were absent, and he was alone with his terror.

And his hope.

Both were fatal, but hadn't he mastered death long ago?

Emrys kissed Galen before he could stop himself. He took his chance before the war in his head erupted, before Galen died of old age and Providence became an empty shell, before the world stopped spinning and he perished by the light of the moon.

He opened his mouth to Galen and allowed everything in, accepting this man and the love he offered, no matter how fleeting, how temporary, how based on lies. His denial disintegrated and unleashed his desire.

Galen clasped the back of Emrys's head and kissed him with his potent hunger. A deep moan vibrated in Galen's throat, the wave barreling into Emrys's mouth and chest. Ravenous, desperate kisses snared him in the grip of this man's passion. Their tongues pressed against each other, delved into one another's mouths, seeking to claim and be claimed. Emrys's lips descended down Galen's neck, sucking that spot that summoned the guttural groans he'd heard in his dreams ever since the locker room.

He lifted Galen, not caring that he showed his strength, not caring to hide how little Galen's weight bothered him and carried him to the bed. He lay him on his back and looked down at Galen's green-flame eyes and kiss-swollen lips. Breath streamed through his nose, enlivening the thumping tension between wanting to capture this moment forever before losing himself in Galen.

"You're right," Emrys said. "I feel it too. I feel what you feel, that this could be something special."

Galen kissed him again, his fervor pressed into him. "We'll make sure it does."

Lust spiked from Emrys's balls to his brain. He wanted Galen naked and on him, but before he could pant out a yes, the apartment door opened. Emrys whipped round to look at Nimue, frozen in the entry.

Galen was out from under him faster than he could say awkward. "Uh, hi, Nimue, how are you?"

She looked from Galen to Emrys and back again. Betrayal softened her features like a Greek theater mask so even the people in the nosebleeds could have seen her performance. Without a word, she ran into her room, leaving behind a couple of wet intakes of breath, and closed her door. She always played moody adolescent well.

Emrys adjusted his trousers to reposition his erection and scooted to the edge of the bed while Galen was busy trying to come up with something appropriate to say. Emrys took his hand and pulled him down to kiss him. Galen melted, and Emrys's heart lifted.

"How about we finish this some other time? I'd better talk about this with Nimue."

As much as she wouldn't care what happened in his room, worry was heavy on Galen's face.

"Do you want me to stay and help?"

He gave a soft chuckle. "I can handle it." He walked him to the door.

Galen kissed him again, but it had the mournful quality of a farewell. The worry for himself had been replaced with the worry for Emrys. "I understand if we can't see each other for a while."

He stared into Galen's eyes and held his gaze. "I'll see you tomorrow. That's a promise." He kissed Galen hard and sent him away. Once the door closed, Emrys rounded and marched to Nimue's room.

She reclined on the bed with her hands behind her head and her feet crossed at the ankles, wearing a pure and devious grin.

He bristled at her nonchalance. "You did that on purpose."

"Of course I did. You can't expect a daughter to be happy her father is fucking someone else right in front of her."

She spoke sense, but he didn't have to like it. "This won't be a problem, will it?"

"Not for me."

Nimue wouldn't have cared what he did with Galen. And considering what she had managed to achieve in Endurance, where the spilled blood was still being mopped up from its halls, he had no doubt she would act swiftly if he threatened her plans for Providence.

The unspoken warning in her minimal words lifted his lust and the ghosts of Myfanwy and Sian rose to haunt his heart. But they weren't enough to scare away his longing to see Galen again. No matter how much they howled.

A TEN-TON TRUCK CAREENED OUT OF EMRYS'S DREAMS AND smashed into his brain, throwing him upright. It continued its violent run, blackening his vision and knocking him out of bed. He collapsed on the floor and gripped his head to keep his skull from cracking.

WHERE IS NIMUE? Ragnar's voice reverberated through Emrys's bones.

Emrys gasped for breath and crawled out of his room into hers. Her bed was empty and made as if she'd never slept there. Fear punched its way into Emrys's throat while Ragnar raged.

He curled into a ball on her floor and tried to wrestle his thoughts into coherence. *I don't know where she is. What's happened?*

Tell me you had nothing to do with this.

What are you talking about?

He couldn't escape from Ragnar's hob-nailed march through his head. Each step crushed Emrys's resistance as if Ragnar ground the bones of his long-dead enemies into dust. Emrys massaged his temples, but it didn't help.

Nimue was the reason Absolon went crazy. She brought Endurance down from the start.

He screwed his eyes shut against Ragnar's bellowing. *I don't believe it. How do you know this?*

From her. I extracted the truth out of that deceitful mind of hers. She fought hard, but I got through. She split a soul with him without us knowing and turned him against us.

That's insane. She wouldn't do that. Nimue might be capable of such things, but she hated Absolon. She'd never share a soul with him, and he would never accept her offer.

She wouldn't? She planted the idea in Clara's head that Yusef would turn traitor.

Clara has always been suspicious. He forced breath in and out of his nose. *You can't blame Nimue.*

It's the truth. She is evil to the core, and I am coming to destroy her.

He froze. *You won't be able to get in.*

I don't care. She is the reason we have lost our home. She will suffer her punishment. She has flaunted our rules from the moment she arrived, and I will have my revenge for her taking Absolon from me. I will see you soon, brother. In the meantime, be wary. She is not to be trusted.

Ragnar stormed out of Emrys's aching mind, and he relaxed as the pain receded like a retreating tide. He rolled onto his back while a multitude of revelations rocked his soul.

Nimue, a traitor.

Ragnar, seeking vengeance.

The Five, tearing itself apart.

And in among it all was Galen.

Had his focus on Galen blinded him to what Nimue was up to? Was she plotting his demise as well, once she was assured the Darisami in Endurance had been exterminated? And now that she knew about Galen, she had a hold over Emrys just as Yusef had had a weakness. If Ragnar spoke true, the depth and reach of Nimue's schemes stole his breath. Nothing was beyond her. Where did he fit into her plot?

He needed to find her but when he did, what would he ask? And would he like her answers?

<hr>

AS MORNING DAWNED IN PROVIDENCE, NIMUE DIDN'T return to the room, and any attempt to reach her was rebuffed. Could she really have caused such destruction? Could she have controlled Absolon and used him as a puppet? And would she do it to him as well? Emrys contacted Clara, uneasy about what she might have to report.

Is Nimue dead? she asked.

No.

Good, then Ragnar can kill her.

Has he left Endurance?

Yes. Wyatt, too. They've got your knife.

So it had begun. Did Nimue know he was coming to kill her? Could they keep Ragnar and Wyatt out of Providence. Did he want to?

I hope they cleaned it first.

Clara recoiled.

Sorry. If it's any consolation, Yusef was always going to be trouble.

But to be so willful, so disloyal. Venom clogged her arteries, but her pain subsided into inevitability. *He has ruined everything.*

What did you say to him?

I said nothing.

He waited.

I only said that it would be better to give Yeleni a peaceful death rather than prolong her suffering. I was trying to be sympathetic.

Why break a three-hundred-year habit? Nimue had done well.

And Denari is dead, too?

Yes, as far as I am aware. Wyatt saw Yusef strike her, and she hasn't been seen since. Clara didn't mourn her.

So, you're the only one left in Endurance.

Her loneliness echoed through her mind, reverberating against the stone walls of her heart. She was doing her best to ignore the fact she would die among strangers.

How many humans remain?

Enough for a few years.

You intend to stay?

For now.

The isolation whistled down Endurance's empty hallways, broken by distant banging and pleading. He recognized the same eeriness he'd discovered in the abandoned arks, a metallic air that took on form the longer it persisted. He had no idea if ghosts were real, but imagination provided ample spirits to haunt the halls of Endurance.

You should find somewhere else, Clara.

Why? So you can come back and take everything from me? Or Nimue? Ragnar? If any of you survive. I have what I need. There is no reason to go elsewhere.

Whether it was the effect of Nimue's assault or if the weeks of stress had taken their toll, her mind took on a furry instability. Those ghosts would get her soon enough, and though she might try to stave off madness, it would eventually claim her. She'd roam the corridors once they'd been cleared of corpses. Once a month, she'd bring terror to the survivors.

Until she forgot to feed them, and they starved.

Then so would she.

Would you consider coming here? He didn't want her there, but it seemed the right thing to say.

No. If there's one thing I've learned these past years, it's that I prefer my solitude.

She retreated, and that was that. She didn't block him, but there was a definite turning away. How long would she last?

He considered hailing Ragnar, but even turning his attention to that piece of soul made his neck sweat. Ragnar was running on jet fuel, and his approach was swift. Would Emrys vouch for the two Darisami when they sought refuge? Or would he call them monsters? Thieves? Murderers?

If Ragnar breached Providence's wall, Galen would be in danger. He didn't trust the barbarian to respect his choice of mate. Not after what had happened to Endurance. Ragnar would not willingly let that threat stand.

And so, he could not enter.

But did his alliance with Nimue hold?

She refused to talk to him, so he showered, dressed, and left for work. The one bright side that day was his move to metalworking in the afternoon. He was distracted as Juliet showed him around, but the equipment was largely foolproof, so he was in no danger of hurting himself or others. He worked like an automaton but when the shift ended and the workshop cleared, he burst out of his dream state.

He pulled out the gold he'd stashed in his pocket and dumped it into the machine. The intricacies and skills he'd gained as a jeweler were hardly called for as the contraption took in pieces of metal and melted them into their respective elements. He pressed a button and waited for it to work its magic.

Half an hour later the machine spat out four ingots—iron, copper, aluminum, and gold. They varied in size, aluminum the largest, but he'd gleaned enough gold to kill a Darisami. With a careful eye on the door in case he was disturbed, he took the four metals, grabbed a hunk of steel, and set to work.

Within the hour, he'd fashioned a handled rod thick enough to resist bending. The end was tipped with an inch of gold, filaments running down for as far as possible for maximum effect. He admired his handiwork, simple and beautiful and deadly, wrapped it in cloth, slipped it into his pocket, and left the Factory satisfied.

That satisfaction paled when he saw Galen waiting for him outside the exit. He was leaning against the balcony wall, his gaze set hard, official, and unimpressed. Captain Galen was waiting.

"This isn't a social visit?"

No smile. "Let's walk." He tilted his head toward the

elevator, and they fell into step side by side. "Why did you ask for a transfer?"

He cursed himself. He should have told Galen about it the night before, but there had been more pressing things to worry about. Isaiah's paranoia was not high on Emrys's list of priorities, but it should have been.

The gold-tipped rod dug into his thigh. What would it be like to tell Galen he'd asked for a transfer so he could make a weapon to kill soul-eaters? What would it be like to live with honesty?

"Tell Isaiah I was getting bored so I asked Juliet if I could move to metalworking and she agreed."

"He'll wonder why she was so agreeable."

"It wasn't easy to convince her, and that's the truth. But I must have showed some aptitude. Perhaps she recognized how skilled I am, something your father should know all about. Is that all you came for?"

They stopped at the elevator, and Galen pressed the button. "Yes."

Emrys opened his mouth to say more but the elevator arrived. They couldn't have this conversation with others around. The journey up three floors stretched. He wanted to take Galen's hand and convey some feeling of comfort, but the risk was too high.

"I'm sorry for keeping you in the dark," Emrys said when they were alone again and walking towards his quarters. "I didn't think it was a big deal."

"The problem is, it wasn't me who told Isaiah you'd been promoted."

"Who then?"

"I'm still trying to find that out."

"Probably Brink."

Galen wouldn't be drawn. "I'm making enquiries, but

next time you do something drastic, tell me so I'm prepared."

They were working with two very different scales of what drastic meant.

"I'm sorry. I'll remember." They arrived at Emrys's door. "Are you coming in?"

Galen gave a slight shake to his head. "I need to go back to work. We're picking up more chatter about the surface since your arrival, which is understandable, but Isaiah and Christos believe Laurence is stoking it so that when the council meeting happens, Providence will be on a knife edge."

"And Isaiah still thinks assassinating Laurence is best?"

"He does."

"Pretty dumb if you ask me."

"Agreed. I'm trying to find a way out of this for you, but I'm not hopeful." Galen picked at his bottom lip. Emrys wanted to kiss it and make this whole situation better. "We need to be more careful about meeting. The fact that I spent so much time in your room yesterday without finding out you'd been relocated has shaken Isaiah's faith in me. It won't take much for him to think I've fallen for another Tristan."

Fallen?

Warmth swept through Emrys's body, but it was followed by a chill. They had a few more days until the council meeting. Keeping their distance would be the smart thing to do, but he struggled to stand a foot away from Galen without touching him. Avoiding him completely would be harder to bear than the last day before a harvest. But if it would keep Galen safe, he could do it.

"Does that mean you won't be dropping by for a while?"

Galen lowered his voice. "Not here. But I've got a better idea that should suit us both." A cheeky grin plumped up his lips, a grin more suited to carefree times.

"I don't want you putting yourself in danger."

"I'd risk a hell of a lot more to make sure you stay safe in Providence." Galen's gaze held him. "With me."

"Then you'd better get to work." Emrys winked.

Galen's neck flushed with heat, and his ears reddened. The radiance of that joy blazed in Emrys's heart, possibility and hope fluttering through its chambers. Galen wrestled his smile under control, slipping back into his military persona. As he turned to leave, his fingers brushed the back of Emrys's hand and caused a spark.

But he had no idea what fires it would light.

When he entered his quarters, Nimue was sitting cross-legged on the couch. Waiting. Her eyes tracked his, her attention pinned on him. All the good feeling of being close to Galen drained. He tried not to think about what was in his pocket.

"I think you and I need to have a chat." She gestured to the chair opposite her.

"I'd prefer to stand." He leaned on the back of the seat, keeping at least one obstacle between them.

She shrugged. "Suit yourself. You're aware of Ragnar's accusation."

"That you split a soul with Absolon and sent him mad?"

She gave a tight smile, like a school principal dealing with a difficult student asking difficult questions. "Yes, that's it. What do you think?"

"I find it hard to believe you would do such a thing with Absolon. But Ragnar must have got the idea from somewhere. Is it true?"

"Yes."

Her admission struck like a gong, a vibration that rippled out from the center of his chest and unsettled any of the beliefs he'd held about her. Was it really possible?

"You…you did it?"

"I did what I had to do for the both of us."

"I didn't ask for any of this."

"Not in so many words, but you didn't have to. We were both rotting in Endurance. We didn't belong with those Darisami. We never have. I split a soul with Absolon—and don't ask me what I had to do to convince him because I never want to relive that—and set my plan in motion."

He gripped the back of the chair, the muscles in his chest and neck straining under the knowledge of her viciousness. "Thousands have died, Nimue. I never wanted that. I wanted them to be free."

"They are now. In a way. We have the chance to do better here. We couldn't have had that in Endurance, not with the others, and you wouldn't have killed them all."

"I might have, if I'd known this was the alternative."

"No, you wouldn't. You'd become too complacent, too comfortable. Look at Denari. You knew what she was like, and you did nothing about her."

"She followed the rules. You, on the other hand—"

"Oh, please. Justify it as much as you like, but you would have done nothing to get rid of them, and then what would happen to us? Endurance always had a time limit, and it had run out."

"But all those people…the waste!"

"Think of it as an incentive for the Darisami to risk their lives for a better future." She got off the couch and came towards him.

He kept her at a distance, whether for his protection or hers. "And what now? You'll kill me too?" She already had access to his thoughts and had no reservations about taking advantage of it.

"I did this for both of us, Emrys. Never doubt that. And now you have Galen." The last she said with sing-song menace.

He froze.

"Don't worry, Emrys. I'm not like the others. If you want to fall in love with a human, you're welcome to, and I could even see a future where he becomes one of us if that is your wish. Provided you help me."

The threat sounded in her words.

"With what?"

"I want you to kill Ragnar."

He spluttered. "If you hadn't pushed him, he would still be locked in Endurance."

"He'd never stay there, not while we had Providence."

"He would have if he hadn't found out what you did to Absolon."

"But he did, and we're stuck with it."

"Then let starvation take care of him. Providence will keep its doors sealed."

"We can't guarantee that. He could kill whoever goes to investigate, surviving on a stream of soldiers. I won't rest easy until I see a gold knife sticking out of his eye."

He looked away from her. How had he allowed himself to be led by this demon? He should have ended her life when they'd first met. But he'd been blinded by her resemblance to Sian and the clawing desperation at having her surrogate in his life. More fool him.

"Galen will never be safe while Ragnar lives." The determination in her eyes was unsettling.

"You're asking me to murder another Darisami."

"And one you would have killed without question before the Fall. Whatever your morals, they are founded on self-hate and loathing. Here, you have a chance for something more, but make no mistake, if Ragnar gets in, then it's over for Galen, me, and you. Ragnar must die."

The gold weapon burned in his pocket. Though this was not what he wanted to do, Nimue's reasoning was sound, no matter how unpalatable.

"Ragnar must die."

✺ 23 ✺

LUNCHTIME THE NEXT DAY, JULIET HELD HIM BACK WHILE the others left. Sweat trickled down his neck and spine. Half an hour out of the heat of the metal workshop would have done him some good, but Juliet guarded the exit. Her skin developed a pink sheen. At least he could handle it better than her.

Five minutes after the room emptied, Laurence limped in, leaning on his cane.

"Hello, Mr. Stone. It's good to see you looking so well."

He grimaced. "Can we get this over with?"

"As you wish." Laurence lowered onto a stool opposite him. "You're aware of the upcoming council meeting?"

Seven days to go, and with Ragnar and Wyatt steaming across the countryside, the timing couldn't have been worse.

"I am."

"I would like you to speak at it."

"What good would it do? You and Kira are outnumbered on the council, and this is a closed session."

A small smile stretched Laurence's lips. "The citizens

may not be allowed in, but they won't be unaware of what you say."

"If this is a propaganda exercise, you hardly need me at all. You're doing well enough without my input."

"Yes, the whispers are turning to murmurs, but your voice will raise them to a clamor that cannot be ignored."

Emrys snorted. "Meanwhile, I'll be shoved out into the wild. Or shot."

"They wouldn't dare."

"They would. Desperate people do desperate things."

"You know all about that." Laurence fixed him with a pointed look. "But sometimes we need to do desperate things to make the world a better place."

He'd heard enough justifications for war during his life to fill a library. "Are you sure now is the right time?"

"You work with metal, Emrys. You know that you strike while the iron is hot."

"Yes, but you must be certain it's hot enough."

"It is." His cane rapped the floor. Argument over. Judgement passed. "Will you support our cause?"

"And say what?"

"Tell them again about your journey and the world beyond, but show what you, as an outsider, have learned during your weeks in Providence. Stress how dissimilar we are to Endurance and the other failed arks. Convey how our way of life is stronger, our science is robust, our hearts are pure. Impress upon them how Providence is fit for a return and that we should be making *that* our goal, but also that Providence shares a similar stifling of attitude and exploration that you worry will lead to our demise." He raised his voice and his cane, the calculating restraint in his eyes consumed with the fire of his faith. Laurence believed, and belief was contagious.

Juliet's eyes tracked the councilor, her mouth set and eyes shining.

Laurence's passion roused the flutters of hope in Emrys's stomach, lifting his heart on the vapors of evangelism. He blinked, and the scales of skepticism slid over his eyes.

"And if I say all that, how will you keep me safe?"

And Galen.

"We will guard you with our lives."

He'd witnessed plenty of revolutions where people died and the regime didn't. But perhaps this time could be different. Providence had cracked before he and Nimue had arrived. They could be catalysts for the right kind of change.

"If you can guarantee our protection—mine and my daughter's—I will speak in support of your cause."

"Thank you." Laurence rose from his seat, using the cane to help him stand. He remembered this time. He was in control—or at least felt assured of his victory. He offered his hand.

Emrys shook it. "But just because I agree doesn't mean I share your optimism. They won't like what I have to say, and they won't like your support of it. You are outnumbered, and very few battles have been won with inferior forces."

"I appreciate the warning, but I've learned that when people have weapons, they tend to rely on them, yet when they're disarmed, they fall."

"I hope you know what you're doing."

"The meeting is in one week. We will collect you the night before to keep you safe." Laurence left the room, and Juliet followed.

Laurence may not put much faith in weapons, but

some enemies couldn't be killed without them. That he knew from bitter experience.

When Emrys returned from work, Galen had been in his room. A piece of white cloth poked out from beneath his pillow. On it he'd written instructions in oil, paper being a relic after sixty-five years in a tomb. He tilted the fabric to decipher Galen's directions to where they could meet without being seen.

He showered, dressed, and committed the instructions to memory before shredding the cloth and flushing it down the toilet. Galen's intricate path led him through different levels. He got confused and retraced his steps, the anticipation of what he might find making his memory falter, but he picked up the trail, his memory firming with his rising heart rate, and found room 8945. As instructed, he bypassed the sensor and knocked.

Seconds dragged, gathering doubts and suspicions. What if the note hadn't come from Galen? Had he been seen? What if Galen had been discovered?

He glanced down the hallway to be ready for a surprise attack. Providence's hum tickled the hair on the back of his neck then dug into his skin as the door opened a crack revealing a blackness that could hide an assassin's blade or gun. He stepped to the side, readied his fists, and the symbol shone at the front of his mind.

Galen stuck his head out of the door and gave him a smile like he was a VIP guest at the most exclusive hotel in town. Before they all got bombed.

A breath exploded out of Emrys's mouth. The symbol dissolved.

"Come in." Galen disappeared into the room.

Emrys slid through the narrow opening, leaving Galen to struggle with the heavy weight of the metal door.

"And this is meant to be safe?"

"The sensor is deactivated, and people won't think to try the door, even if they wanted to come in."

The lights didn't work, but Galen had placed a few lamps deep in the room to provide them some illumination. Crates and shelves created a maze of barriers to hide behind.

Galen circled his arms around Emrys's waist. "I'm glad you came."

"I may have got lost." He kissed Galen, the last of the tension fading away. "What is this place?"

"It doesn't matter. All you need to know is that thanks to a few modifications, no cameras tracked you along the route you took. Some skills I picked up from Tristan."

He hoped Galen's former lover approved. "They won't like me disappearing. What if they realize it was you?"

"Then I'll handle it. But for now, I want this moment where we don't have to worry about what's going on in Providence." Galen broke out of Emrys's arms, took him by the hand, and led him to the back of the room. Outside the edge of light lay a single cot bed covered with a blanket.

"You thought of everything, didn't you?"

Galen stopped him from slipping down onto the bed and pulled him back until Galen was propped against one of the crates.

"That's for later." His hand slipped into the waist band of Emrys's trousers and tugged him close. "Unless you'd rather not?"

There were many reasons to not proceed. The worry over whether Nimue could be trusted. Laurence's request to be in the vanguard of a revolution. Isaiah's surveillance over him and possibly Galen. The impending arrival and execution of Ragnar. Plenty of reasons to take things with Galen no further.

But the proximity of this living, breathing human, the leather and man scent that filled his senses, and a clawing need to have something that was his and his alone swept all those excuses aside.

He grinned at Galen and saw his desire reflected in Galen's devouring gaze. "I definitely rather would."

Galen moved fast, lifting the shirt off Emrys's body and pressing his lips against Emrys's neck. He mouthed down to his chest, hard kisses enlivening his skin and sparking in his balls. He wanted Galen naked five seconds ago.

Hands dove to unbutton trousers. Hardening cocks exposed, asses bared, mouths greedy for more. Emrys sank to his knees and took Galen in his mouth, suppressing his gag reflex and relaxing his throat to swallow every inch of his thick, long cock.

Galen groaned. "Fuck." His fingers twisted into Emrys's hair, and Emrys relished the sting in his scalp.

He raised and lowered his head, tongue swirling, mouth sucking up and down the length of Galen's shaft, flicking at the head, spit coating his cock. He dove again, wanting more of Galen's moans, wanting his cries as his thighs tensed and he bucked deeper. He slid in and out as the rhythm of his thrusting fell in sync with his heartbeat, his desire for more, more, more, to give everything he could to bring Galen pleasure.

Galen's fist tightened and he pulled Emrys up like he was forcing a dog to leave a bone. Held aloft, lips wet and swollen, Galen's mouth was on his, his tongue deep and probing, tasting his salty slickness. He broke the kiss with a wet smack. Galen held his gaze. Even in the shadowy light his desire blazed strong.

"I want to fuck you," Galen said. "I've wanted to fuck you since the moment we picked you up."

The words shot down Emrys's body and crashed into his taint. It had been a while since he'd had sex with anyone, even longer since he'd been fucked, but there was nothing he wanted more. "Do it."

Galen switched places with Emrys and pushed him back onto the hard edge, keeping on until Emrys was lying down with his cock twitching and dripping onto his stomach. Anticipation thrummed beneath his skin and shortened his breath. Galen grabbed a small bottle, flicking its lid open and tipping the viscous fluid onto his fingers. He coated his cock before reapplying to his hands and ditching the bottle. Coming between Emrys's legs and positioning them on his hips, Galen's wet fingers circled his hole, enticing it to relax.

Emrys breathed in. He was tight but not from fear it would hurt. Tight from wanting to feel Galen inside him. Tight from wanting to make this last as long as possible. As Galen slid a finger inside, he forced himself to relax, and desire rippled up his body. He arched his back and clenched, growing accustomed to the feel of Galen probing him.

Galen waited until he was calm enough to go further, stretching him, preparing him for the rest of his finger, even as Emrys started to rock his hips. First one finger, then a second. Emrys moaned, his breath quickening and cock pulsing.

"How does that feel?" Galen said.

"Good." Emrys forced the short sharp sound from his mouth. "Good. But I want more."

Galen smiled, a half-cocked grin that was pure sex. He leaned over and kissed him, pushing his finger in further and stroking his prostate.

Emrys's moans exploded into Galen's mouth. "Do it. Please, Galen. I want you in me."

Galen slipped out, then with one hand on Emrys's chest and the other holding his cock, Galen pressed against his hole. They breathed together, the muscles relaxing to allow Galen entry, and with a few jerks and spasms, Galen slid into him inch by breathtaking inch until it felt like the head hit his heart.

"Are you okay?"

The last time it had felt this good, this free and easy, had been with Lysander. The thought was fleeting, the silken touch of his caress that turned to sticky spiderweb. But Galen was not Lysander and that remembrance was enough to return him to the beautiful man over him.

His whole body tingled, sparks radiating out from his ass, through his legs and stomach and arms. His scalp was afire with electricity and his breath alive with the energy of the stars. He couldn't speak. He nodded. He shivered.

Galen moved his hips, pleasure-pain rippling through him with each slow stroke. He didn't dare touch himself.

"Keep going?"

Emrys nodded again, barely able to think beyond wanting him to go harder. His hand locked onto Galen's as he fucked him. He did a poor job of stifling his moans, even louder when Galen went that little bit faster, little bit deeper, little bit harder.

He released Galen's hand, lifted his hips more. Galen held his legs wide and hit *that* spot, forcing his eyes to roll back into his head.

He gasped. "Like that. Just like that."

Galen kept at it, kept at him, connecting every time. Emrys forced his eyes open to look at the towering man above him, eyes intent on his face, strain across his forehead, sweat matting his hair and glistening on his chest in the half light. Galen watched him with a deep need that heightened the rapture running rampant through Emrys's body.

This man…

This man offered him a chance at the love he'd been missing for centuries. This man made all the fights ahead worth fighting. It was no longer just about his survival but about Galen's too.

The surge of emotion gained from that knowledge detonated, starting with his heart and catching fire to the powder keg in his balls. He froze, all muscles tensing, straining through his neck, his groin, his ass. His hand shot out to clasp Galen's arm, and with a strangled shout he came, the orgasm rolling wave after wave through his body, everything destroyed and cleared.

He collapsed onto his back, his stomach wet and hot with his own come, his spine bending as another orgasm rolled through him. Breath galloped out of his lungs. He attempted to raise his head as Galen fucked him hard and released deep inside him with sure, steady, strong thrusts. Warmth blanketed him from top to bottom before Galen pitched forward at the waist and rested his forehead on Emrys's chest. They breathed together, long and labored, content. He stroked Galen's hair and drifted on the afterglow.

Everything was still except the rise and fall of their chests.

He didn't know how long it was before Galen slipped out of him and returned with a towel to wipe him clean. Galen interlocked their fingers and took him to the bed where he wrapped Emrys in his arms. He drifted until the haze cleared from his mind and the shadows of the room and their situation returned.

"How long do you think before they find us?"

"Emrys, please. Why ruin this?"

Because I don't want to lose it.

"I don't mean to, but we have to be prepared." He used to be so good at letting humanity's petty squabbles fade into the background. As long as he could feed, everything was bearable, but times had changed.

And so had his heart. Now he had much more to lose than his life.

Galen shifted and sat up. "Things will ease after the council meets."

"I'm not going to kill Laurence."

"I know."

"So how can you possibly think things will get easier? Isaiah must be getting frantic now only a week remains."

Galen stroked his chin with his thumb, his mouth bunching in one corner. "He's even worse after your meeting with Laurence today."

He dropped his head back onto the cot. "I was going to tell you, but there wasn't time."

"It's okay. Everything's going to be okay."

"I don't see how. There's nothing secret in Providence."

"Only this." Galen kissed him, but his lips weren't warm enough to stop the chill sliding down Emrys's spine. He didn't share Galen's confidence in their rendezvous remaining a secret for long, or even that it still was.

He brushed his knuckles against Galen's cheek. "Don't you see that the risks we're taking make you more of a target? I'm terrified they'll use you to get to me."

"They can't. They don't know about us."

He couldn't make Galen understand. And part of him didn't want to. "Promise me you'll be safe."

"I promise. But I won't stop seeing you."

"How will I know when we can meet?"

"On the days I can't, I will be waiting for you outside the Factory for a report. The days I can, I'll be here at seven. Will you come?"

Emrys hesitated. The more often they met, the greater the chance of discovery, but the thought of not coming soured his stomach. "I'll be here."

Galen smiled and kissed Emrys, stirring a desperate desire that demanded the desperate attention of the damned.

❧ 24 ❧

THE TEMPERATURE IN THE WORKSHOP SOARED. IT HAD BEEN nineteen days since Emrys had taken Jared's soul, but the symbol flickered in and out of the front of his mind at random.

The only moment he was calm was when he was with Galen.

So far, he'd not shown up at the Factory. Emrys held his breath every time he walked through the door, hoping to see him, hoping to not. And when he wasn't there, he expelled a long sigh that hitched high in his throat as the thought of putting Galen in jeopardy rushed in. Only temptation and desire kept him afloat.

When they made love in 8945, they floated on rough seas. The fear of discovery rocked them and added something primal, something dangerous that intensified their fucking, making it harder for his doubts to get air.

What was he doing with Galen? Did he deserve this? When would it all break apart?

Every fear was pushed beneath the surface and held down

until it drowned…only to bob up later like a bloated corpse when he and Galen parted ways and he returned to his empty quarters. He didn't sleep, and his days blended into one.

Juliet encouraged him out during lunch to break the monotony three days before the meeting. When he reached the mess hall, the eyes of the workers landed on him. He should have expected his presence was orchestrated to serve Laurence's propaganda, not to improve his mental health.

People crowded in and sat at tables as if they were in some old school. Nourishment was doled out with wan expressions, eaten without relish, and little laughter accompanied the communal meal. There was no feast. No eat, drink, and be merry. Tension hummed through the room, a few friendly smiles but most watched to see if he faltered. Did he measure up? Did they believe his involvement was really going to make a difference?

He and Juliet collected their food and found a table. He made small talk with the man and woman sitting beside them. In their thirties, their skin was sallow and their eyes haggard. They hunched like they sheltered beneath low ceilings despite the space in this subterranean city. The designers had been generous, had had the luxury of time, knowing one day they would need to descend to survive. But their dejection was not due to architecture. It was a weight they bore in their souls.

The couple left.

"I thought they'd ask me to do tricks or something."

Juliet smiled. "No, but they're aware of who you are and what's at stake."

Two large men took the couple's places but at a distance from him and Juliet. On their other side sat another two large men. None talked. Bodyguards.

Emrys leaned closer and kept his voice low. "What if nothing changes and there is no way out of Providence?"

"We will make one. Have faith."

He snorted. Faith was one of those fancy words people used when they weren't willing to face the true horrors of the world.

One of which was him.

He tucked into the slop and made a show of eating. Juliet ran through the proceedings before and after the council meeting. She risked much doing it in the open, but when he stressed caution, she dismissed his concerns. The people needed to see him. It also made it harder for surveillance to track what was being discussed. He almost told her Galen said audio recording wasn't as widespread as video surveillance in Providence, but then Emrys would have to answer her questions about how he knew that. His cheeks heated. He focused on his food.

They were three days from the council meeting. The plan was for him to not go home after work the day before it and for Nimue to be collected from school by some of their followers. From there, they'd be secreted somewhere even he wasn't allowed to know about. He'd rather Galen was in charge of his protection, but again, disclosing that would be a problem. As far as Juliet was concerned, Galen was on the enemy's side. And speaking of enemies…

"What does Brink think?"

"Nothing. I haven't told him any of it."

"But what's going to happen after? He'll have an opinion, and I don't think it'll be the same as yours."

She pushed her plate away after a half-hearted attempt at eating. "Don't worry about us. We've been through worse before, and we managed to find each other."

"Sounds more like a hunter catching its prey than two

lovers. Honestly, what is the attraction? I've seen the way he is with you. He's a possessive, overbearing creep."

She shrugged and brushed a lock of hair from her forehead. "I love him. I always have. Ever since we were kids." She said it like a burden that had to be endured, cumbersome, unfair, and destined for the hill at Golgotha.

How much did she know about Brink's obsession with Galen?

"Does he feel the same about you?"

"Of course. Why wouldn't he?"

"I think he wants to own you rather than love you."

"Look, Emrys, I know you two—" Her sights shifted over Emrys's shoulder to the entrance. "What the?"

Emrys turned. Brink. "Well, speak of the devil."

Brink stormed through the mess, pushing workers aside as he fought to get through. He was dressed in his uniform, and his eyes locked onto Emrys with the prejudice of a nuclear warhead.

Emrys stood. No way did he want to be an easy target. "Brink, what's—"

Brink's fist connected with Emrys's jaw, the surprise of it knocking him back onto the bench. Brink launched, granting Emrys no space or time to retaliate, dragged him to the ground, and kicked him. Emrys tensed his stomach and covered his head while Juliet shouted for Brink to stop. The four bodyguards wrestled Brink back, and Emrys regained his feet and massaged his jaw.

Brink broke out of the bodyguards' restraints, but they formed a wall between him and Emrys. "Let me through or you'll all be thrown in a cell for assaulting an officer."

"What's this about?" He indicated for the bodyguards to let Brink pass.

The soldier shoved his way through and reared up to Emrys. "I've been watching you two."

"We're just talking." Juliet appeared beside him.

"Not you. Like I give a fuck what he does with you." Brink sneered and turned back to Emrys. "I'm talking about Galen. I know what you two have been getting up to, and it's going to stop, or you'll be sorry."

Emrys's heartbeat slowed, blood pounding a warning through his body, every pulse pumped with primal dread. They'd been exposed. Galen was in danger. A sour taste burned at the back of his throat that had nothing to do with the food. He swallowed it down and held onto a thin thread of nonchalance. "What I do is none of your business."

Brink narrowed his eyes. "You'd better believe it's my business, Stone."

Cold fire sucked the oxygen from Emrys's lungs. He put his hand on Brink's shoulder. "Listen, Brink, why don't we talk in private?"

Brink answered with his fist. The blow wasn't strong enough to knock Emrys to the ground, but it knocked out the last of his patience. Rage coiled in Emrys's belly and released in his fists. The impact sent Brink flying across the room as if he weighed nothing and he landed on his back on one of the tables.

Emrys raced over and grabbed the front of Brink's uniform, pulling him to stand on shaking legs, and punched him in the face with enough force to wet his knuckles. Brink's head lolled back, the man dazed and barely conscious.

"If you ever threaten me again, I will kill you." Emrys didn't unclench his fist, but Juliet forced Emrys to release his grip.

She ordered the bodyguards to take Brink to the hospital. Nobody else moved, and an uncomfortable silence prickled through the crowd. Wide-eyed expressions formed a circle around him, but Juliet's stricken face was the one that made the most impact. Though he hadn't been explicit, there was no doubt Juliet knew what he and Galen had been up to. And absolutely no doubt that Brink cared more for Galen than her. He wished he could have kept her from that knowledge and hurt.

"Juliet, I'm—"

"We need to go." She hurried for the exit, her face doing a good impression of looking determined and in control.

He followed, and the eyes of every person tracked him. He didn't turn around, afraid to see their hopes dashed as they realized they'd trusted their future to a violent troublemaker.

GALEN WASN'T WAITING FOR HIM AT THE FACTORY AFTER work finished, but Emrys had only been back inside his apartment for five minutes before he appeared at his door cloaked in his black uniform. He swept into Emrys's apartment, a storm flashing across his face.

"I guess this isn't a social call."

"You put him in the fucking hospital."

"He attacked me first. You're saying I shouldn't fight back?"

"That would have been best."

Galen checked Nimue's room, but it was empty. He continued to pace around the apartment, nervous energy sparking off him like a diesel lawnmower, back when lawns were a thing. Emrys stayed still, watching Galen circling and cutting up the floor.

"Is he all right?" He'd hit Brink very hard. Could have hit him harder. Maybe next time. If there was a next time.

"The doctors wanted to keep him in overnight, but he's been discharged."

"I didn't hit him hard enough then. At least tell me he's lost a tooth or three."

"This isn't funny, Emrys. You're lucky I'm not here to arrest you."

"Perhaps that would be better. Then I'd get some protection. What did Isaiah say about the fight?"

Galen sputtered to a stop and slumped onto the couch, but his right leg stayed active, bouncing up and down. "He laughed, actually. Thought it was amusing. He's decided to be lenient."

"That's big of him." Emrys sat opposite, clasping his hands together to hold himself still out of fear that Galen wouldn't let him get close.

"It doesn't come from the goodness of his heart. He's still waiting for you to murder Laurence, but he did tell me to pass on a warning that he wouldn't stand for you beating up soldiers and Providence-born citizens."

"Then Brink needs to stay out of my way, or I can't be held responsible for what happens to him."

Galen flinched. When Emrys furrowed his brow, Galen's gaze dashed away. Was Galen worried he'd kill Brink? After what they'd been through and what Brink had done to him, Galen cared more about Brink's safety than his? Even when Brink was a threat to Galen's safety too. Or maybe he didn't know that.

"Brink knew about us meeting. He knew about all of it." Emrys spoke calm and slow. Galen wasn't his enemy.

Galen jerked back to face Emrys again. "What are you saying?"

"That's what the fight was about. You must know by now. Hell, the whole of Providence probably knows we're fucking thanks to Brink."

His eyebrows pulsed in confusion. "That's not what Isaiah said."

"What did he say?"

"He said you attacked Brink because of Juliet."

Emrys blew breath across his lips, a breath propelled by disgust. "He's lying. Brink knows about you and me. He implied it to everyone in that mess hall. He didn't care about the effect. He didn't care who knew. All he cared about was warning me away from you."

"That's not the message that's being spread. They're saying it's a fight over Juliet, about Brink trying to keep her to himself."

"And you believe that?" Emrys dropped his chin, raised his eyebrows. Surely Galen couldn't believe that.

"I believe Brink is crazy enough to think you're a threat to his relationship with Juliet."

"But not crazy enough to punch the living shit out of me because of my relationship with you? Wake up, Galen."

The propaganda machine was working overtime to turn this into something that worked in Laurence's favor. The workers must have all been fed lines about what to say throughout Providence. It looked better for them that Emrys was protecting one of their own from the might of the military faction—not so much that he was meeting in secret and fucking one of its highest-ranking officers.

It also worked in Isaiah's favor. Who would trust the volatile workers—and their leader—with Providence's future?

"If what you say is true—"

"If?" Emrys cut Galen off with the same sharpness that Galen's mistrust slashed through him. "You really don't believe me."

"I've seen the footage, Emrys."

"And I was there. I know what happened, and I know what Brink said." He slammed his hands onto his knees and pushed to his feet. He walked away from Galen's mistrust, but the apartment was small. "I can't believe you'd take Isaiah's word over mine."

Galen looked to the ground. Was he jealous? Did he think something was going on between him and Juliet?

"What's this really about, Galen? Is it you don't trust what I'm telling you? Do you think I'm fucking Juliet?"

Galen kept his eyes downcast.

"Or are you frightened of me?"

Galen's eyes shot up and stuck him like a blunt needle.

"You're afraid of me." The words came out whispered as if speaking them too loud would make them real.

"I'm afraid of what you can do and what you're capable of. You nearly killed him, Emrys."

"He deserved it but he's not dead because you wouldn't like it, which right now makes me wonder where your loyalties lie."

Galen bolted to his feet. Righteousness carved his face into something unbending, unfriendly, and unlike Galen. "You think because I don't want you to kill another human being, I'm somehow unfaithful? And you say Brink's the crazy one. I don't want to be the only thing standing in the way of you killing someone. I don't want that responsibility."

Emrys wanted to say he derived no pleasure from killing. Surely that was evident in his reluctance to kill Laurence. He wanted to say he killed only out of necessity, but what reason could he give for that without revealing what he was? He didn't want to lie, but he couldn't tell the truth, even if it meant losing Galen.

And the truth was he brought nothing but death.

"So what now?" Emrys straightened his back, clearing

the strain from his face while inside his heart unthreaded, sinew by sinew.

"I can't do this. I don't have what it takes to be with you and join in your fight for a different future for Providence. It's too dangerous. *You're* too dangerous."

"Something Tristan and I have in common then. I guess I shouldn't have expected you to treat me any differently."

Galen blinked but where Emrys anticipated recriminations and a violent denial, Galen offered the blank face of antipathy. There was nothing more hurtful, and Emrys wished he could take back the words he'd uttered.

"Galen, I'm—"

He held up his hand. "No, you're right. I'm a coward and need to accept that no matter what I feel for you, I do not have what it takes to fight. Your secrets are safe with me, Emrys, but I can't be the man you need me to be. I can't lose again."

Galen left the apartment and took with him the tattered remnants of Emrys's heart.

$\maltese$ 25 $\maltese$

Emrys blinked awake as a squad of helmeted and armed soldiers charged into his room. The lights flickered on, and he scrambled up in his bed, ready to fight, but slowed as eight machine gun muzzles zeroed in on his chest where his heart was struggling to escape through his ribcage.

Three soldiers rushed him, pulled him out of bed, and forced him to the ground. A gun barrel jammed into the spot where his spine connected with his skull. They slapped handcuffs around his wrists and hoisted him to stand naked among uniformed men.

"What's this about?"

Isaiah entered his quarters. "You're under arrest for the murder of Brink Ford." He barked at the soldier beside him. "Get him some trousers. I've seen enough ugliness for one morning."

Brink's dead?

A soldier rifled through his drawers and pulled out trousers for him to wear.

"Where's your daughter?" Isaiah said.

"Somewhere you'll never find her." Emrys allowed himself a grin which got bigger the more Isaiah sneered.

"Take him to the cells." Isaiah's head jerked towards the exit, and Emrys was half-lifted and half-shoved out of the room.

Providence hadn't roused yet. He was escorted down the corridors to the military complex. The warren twisted and turned until he was thrown into the cell he'd occupied on arrival. They removed the handcuffs and locked him inside.

Isaiah dismissed the soldiers. Whatever treason he was about to spout wouldn't be heard by a subordinate's ears.

"Where's Galen? I want to talk to him," Emrys said.

"You're in no position to make demands considering what you've done to embroil him in your actions." Isaiah neared the glass. The wrinkles around his eyes deepened as he smiled. "You've implicated him in a plot that could result in his execution."

"You wouldn't do that to your son."

"You have no idea what I'd do to ensure Providence's survival."

"To ensure your stranglehold on power more like. Where is he?"

"He's here. In a cell. We need to ask him some questions."

"I didn't kill Brink."

Isaiah frowned and tilted his head. "That's not what it looks like."

"What do you mean?"

Isaiah tucked his hands behind his back, marched left. "Well, the whole of Providence knows you two had a fight in the mess yesterday."

"That doesn't mean I killed him. Surely you've got enough surveillance in this place to know who did."

Isaiah kept pacing. "That's the thing. Where he was found, the cameras don't quite follow, although we've been able to piece together a few things, such as the way Galen set it up so you two wouldn't be tracked." He returned to Emrys and stopped. "Room 8945 ring a bell? There's a lot of evidence about that. A lot of damning evidence."

A realization entered Emrys's mind, as steady and inescapable as the touch of the Darisami's symbol. "You've known all along."

"I know my son, Stone. I know where his sympathies lie, and I knew you would be someone he could not resist. Just as he could not resist Tristan."

"You're a monster."

"I've been called worse. Brink was found earlier this morning in much the same fashion as Jared. Not a mark on him. Seemingly died of natural causes. And your fingerprints and DNA were found at the scene. The evidence is solid. I'm certain you were able to pull this off by yourself, but perhaps you convinced my son to go along with you." The faux charm sloughed off Isaiah's body, revealing the wolf Emrys should have made it his mission to skin. "You had a choice. You could have done what we asked and none of this would be happening. We'd be all having a good laugh and toasting Providence's salvation. But the council meeting is in two days, and you have not done as instructed."

"I was going to kill him today."

Isaiah laughed. "I'm sure. No matter. I have no desire to see Laurence killed now that another way has become clear."

"What do you mean?"

"Within a few hours, the whole of Providence will know that you are a murderer and corruptor. Ordinarily, we would execute you, but considering you're not one of us, we've decided to put you back where you came from. We'll see how well you survive in the wild a second time around. Word will filter down of your eventual starvation and death, and that will be the end of Laurence's revolution. He will be discredited, and you will be dead."

"You really think I'll go that easily? Surely the people will demand a trial. They'll demand some evidence."

"They'll have it. Enough to dispel even the thinnest shadow of a doubt. But you'll plead guilty and make this a lot easier on everyone involved."

"Why would I do that?"

"For Galen and Nimue. If you fight this, Galen will be your co-accused and executed alongside you. The evidence is equally damning for him." He directed Emrys's attention to the screen beside him.

A video played of spliced-together footage showing Galen and Emrys entering the room separately followed later by Brink. The time stamps had been doctored to show one followed the other without much break in between. Galen left looking disheveled, and Emrys followed soon after. Brink never reappeared.

"No one will believe it," Emrys said.

"They'll believe what I tell them to believe. But if that's not enough, then there's always Nimue."

He bared his teeth. "Stay away from her."

Isaiah's thin lips curved. "You'd rather she had a chance at life, wouldn't you? Plead guilty, and she can stay. She'll have a home. If not, she'll be expelled with you, and you won't have your pack of supplies like last time. She'll be lucky to survive the first night." His smirk chilled Emrys's heart. "The choice is yours."

"Some choice."

Nimue would be fine, but Galen was another question. No matter their argument the night before, he wouldn't let

Galen suffer for his missteps, his failure to see how dangerous this web had become. He'd known he wasn't designed for cohabiting with humans, and he should have stayed separate. He was wrong to have fallen for Galen and put him in danger.

The few moments they'd shared, bright as they were, had burned them both. He could fight his way out, suck out Isaiah's soul, and leave Providence behind. But then he'd be leaving Galen with the thought Emrys had killed Brink. He didn't want that. And he didn't want Isaiah's death on his hands, even if harvesting his soul would give him an extra month to find another food source. Death couldn't answer all his problems.

"Well?"

Isaiah would never know how close to death he'd come.

"I accept, but under the conditions that Galen is absolved of any crime and released, and my daughter is accepted as a citizen of Providence without prejudice."

"You are in no position to bargain."

"And you don't really want to see your son die. You can easily re-edit the video to remove Galen, so agree to this, and you get to keep your ever-grateful son."

A muscle in Isaiah's cheek twitched, prodding his eye into a squint. "I agree to your terms."

"In that case, I am guilty of the murder of Brink Ford."

Isaiah clapped his hands together. "Excellent." He indicated to the screen inside the cell, meanwhile pressing a few buttons on a panel on his side of the glass. A statement appeared on the screen in which Emrys admitted to the crime. "Sign that, and this will all be over."

He didn't hesitate. The signed statement vanished.

"Now that that's out of the way, Stone, I'm prepared to

make another deal."

"Don't you get tired of deals?"

Isaiah ignored the comment and got close to the glass. "Tell me how you killed Jared, and I'll let you stay."

"You can't be serious."

"I've never been more serious about anything."

He neared Isaiah, his gaze hardening and his fingers curling like a cat flexing its claws. Isaiah's Adam's apple bobbed in his throat. "That secret is mine and mine alone."

Isaiah flared his nostrils and stepped back. "So be it." His lips parted to let the pronouncement slip through his teeth. "You'll be escorted out in a couple of hours. Now, I'm going to look for your daughter. Perhaps if you see her, you'll be willing to give up your secret." Isaiah walked away.

Emrys banged on the glass. "I want to see Galen before I go."

"But he doesn't want to see you."

Isaiah left. Emrys reached out to Nimue when all he wanted to do was speak to Galen.

You could break out and get your revenge.

Then what? Become another Absolon? I won't have that on my conscience. Galen wouldn't want anything to do with him once he saw what horror he was truly capable of.

So that's it? You'll go quietly? Won't make a fuss?

You should be happy. You'll have Providence to yourself. With my expulsion, they'll never let any survivors back in. You're safe from Ragnar.

I wish it hadn't come to this, Emrys. Enough emotion laced her words that he believed her.

It's not your fault. Or at least he hoped it wasn't. Perhaps there was some hope they'd meet again. *We had a good run while it lasted. Longer than most.*

We did. Thank you, my friend.

He didn't respond but she stayed with him, a comfort nestled at the back of his mind.

THEY BROUGHT CLOTHES AND BOOTS, BUT NO PACK FILLED with supplies. He'd be kicked out with less than he'd had when he came in.

Much less.

But Galen was safe. He wished he could speak to him one last time, to tell him what he meant to him, and that he'd not done what Galen thought. He didn't want their fight to be their last memory together.

His long life had started with hard goodbyes. It couldn't end with them as well. A failed relationship, bitter words, and his lover thinking he was every bit as evil as he truly was. Galen was better off without him, of that he had no doubt, but Emrys?

He'd have given up a few centuries to have one more day with Galen.

Isaiah returned. Emrys was waiting, prepared to meet his fate.

"I had hoped to bring Nimue to say goodbye, but she has proved elusive and time is pressing." Isaiah's voice strained, not out of any compassion for a father to say farewell to his daughter but at his inability to hold onto a hostage.

"She's good at hiding."

"A skill she no doubt learned from you. I wonder if she learned any of your other skills."

"She knows nothing of what I did for you or of my methods."

"Luckily for her, I believe you. But soon she will know

about your betrayal of our ways, and that will be a lesson that will stand her in good stead for the rest of her natural life in Providence."

The thought of any child, let alone a Darisami, stuck beneath the ground for another eternity grabbed at his throat and squeezed, stuffing his windpipe full of dirt and rocks.

"We will find her eventually. But for you, time has run out." Isaiah signaled down the corridor, and a team of soldiers appeared, their faces masked, their weapons armed. Emrys could kill them all.

But I only need one.

Isaiah ordered him back from the door, and it slid open to admit three soldiers. Two aimed their guns at his chest and the other cuffed his wrists. The symbol blazed. He didn't care who he took. He needed to harvest, or he'd be dead in eleven days.

He stepped into the corridor. The soldiers flanked him and marched him out. He swayed to the right, toward the soldier nearest him, and reached out his shackled hands as if to steady his step. He extended an inch further, and with the barest touch to bare skin, the symbol propelled forward, snaring the soldier's soul.

The soldier staggered, the one behind bumping into him. Emrys lost the connection but the soul was his. He sucked it in as fast as he could, while the soldiers rushed to their mate's aid as he collapsed to the floor. The soul slithered into Emrys's body and burst into a billion stars. His head reeled with the joy of singing angels, but he ground his teeth, and in the confusion of the soldier's downfall, sprinted in the opposite direction in search of Galen.

"Stop or we'll shoot!"

Go ahead.

He found Galen three cells down from where he'd been

imprisoned. No gunfire followed but footsteps pounded after him. He thumped Galen's glass cell wall.

Galen startled, and his eyes locked on Emrys's. Sadness streaked through them and he made to turn away. He believed Emrys had killed Brink.

Emrys banged on the glass to get his attention, but Galen refused to turn, the denial a boot heel that ground his heart into the dirt.

"It wasn't me, Galen. I didn't kill Brink. Please trust me. I wouldn't break my promise to you."

The soldiers tackled him to the ground, and boots battered his body. An electric shock zapped his kidneys, and he spasmed. He tried to keep his eyes on Galen, and in the moment before he was wrestled back, Galen glanced his way. Emrys's throat closed, jammed shut with the uncertainty in Galen's expression. But he found hope in the face of that doubt.

They marched him down the corridor, keeping him in their center with electric probes, Isaiah warning them not to let him get close. They passed the dead body on the ground. The soul had given him one month's grace from death, one month more to starve.

They took him to the transport elevator. Isaiah did not enter. He didn't speak, and though he tried to appear strong and in control, he couldn't keep his eyes free of fear.

Emrys went quietly.

They reached the little room in the broken-windowed warehouse and led him outside. They removed his cuffs but did not shift the sights of their rifles off him. They directed him away, demanded he turn and walk. He needed to find a place to hide when the moon showed her face.

And when Ragnar and Wyatt reached the city.

❧ 26 ❧

Night fell with the suddenness of a guillotine, and the world never seemed deader. Emrys sought the shelter of the jagged skyscrapers that provided a good vantage point back towards the warehouse and beyond to Providence, as well as to all points into the ruined city.

He didn't sleep. Couldn't. He kept away from the windows and the waning moon. He watched the west for Wyatt and Ragnar's approach. They were coming. The pressure in his mind swelled as Ragnar's fury rumbled across the country towards him.

And towards Nimue.

Ragnar would have no satisfaction. He'd die out there. They all would. No Providence welcoming party would dare venture out of the ark and collect another couple of strays. Laurence would not be able to put forward a murderer as the hope of their salvation. Much of his support would collapse. The part that didn't scatter would harden into a revolutionary faction that Isaiah and Christos, and perhaps Elaina too, would delight in exterminating.

All for the good of Providence.

Nimue would feast on the strife and cleanse Providence of souls.

Emrys, however, would attempt to move on and seek another home. He could return to Endurance and shelter with Clara until he worked out a better alternative. He would leave the next day, or the one after that, when his desire to stay wasn't so strong.

As the night got colder and the world died a little more, that hope flickered in a stinging wind. Was Galen safe? Would Isaiah stick to his bargain? And what of the other threats?

He sought Nimue's mind.

How is the outside? she said.

Cold.

I'm sorry about all this, Emrys.

Would you have done anything differently if you knew it would end this way?

She didn't answer.

Why did you do it, Nimue? Why share a soul with Absolon? There would have been other ways to get what you wanted.

I never get what I want.

You've got it now. You've got your freedom.

I want more than that. With a surge of power that propelled the air from his lungs, she dragged Emrys into her memories.

She sat on Absolon's lap, and this memory of Nimue stroked his face and touched his chest, while he held her.

Emrys recoiled. What was this? They had never been anything but enemies. What game was she playing? But when his judgement eased, he felt her true emotion and almost wept.

That is what I wanted, Emrys. I wanted him.

Her heart floated whenever she saw him. She grew

addicted to the way he held her and made her feel like the adult she knew herself to be. He said they couldn't let anyone know about them, but she was addicted to him. The more they maintained their icy distance in front of the other Darisami, the more obsessed she became with keeping him close. She insisted they share a soul, and he relented. None suspected them. None suspected her.

For a little while she basked in their intimacy, and he did too, but that intimacy didn't last. Ragnar was still at the core of Absolon's being and no matter how deep she went, she could never supplant him.

The scene shifted.

She snuck into his room through the back tunnels. She'd come to confront him over his unfaithfulness, sensing it through the soul shard while trying to deny it. But he told it to her true. He didn't want her. He didn't love her.

Her heart hardened into coal, and she left.

But she didn't leave his head.

I did it subtly. I didn't want him to warn any of you about what was happening to him, so I got into his mind and laid my traps. He thought the soul shard had faded because of how I cloaked my mind. He sought me but couldn't find me. When I was ready, when I was certain he would suffer for what he'd done to me, I let it all out and his mind was consumed with hunger.

Nimue, you didn't—

Didn't what? Didn't have to feel that way? Didn't have to destroy Endurance? No, I didn't. But I wanted to. I wanted him annihilated just as he annihilated me. I wanted him to feel such hunger that he'd know how I hungered.

Her memories faded and they floated in a void. There was a sense she wanted to say more, that the stillness of her mind hid a turmoil, but that may have been misplaced sentimentality.

Do you regret it?

Do you regret killing him?

Did he regret killing Absolon now he knew why'd he'd gone berserk? A little. But he also felt Nimue's pain deep in his marrow. He regretted killing Absolon, but he'd had no choice at the time. And as ever he'd have done anything for Nimue.

I'm sorry, Nimue.

Don't be. I was a fool to expect more.

And Clara? Why push her to destabilize Yusef and destroy what little remained? We could have been fine here, and they would have stayed there.

I don't want them to survive. Her words scuttled beneath the surface of his skin and he shivered. *I want Ragnar dead for consuming all of Absolon's love. I want all those Darisami who ever disregarded me slaughtered.*

And what about me, Nimue?

I still want you to kill Ragnar.

A laugh exploded out of his mouth. *To what end?*

To ensure Galen remains safe.

Ragnar will never gain entry to Providence, of that I am certain. And as for Galen, he's better off where he is.

Then do it for me, Emrys, because I can't. You know Ragnar won't rest until he's killed me and that will forever put Galen in danger.

Where is Galen now?

As far as I know, he's still in a cell, which is the safest place for him, what with the straining tensions in Providence. But it'll all be for naught if you don't kill Ragnar. Especially after what happened to Yusef.

Yusef. What had he said to Clara about Yusef's failings? He'd fallen in love with a human and ruined everything.

It's nothing that you haven't done before, Emrys.

Why should he care? Galen had finished with him

before Brink's death. He could not love a murderer. The most Emrys could wish for between them was Galen's safety. There had been little else to hope for, especially not a love built on his lies. But he had to do whatever he could to keep Galen safe.

I have little choice.

He'd been the Darisami's executioner for centuries. He could kill a few more if it meant keeping Galen alive.

Excellent. I will do what I can to help you. We are still linked, and while Ragnar is strong, my mind is stronger. You will be victorious.

Not without gold.

Ragnar has your knife. You can best him and take it from him. But you should get some sleep. He will arrive tomorrow.

She vanished from his mind, extinguished like a pinched-out candle flame. But scorch marks stained the inside of his head, and his tongue was blanketed in ash.

27

Emrys rose with the sun and sought a location to
serve as a battleground. He searched for Providence's
surveillance of the ghost city, retracing the steps he and
Nimue had taken when they'd arrived less than a month
ago. Unobtrusive cameras jutted out from several stories
high, wires connecting them to solar panels. He clocked
about twenty placed to minimize the need for a wide-
ranging network.

He deviated from the path and found what used to be
an inner-city high school. Brown brick and concrete block
buildings of no particular architectural merit hunkered
down beneath the umbrella of skyscrapers. The sports field
had long ago turned to dust, and he spied yellow weeds
cracking through the dirt.

At the center of a maze of two and three-story class-
room buildings, he found a quad and a basketball court.
The net had rotted but the metal hoop remained like a
scaffold waiting for a noose.

He had the choice of multiple exits and high vantage
points to watch Ragnar and Wyatt's approach far from

Providence's eye. Throughout his search, he beamed to Ragnar, hoping to gain an audience.

His gentle, rapid knocking against the gates of Ragnar's mind grew into the heavy and forceful blows of a battering ram. He wore down Ragnar's resistance until the gates opened onto a mind in turmoil. The barbarians had already gained access and ransacked the place. Ragnar's mind writhed at his futility, at his blindness, at having lost something that belonged to him.

That was the only way Ragnar could process the loss of Absolon and having had him in the first place. An object that had been stolen from him. If he could not have it back, he would have restitution.

WHAT IS IT?

Ragnar's thoughts rolled through Emrys. He gritted his teeth and forced himself into the fray. Ragnar didn't need to know the truth. He only had to believe he had an ally.

Nimue has betrayed me. I'm waiting for you in the city so we can plot our revenge.

YOU ARE OUTSIDE PROVIDENCE?

I have been expelled for a murder that Nimue orchestrated. The lie landed true.

THEN HOW ARE WE TO GAIN ENTRANCE? WE NEEDED YOU INSIDE. YOU HAVE FAILED.

You should have responded to my hailing sooner. This would not have come as such a surprise.

THE ONLY THING THAT SURPRISES ME IS YOUR INCOMPETENCE.

Berate me all you wish, Ragnar, but we need to work together to get back inside.

WYATT AND I WILL CLAIM ASYLUM.

Emrys explained why that would not work.

Rage rendered Ragnar's response incoherent.

Meet me and we will discuss this.

THERE IS NOTHING TO DISCUSS. YOU HAVE FAILED. WE WILL APPROACH THE MAIN GATES OF PROVIDENCE.

I suggest a different course. Meet me and I can tell you all you need to know. I have little hope of returning to Providence, but I will do everything to ensure you do so you can have our revenge.

Ragnar struggled to restrain the battle that raged through his mind, spurred on by the speed with which he raced across the country. He would arrive in a few hours, gathering beyond the horizon and streaming towards Providence like a vengeful horseman.

Very well. We will meet with you before pressing our case with Providence.

Emrys instructed him on where to rendezvous and how to avoid the cameras. It would not do to have surveillance pick them up, and even less well to show them meeting Emrys. He advised them to limp into town like weary travelers.

Ragnar's mind slammed shut.

Emrys explored the surrounding buildings. The class-rooms had been ransacked, the windows blown out, and chairs chopped into firewood. The shadow of a world destroyed, torn and tattered and blowing in the hot breeze peppered with dust. If his plan did not work, in a month he'd join it.

It struck him that he would not be there to witness the end of the world. Immortality had dogged him for so long that he'd assumed—especially when the world fell—that he would be one of the last to see it shudder to a stop. But those humans in Providence had a greater chance of seeing this through. He was a relic from a time of abun-dance and would be forgotten along with all he had beheld —the arrival of steam engines and automation, of elec-tricity and wars too terrible to comprehend. So much existence was enshrined in his body, the lives of thousands etched into his soul, filling him with life, good and bad.

He did not want to die, but the odds were not in his favor. Ragnar had always been the better fighter, and though Emrys had recently fed, he was outnumbered and lacked a weapon.

He would die.

Just when he was beginning to live again.

Five hundred years, and he would end it on a cracked basketball court. Would Galen mourn him? Not if he believed Emrys had killed Brink. But Emrys would fight until the end to save Galen from the Darisami who threatened his life. He trusted that Nimue would not harm him, but Ragnar could not gain entry to Providence.

A Darisami had destroyed Emrys's life and love once before, and he would not allow it to happen again. He would protect Galen, even if it meant he died in the process.

Footsteps thudding on asphalt turned his head to the corridor between two buildings. The shadows had lengthened and though Ragnar had not warned him of his arrival, now would be the time that—

Galen, dressed in his uniform and armed with a machine gun, hurried down the laneway. He'd foregone his helmet. His mouth was set in a hard line, his glances furtive. He slowed his steps, searched ahead and around him like he wasn't sure he was alone. Galen kept moving towards him, but Emrys's heart had stopped.

"What are you doing here?" The words struggled to escape his constricted throat. "How did you get out?"

"Are you alone?"

How much to tell him? "For now, but you shouldn't be here."

"I had no choice. Nimue—"

Mercury sluiced through Emrys's veins. "Nimue what?"

He came close to Emrys, lowered his gun, and looked around for any signs of ambush.

"Nimue what?"

Galen licked his lips, and for all the fear flooding through Emrys's body, he wanted to press his mouth to them.

"She broke me out."

He flinched. *What was she doing?* Just once it would be nice if she stuck to the bloody plan. "She what?"

"She freed me." He lowered his gun and reached behind his back to pull out something wrapped in black cloth. "And she told me to give you this."

He took it from Galen and unwrapped it. Inside was the weapon he'd made. Clever. She was giving him a fighting chance at least—and making it impossible for him not to fight on her behalf. If Galen were outside, he'd be a target that Ragnar could not ignore.

"She said if I didn't get you that, you were going to die. What is it?"

"I can't explain, but you must go back to Providence."

"She said you were in danger. Though how she knew, I have no idea. And the way she got me out… There's something about her I don't know, isn't there?"

"Yes. She's not my daughter, and she's a lot older, a lot smarter, and a helluva lot more devious than she looks." He spoke fast, grabbing Galen by the arm and marching him back the way he came. "It's not safe. You must leave."

Galen resisted. "I'm not going anywhere. You're out here because of me."

"I would have thought you'd be pleased to see me gone after Brink's death. I know you don't believe me, but I didn't kill him."

"I know. Isaiah showed me a video of the two of you going into our room, and I knew it was faked."

"That was enough?"

"That and what you risked trying to see me before you were marched out. I had to come help you, so when Nimue said she had to get to the surface—"

"Nimue's here?" Emrys spun, searching for any sign of her, reaching for her mind. What was she playing at? Was she helping him or ensuring his death? It was too much to hope for her aid, yet there Galen was.

"I said I'd go get you, but she refused to stay in Providence. She's safe, though. She told me this was the place you'd said to go if you ever got separated." Galen pulled at him. "Emrys, please, I'm not going back in there without you."

"But I can't. Not with the way things are in Providence. I signed a confession."

"A lot has happened since you left. There are protests. It's chaos."

"Why?"

"Everyone knows you've been evicted, but they're demanding a fair trial. They want proper justice. Isaiah's plan has backfired, and it's turned people against him. That's how we were able to get out, the confusion acted as cover. And if you come back, you can help quell the unrest."

He shoved the weapon into his back pocket. "I can't, Galen. Not yet. There's something I have to do, but you must go, please."

"I'm not leaving you. I failed you in Providence. I won't fail you again." The ferocity in Galen's eyes brought Emrys a second of stillness in which he almost believed he could accept Galen's help. But it would be futile, and he'd lose even more than he already had. Galen had to go.

"You didn't fail me. You told the truth. I may not have killed Brink, but I did kill Jared, and I did kill that soldier when I was being led out. I'm a killer. I don't want to be, but it's something I have to do in order to survive. I can't explain it all now, and I probably can't explain it in the future, but you are better off without me. You're safer." He fired off his words or else he'd never get everything out. Already it felt like his chest was caving in and he was only narrowly avoiding tumbling into the abyss.

Determination took root on Galen's face, his feet planting firm on the asphalt.

"I don't want safe. I understand you more than I want to. You do what you have to to survive. And it's in me, too. I wanted to resist it, to reject it, because I was scared I'd get it wrong, but being with you made me face up to the reality that there is nothing I wouldn't do to survive. What I feel for you scared me because of the lengths I'd go to keep it, but the time I had in the cell made me realize that whatever threats there are, whatever battles we must face, I want to face them with you."

Galen kept trying to throw him a line, but Emrys couldn't take it or he'd pull Galen down with him. "You don't know what you're saying. You have to leave. Please. I can't protect you if I have to worry about you."

"I can handle myself, Emrys. No matter what happens." Galen put his hand against Emrys's cheek, and Emrys resisted leaning into that comfort and everything—all the hope and potential and love—that came with it. "Don't you see? There is no life without you. Until you came along, I'd been existing but not living, like most of us in Providence. But you've given us, you've given *me*, another chance at life. You've given me hope. You've given me my heart back, you've awakened my soul, and for that,

I will be beside you. If anything happened to you, that would be the death of me. Please, Emrys, let me help you."

Galen had already helped him more than he could know, but this was not a fight he could be a part of. He put his palm on the back of Galen's neck, and Emrys's eyes closed as their lips met. Emrys's heart balanced on the precipice. Galen had to go, or he'd risk losing him for good. But now he had something to fight for. Lost in Galen's affection, his heart teetered and fell, only to be rescued by Galen.

"An ambush, Emrys? Really?"

Emrys broke the kiss and pivoted to the sound of Ragnar's voice as he stalked down the darkening laneway. Wyatt loped a few steps behind. Dressed in torn and tatty clothes, dirt and sweat streaked their faces like they'd spent months roaming the wilderness. Neither carried packs. The gold knife glinted in Ragnar's fist.

Emrys stepped in front of Galen. "Well met, Ragnar. Wyatt. I didn't expect you so soon."

"Clearly. So, what is this? A welcoming party? That wasn't part of the arrangement." Ragnar's fist flexed on the hilt of the knife. Emrys's hand stayed clear of the weapon in his pocket. "Or perhaps he's a refreshment."

Galen stepped to the side and pointed his gun at Ragnar. "Who are you, and what are you doing here?"

Ragnar's lips twitched. "My name is Ragnar. We are from Endurance and seek asylum."

"You are not welcome within our walls."

"From what I hear, neither is our brother."

Galen stiffened, enough for Ragnar to assume he was correct. How could Emrys protect him? With one touch, Ragnar could rip Galen's soul from his body.

Ragnar went to Emrys's left, Wyatt to his right. Galen

would be his weakest point, but Emrys dared not take his eye off Ragnar.

"You should keep moving, Ragnar," Emrys said. "Providence will not welcome you."

"I'll test that theory myself. You and Nimue have been working against us for so long, I don't trust anything you've said."

"I'm sorry for what Nimue did to you—and to Absolon."

Ragnar slashed the knife through the air. "Keep your platitudes, Emrys. I'm not in the mood."

Galen braced the rifle against his shoulder. "I think you two should back off."

Ragnar smirked. "Your gun means nothing."

While the bullets would slow the Darisami down, they wouldn't stop them completely. And when the bullets ran out, they'd harvest Galen's soul.

Emrys's tongue wet his dry lips. "How about we make a deal, Ragnar? You let us go, and you can have Providence."

"You think to make me a fool again? The way you and Nimue slipped out of Endurance...I should never have trusted either of you."

"And you think you can trust Wyatt?"

Ragnar didn't pause. "He's more loyal than you ever were."

"Because he needed you to protect him from the others. But once you're inside Providence, how soon before he turns on you?" Emrys turned his head enough to catch Wyatt's eye. "Or him on you, Wyatt?"

"We are brothers, and the only traitor is you," Ragnar said. "But there's one thing you can do with your final moments. Tell me where Nimue is."

Galen kept silent.

"She's safely locked in Providence, you know that," Emrys said.

"No, she's not. She's here. I can feel her watching me and trying to get inside my mind. She thinks she's clever. Don't you, Nimue?" He shouted to the surrounding buildings, and his voice echoed. "Ferreting around in my mind as if I wouldn't know."

Ragnar addressed the empty and chipped-toothed windows as if he were orating at a trial and trying to woo the jury, but his voice cracked on his arguments. "I loved him, Nimue, and you took him from me."

"Ragnar." Wyatt didn't dare move from his position. Arms primed, hands open, the symbol must have floated in his mind, his hunger driving him to kill Galen. But his fear of Ragnar, or the plan for their last hope at survival, stayed his attack.

"You're a vengeful bitch, Nimue, and I should have killed you the moment you came into our lives. He loved me, and you knew it. You couldn't bear to let another be loved, could you? Your heart never grew, you pathetic child!" Ragnar punched out at the phantom Nimue.

"Ragnar!" Wyatt shouted at him, but Ragnar was locked into his rant, hate flaring in his eyes, spit flying from his mouth as he read the charges against Nimue and demanded vengeance. This was Nimue's doing, but it wouldn't occupy him for long.

With one hand, Emrys pulled Galen behind him, leaving enough space for him to keep his gun pointed at Wyatt. Emrys's other hand was free to grab the weapon from his back pocket.

"I didn't want to do this, Emrys, but you had no idea what you left us with. It was hell. You left us in Hell, and I can still hear the screams." Pleading and panic quavered in Wyatt's voice.

"Then walk away, Wyatt. Find somewhere else." *Please, walk away.*

"There is nowhere else!" Wyatt snarled, hunger stalking his anguished face. "You know it and I know it. We're all going to die, but the one hope I have is that I can get into Providence and the screams will stop. I'd do anything to make the screams stop." Wyatt charged.

Adrenalin surged through Emrys's body. He picked up Galen and threw him across the basketball court, far from the Darisami. He hit the ground, gun firing into the air and startling Wyatt enough to slow him. In that microsecond of hesitation, Emrys ripped the weapon from his back pocket with his right hand, raised it up, and met Wyatt's force with all of his strength.

Emrys slammed into the Darisami, the fresh soul giving him the power to knock Wyatt back and throw him to the ground. Jumping on top of his brother's body quicker than Wyatt could respond, Emrys stabbed the rod into Wyatt's eye through to his brain. He pulled it out and sprang off Wyatt.

It was over so fast.

Death rattled in Wyatt's chest as he fought for breath. Sadness clouded his undamaged eye, his face dropping and his mouth begging silently to be saved before he collapsed to the ground.

Emrys backed away from Wyatt's corpse as the souls he'd held captive for two centuries burst free. He was out of the souls' flight path, but even so, they brushed against his skin and fluttered—

Ragnar tackled Emrys from behind, and the two of them flew into the tornado of freed souls. Emrys lost the grip on his weapon, and it skittered across the concrete. He reached for it as the stream of beautiful souls overwhelmed his fight, and he writhed beneath Ragnar's body, resisting the ecstasy coursing through his system.

He spun beneath Ragnar, gritting his teeth until the last of the soul rush fled. The rage in Ragnar's eyes cleared the fog as the Darisami bore down on him with a strength Emrys struggled to match. He gripped Ragnar's wrists as the point of the gold knife in Ragnar's fist came dangerously close to Emrys's eye. It lowered and nicked the skin on his cheek, burning as it drew blood. He hissed and turned his head, then gathered power in his arms and threw Ragnar off and away.

Ragnar flailed but regained control of his momentum, flipped, and landed on his feet. Emrys charged Ragnar, meeting him in mid stride. Emrys narrowly avoided the knife, the blade cutting through his shirt but not piercing his skin. He threw him back and charged again, fists raised, ducking and weaving as the knife flashed through the air and Ragnar sought desperately to stab him.

As they danced and fought, Laurence's words came back.

When people have weapons, they tend to rely on them, but when they're disarmed, they fall.

Ragnar fought with a weapon, his whole focus on trying to stab Emrys, whereas Emrys had his fists, strength, and agility. He avoided the knife because he was using everything he had, while Ragnar was the knife and the knife alone.

Disarm Ragnar and he'd win.

He ducked low under Ragnar's swinging arm, driving up with enough force to knock his hand out of the way, and pummeled Ragnar's gut with his fists. He swerved out of the Darisami's desperate overreach, avoiding the blade as Ragnar went from the wide strokes of a swordsman to the dirty tricks of a knife fight.

Emrys parried and crouched, swung his legs, and landed rough kicks to Ragnar's stomach, his shoulder, his knee. And as Ragnar staggered backward, Emrys rose to his feet and knocked the knife out of Ragnar's weakened grip. The dagger went flying, but while Ragnar watched it, Emrys struck him hard against his temple and brought him to his knees. He gripped him by the hair and drove his fist again and again into Ragnar's face. Ragnar swayed, and Emrys let him go.

Emrys raced for the knife and grabbed it. Dazed, Ragnar staggered to his feet, but Emrys returned and slammed his fist into Ragnar's face, knocking him to the ground. The fight for Galen's life overrode any qualms at ending Ragnar's.

He wound his fingers through Ragnar's sweaty, matted hair, lifted his head, and drove the knife deep into Ragnar's right eye.

Ragnar roared, but his death was inevitable. Emrys retracted the knife and let go of the Darisami, leaving him to thrash and scream. Ragnar tried to stand, but he fell face down and shuddered to his end.

The adrenaline trickled out of him, leaving him empty. "Rest easy, brother."

Ragnar's soul fled, bursting out and starting the exodus of all those other souls he'd harvested. Now they flew home.

Ragnar and Wyatt's names joined the forty-seven others on Emrys's list.

Ragnar's body flaked. Wyatt's was almost gone. Galen lay where he'd been thrown, knocked unconscious on the other side of the cracked basketball court. Emrys raced to him, relieved at the sight of Galen's chest rising and falling.

He sank to the ground, brushed Galen's hair off his forehead and checked for wounds, for blood. He didn't find any, and the way he'd landed didn't lend itself to any spinal damage. His heavy uniform had protected him. He cradled Galen in his lap, taking the gun strap off his shoulder. The movement stirred Galen, but he winced and shot one hand to his head.

His eyelids blinked open, and he looked up at Emrys. "Where are they?" He fought to stand.

Emrys held him down. "Don't worry. We're safe."

Galen looked for Wyatt and Ragnar. "They're…they're gone?"

"Yeah."

"And they left their clothes behind?"

"Couldn't take them where they were going."

Galen frowned. "What aren't you telling me?"

Maybe one day he could tell Galen the whole truth. "A lot, but you're going to have to trust me on this. They're gone, and they'll never hurt you again."

"You did this? All by yourself?"

"I told you, Galen, I'm a killer. It's what I do."

"But still…two against one."

If he didn't count Nimue's control of Ragnar's mind. "All you need to know is it's over."

"Does that mean you can come home now?"

He hesitated. Could he really do it? He wanted to. Badly. Could he have another chance at love? "You still want me? Even after this?" Funny that asking that was harder than killing Ragnar and Wyatt.

"How about this for an answer?" Galen pulled Emrys to him and brushed his lips.

The press of his lips sealed his fate. He hugged Galen to him, kissed him hard, his tongue diving and caressing Galen's as one kiss became many. The rapture of souls paled beneath the hellfire of his love for Galen, incinerating his final doubts, his last fears, and out of their ashes rose a new hope and a new heart.

Emrys broke the kiss with labored breath. "I guess that's a yes?"

Galen laughed. "A thousand times over."

Emrys kissed Galen again quickly and helped him to his feet.

They passed the two heaps of clothes, Galen wanting to examine them, but Emrys pulled him away. He pocketed the golden knife and searched for the weapon he'd made in Providence. He was certain he'd thrown it somewhere near the northern end of the basketball court.

Dread stilled his blood. Emrys looked around the buildings. Nimue must have watched from one of the windows and listened to Ragnar's ranting, her proximity making it easier for her to plan her attack. And when it was all over, she'd snuck down and taken his back-up weapon.

"Where did you leave Nimue?"

"She's back towards the warehouse. I wanted her to stay close to safety."

She'd return to Providence before them.

Emrys held Galen's hand and hurried him through the deserted streets. The shadows were getting longer as night crept closer. They'd have to get inside soon.

He hailed her. To his surprise she answered.

I'm not coming with you.

Emrys halted at Nimue's voice.

Galen stopped, gave him a quizzical look. "Everything all right?"

He nodded dumbly and kept going, but his steps faltered.

What do you mean?

Providence is yours, Emrys. I did this for you.

Why are you leaving? We could both stay in Providence.

I can't be your daughter any longer.

You're not. You're my friend. Desperation pushed him to run faster.

But every time you look at me, you think I'm Sian, and I can't be that for you, Emrys. Don't deny it, please. I've seen inside your mind. She died a long time ago, and you have to forgive yourself and move on.

But why do this?

I can survive out here, Galen can't. And seeing what you have, I don't want you to lose it. Lysander broke you but Galen can piece you back together.

Loss bubbled into his throat, cutting off his oxygen. He was drowning. *No, you need to come back with us. What will I tell them? What will I tell Galen?*

Tell him he's a good shot.

He'd shot her? *Is that why you lost your grip on Ragnar?*

It was slipping anyway but getting shot in the shoulder didn't help.

I can't tell him. He'll think he killed you.

Then tell him the truth. After what he's seen, after what I did for him, he'll believe I'm not some child who can't take care of herself.

The truth about him being a Darisami? One day maybe. After they were safe inside Providence.

I don't think I can.

Then say survivors from Endurance came and took me away. Say you were my guardian but I have gone with my real father.

She'd thought of everything. She always had.

I don't want you to go, Nimue. Please, come back.

I can't, Emrys. I'm sorry, but I want you to let me go. I want to go find my own life again, far beyond the Darisami.

What if there's nothing out there for you? What if you can't find another soul?

Then so be it. Please, Emrys, let me go.

Galen stopped outside the building where he'd left

Nimue. Emrys hoped this was another one of her ruses, but when Galen shouted for her to come out, he knew she was gone. Galen was frantic, begging Emrys to believe he'd told her to wait, and left the building to search another and another.

All while Emrys held his breath.

Emrys, it's time to let go.

He'd held onto her and Sian for so many centuries, they were enmeshed into who he was. He'd grown used to the pain of reliving her demise and his failure. He'd kept it through the long years. But when Galen stuck his head back around the door, imploring him to look, he knew that Sian and Myfanwy and Nimue and even Lysander were all gone. He had to let go of his pain and his guilt and his belief that all he brought was death.

He could bring life to Providence as Galen had brought life to him.

"Are you going to help me look?"

He took a deep breath and closed his eyes. She was right. Five hundred years was long enough to grieve. *Thank you, Nimue. I hope you find what you're looking for.*

May we meet again in more prosperous times.

She left him then, but her loss was a scar he knew he could brave.

"Emrys! We need to find her."

"No, we don't. This is what she wanted."

"I don't know how you can say that. She's a child."

"But she's not. With what you saw today and what she told you, you know she's something else. She's something special. And this is what she wanted."

Galen gaped at him like he'd lost his mind. "I'm going to look for her." He returned to the street.

Emrys followed. How could he explain what had happened to her? What she had done? But the more Galen shouted, the less Emrys had to say. He kept with him but didn't search for what he knew he'd never regain. He had what he needed and what he wanted. Galen was there, whereas all else had passed away.

Futility ceased Galen's search. "I don't know how you can be so calm."

"Because I know she's safe, and I know you won't find her." He took Galen's hands. "She will be fine, have no doubt about that."

"But what is she?"

"She's no child, but beyond that, I can't say. Please, trust me."

"You're expecting me to take a lot on faith."

"And hopefully love. Because while I can't tell you anything about Nimue's nature, I can tell you that you're the one I'm meant to be with, and that's the truth."

"Do you mean that?"

"I do. There has been far too little love in my life. I spent so much of it afraid of the damage it could do that I never believed it could bring me happiness. Until I met you." He kissed the back of Galen's hand. "And because of you, I want to change Providence and change it for the better. Now I'm with you, I know we can do that, and I want to. There's no point in surviving if there is no love. And there's no love if I'm not with you."

Galen kissed him, and Emrys's heart opened so wide it felt like all the souls he'd fed on in five hundred years broke free.

Galen held tight to his hands, his forehead resting against Emrys's. "You do know once we're back in Providence, there's going to be little time for us to be alone. You might have to go back to a cell."

"No such thing as conjugal visits?"

He chuckled. "Not likely. But what I'm saying is we

don't have to go back if we don't want to. We could take our chances in the wild."

Emrys could do it, but Galen would die in three days if they didn't find fresh water. He couldn't even make him into a Darisami. Galen would need to feed within a day of the change, and the surrounding countryside lacked human souls.

"We need to go back," Emrys said. "We can't run away and leave everyone to die."

"Spoken like a true hero." Galen turned to the warehouse gate and keyed in the code to unlock the door. And without a moment to spare. The sun had gone, the sky a dark blue with a hint of sunset. The moon would show her face soon if—

The door wrenched open. Black-gloved hands grabbed Galen and threw him to the ground. Soldiers poured out, and Emrys staggered back. He had to resist the temptation to kill them all to defend Galen. He might need them in Providence. They fanned out, forming a half circle around him, and raised their guns.

"I'm unarmed." He showed them his hands.

Their grips tightened on their weapons, but then they started to dip. A soldier raised the visor on his helmet, and his mouth gaped open.

Emrys's heart sank. He looked at his bare hands and forearms, at the light shining bright out of his skin. He tilted his head to the sky and swore the moon was laughing.

"What the…" Galen said.

Emrys lowered his chin to look into Galen's eyes stretched wide. Fear knotted his forehead. "Emrys? What's happening to you?"

"I can explain."

But he couldn't. Not in any way that could make this right. Too impossible. Too strange. Too late.

Then a soldier put down their weapon, sank to their knees, and began to pray.

And another.

Then three more.

And Galen…

Galen looked up at him, ecstasy blazing on his face.

Emrys closed his eyes and wished it were all a dream, but when he opened them, the nightmare remained as the soldiers basked in the light of revelation.

Fuck.

ABOUT THE AUTHOR

Daniel de Lorne writes about men, monsters and magic.

In love with writing since he wrote a story about a talking tree at age six, his first novel, the romantic horror *Beckoning Blood*, was published in 2014. At the heart of every book is a romance between two men, whether they're irresistible vampires, historical hotties, or professional paramours.

In his other life, Daniel is a professional writer and researcher in Perth, Australia, with a love of history and nature. All of which makes for great story fodder.

And when he's not working, he and his husband explore as much of this amazing world as they can, from the ruins of Welsh abbeys to trekking famous routes and swimming with whales.

Connect with Daniel and get a FREE short story. Be the first to know about new releases, cover reveals, giveaways and more.
www.danieldelorne.com

ACKNOWLEDGMENTS

Soul Survivor started out as an idea way back in 2010. I was working on *Beckoning Blood* and toying with the idea of writing something that wasn't about vampires but was *like* vampires. I also worked for a zoo back then so issues of conservation and extinction were front of mind. Combining those two topics—of not-vampires and extinction—brought me to consider what would happen to the creature that fed on humans if humans became scarce.

A lot of this story has changed since I first wrote it. And I mean A LOT. That's largely due to the frank and fearless feedback of my friends, Nikki Logan and TJ Nichols. They helped me make this story even better—as they do with everything I write. Thank you for your help with this series.

I'd also like to thank my editor, Charlie Knight, for getting *Soul Survivor* up to publishable standard (and picking up my Australianisms), and to Lana Pecherczyk for her graphic design advice.

And thank you to my husband, Glen, who can finally get an answer to the question, "Who is Galen?"